The ultimate road trip and sudden death, passion and panic, desire and decadence, hope and pity, laughter and longing, infinity and more – all in *Don't Think of Tigers* a glittering collection of work by fourteen prize-winning new writers. The future of fiction is here.

The writers featured in this anthology are all winners of First Edition, a writing competition and mentoring scheme run by the Asham Literary Endowment Trust, supported by the National Lottery through the Arts Council of England.

The work in this anthology is a consequence of collaborations between the writers and their mentors. The mentors involved in First Edition were: Alan Brownjohn, John Burnside, Chaz Brenchley, Stella Duffy, Suzannah Dunn, Robert Edric, Sophie Hannah, Selima Hill, Tobias Hill, Russell James and Shena Mackay,

DON'T THINK OF TIGERS

THE FIRST EDITION ANTHOLOGY

EDITED BY PETER GUTTRIDGE

First Published in Great Britain in 2001 by
The Do-Not Press Limited
16 The Woodlands
London SE13 6TY

Casebound edition: ISBN 1 899 344 67 5
C-format paperback: ISBN 1 899344 66 7

British Library Cataloguing in Publication Data. A catalogue record for this book is
available from the British Library.

h g f e d c b a

Printed and bound in Great Britain by
The Guernsey Press Co Ltd.

CONTENTS

INTRODUCTION

I t reads like a wish list of some of Britain's most exciting poets, novelists and short story writers: Alan Brownjohn, Chaz Brenchley, John Burnside, Suzannah Dunn, Stella Duffy, Robert Edric, Sophie Hannah, Selima Hill, Tobias Hill, Russell James and Shena Mackay. It *was* a wishlist for the fourteen writers whose work appears here, a wishlist of the writers they most wanted to act as their mentors in a unique project which began in 1997 and concludes with the publication of this anthology.

In 1997 The Asham Trust (Who that? See page 245) ran a writing competition in the south-east for people between the ages of 18 and 25. The trust's office in Lewes was inundated with poems, short stories and excerpts from novels. The work was of a high standard but certain writers stood out.

These writers were invited to attend a week's intensive writing course in Ty Newydd, the Welsh writing centre, under the tutelage of one of Britain's finest novelists, Robert Edric, and finest poets, Gillian Clarke. That was the first part of their prize.

The second part was for each of them to be mentored for six months by a writer whose work they admired. I facilitated the mentoring scheme. I thought getting the mentors would be the hardest part since there was little in it for them but hard work.

But in fact the writers listed above embraced the idea with enthusiasm and, despite their other commitments, went far beyond the mentoring scheme remit in the time they put in and the advice and encouragement they gave. Some real friendships were forged between mentor and "mentee".

The writing in this anthology is a product of that relationship between mentor and mentee. It's in a range of genres, a variety of forms. All it has in common is its excellence.

You won't have heard of any of these writers in this anthology. Yet. But as Russell James – who mentored both Robin Hill and Adam Hays – points out, albeit erring on the cautious side: "Out of all the hopeful writers in this book, some you will never hear of again, some will reappear occasionally, and perhaps one or two will break through into longer, hard cover works. One of them might become famous. So today you might be holding in your hand the first edition of the first published work of one of the top literary names of the twenty-first century. Let's hope so."

No doubt about it. The future of fiction is here.

Peter Guttridge
Coordinator, First Edition mentoring scheme.

Chantele Bigmore

Poems

Lines and Angles

When she was younger
she used to lift her T-shirt
to see how much her belly stuck out,
but now, she takes time
to undress and observe
from one angle then another
like an artist
about to sculpt herself.

Dance Tent

Her eyes say 'fuck me',
but her hand motions don't.
She'll let me lay her down
before she says no.
I'm already inside
before I let her have her way.
Teasing me to stop
is all part of her game.
She'll surrender in time.
Too drunk to argue with.
She's needy and I'm full on.
She's all I want and I'm all give.

Don't Think of Tigers

I will deliberately not think of you,
not taste you on my skin,
not feel you in my mouth.
I won't run my fingers
through your hair,
or watch you smoke
your French movie star cigarettes,
as I pretend to not be awake.

And there will be no bare back
to place my hungry kisses on.
No breast as pillow
I can rest my head against.

As I hunt you in my sleep
I'll cause danger to your safety,
but I won't think of the tigers
as your body won't embrace me.

Paranoid Android

She's been sleeping in our bed.
The very same
who flirts with you behind my back.
Is this what I get for my trust in her?
Only a day since the cat went away.

Might it be expected of me?
Am I the tempter or the tempted?
I have spent few hours testing you,
dropping names and sly comments,
like used knickers on the floor.

A Rock and a Hard Place

You whimper like a dog.
Your back is turned,
but my gentle touch is hard this time.
I show you the stars
and you turn to me.
I am a child cradling a child.
The bedclothes capture like nets.
It's quarter to five
and sleep won't let us join in.

Pulse

I sit observing through cigarette smoke,
at a girl passed out in the corner.
She moans from time to time,
but her mumbles are ignored
as she has already been sick three times
successfully out of the window.
Her brother is one of the men in here,
and I dare not make a move.
I pretend to be interested
in taking a joint from a stranger
agreeing that *The Wall*
was the best album ever made.

The Inclination of the Longing

The inclination of the longing, tiredness of the sad, weeps
the tears of an ocean.

All summer long in an empty house
alone staring out to the shipwreck of our love.

Wildly roaming without you, I drank for amusement.
Crying into the pillow of the sea like a savage.

Some guards with tiny bald patches stood a distance from me
in a watchtower, emerging slowly on the Spanish beach.

The inclination of the longing, shows my sadness. It weeps
to the sound of the sea with the sacrifice of the oceans.

The people woke at night and pecked like big birds
at the hundreds that came to command love.

They galloped to the wedding in yellow sombreros
desperate, mischievous and restrictively camp.

The last days of Disco

Torremolinos was your escape,
I thought trouble, much like before.

It reeked of the bright lights,
the music and the girls

of the childhood and the secrets
we shared in our minds.

I knew of your frequent trips home.
Of the raped prostitutes in Plymouth and Bristol,

but your guilt left with you,
back to the discos and the rohypnal cocktails.

Rearing its head in Crimewatch reconstruction's
of your own twisted ploys.

So I called gave them a what where and when
And now I will never see you again.

Rowena Macdonald

Infinity

It was early evening and the coast road looked at its best. In the low sunlight the glitter of the sea danced like television static. Lois leaned her cheek against the window, feeling tremors in her head from the vibrations of the bus. She noticed herself smiling, then wished she hadn't noticed but carried on smiling anyway. The bus drove past long arcs of pale houses overlooking empty squares of grass. Balconies stretched along the facades and Lois could see people basking in the late sun and sipping early drinks.

Lois unfolded the three sheets of airmail paper with Maggie's closely written instructions:

"...Rover will be with Jackie next door at No. 39. She will also have the keys. The silver one is for the outside door, the gold Yale key is for the front door. The big silver one is for the back door. Make sure you take off shoes every time you come in. Rover likes to be fed at 8 o'clock in the am and at 7 o'clock in the pm. All his food is in the utility room next to the washing machine. He likes to be walked every am at 9 o'clock. Make sure that he has a nice run on the green for at least half an hour and that he does his business. I would be very grateful if you could record Home and Away every day and also The Bill for Roy..."

The prospect of long days regimented by recording soap operas and Rover's feeding, walking and crapping routine took the smile off Lois' face.

She gazed out at the huge solemn edifice of Roedean school and further on at St Dunstan's, momentarily wondering why they had built a home for the blind with such a fantastic view.

The bus turned just before the Lido and drew up by the green where Lois got off. As the bus trundled away an unnatural Bank Holiday silence settled over the village. White seaside bungalows stretched up into the sloping green of the Downs. Each sat in the centre of a lawn like a pool table, edged with violently bright rose beds and neat dwarf conifers. Double glazing was polished and sealed to the evening breeze and York stone cladding looked as fresh as it had in the estate agents' particulars in 1974. Lois lumbered along with her suitcases to Glyndebourne Avenue without seeing a single person.

Maggie and Roy lived at number 37, a small bungalow with an oversized chimney and a wrought-iron sign curling out the name "Strathmoore". Maggie and Roy never referred to their home as "Number 37" – always "Strathmoore" as if it were a huge Highland estate. Lois had been twelve when she last stayed there. She had padded around the deep-pile carpet; Maggie's sheepskin slippers feeling like a pair of powder puffs on her feet. She had won a Terry's Chocolate Orange at a beetle drive in the church hall and proudly walked Rover round the village as he strained at his lead and cocked his leg at every other lamp-post. On balance, her last stay at Strathmoore had been an unqualified success.

The house next door had a more proportionate chimney and, hanging from the gate, a piece of slate with the name "Rexequus" carved in Grecian lettering. Lois slipped through the gate and pressed the doorbell. Dark shapes moved beyond the frosted glass before the door was eventually opened by a woman with a deep tan and an excess of gold jewellery. Expensive perfume surrounded her like a scented forcefield.

"Hello", she said, looking at Lois blankly.

"Jackie?"

"Yes?"

"I'm Lois – Maggie's niece,"

"Oh!" Jackie smiled vaguely and ushered Lois into the hallway. "Rover's out in the garden – I'm not good with dogs."

She led Lois into a living room which smelt of air freshener and out through a French window onto the lawn. Rover skulked by a clinical-looking fishpond. He was a rather subdued white Labrador; the sight of Lois and Jackie barely registered any reaction.

"Thanks very much for looking after him," said Lois, patting Rover self-consciously in an attempt to look at ease with him. Like Jackie, she was not good with dogs.

"Hello Rover. How are you?" She did not relish the prospect of calling him Rover in public. Why hadn't Maggie and Roy given him a less ridiculous name? Jackie stood in the French window and looked at Lois in a considering way. Lois wondered what Maggie had told her.

"Drink?" said Jackie abruptly. "G&T, Martini...? I'm going to have a little vodka," she said, veering towards the drinks cabinet.

"A gin and tonic would be nice," said Lois weakly.

She watched as Jackie unscrewed bottle tops with dainty concentration and set two glasses on an occasional table from a nest of three. Jackie's nails were peachy beige and tapered into long points.

"Come in and sit down."

Lois sank into a large cream leather sofa. The living room was tidy but areas of ordered clutter pointed to the pattern of Jackie's day. Lois noticed, like props in a photo-shoot, a marble ashtray filled with lipstick-smudged cigarette stubs, a packet of Consulate lying open and nearly empty, the Daily Mail, a saucer of crumbs, a maple-wood effect mobile phone, several empty glasses and a bottle of handcream. But above all she noticed the walls. Every available space on every wall was covered in large gold-framed photographs. Every photograph showed the same blonde girl. The girl lay in a field of poppies in a blue sundress. She reclined among breaking waves in a pink bikini. She stood by a balcony, toying with an arum lily, in a silver evening gown. She sprawled on a four poster bed in a diaphanous negligee. Her image was repeated endlessly in a kaleidoscope of clothes and scenarios: miniskirts, halternecks, high heels, fur coats, feather boas, jazz bars, jacuzzis, ski slopes, speedboats, sand dunes. But her only pose was an indolent loll and her only expression was a vacant pout. Sometimes her eyes slid sideways to an unseen observer. Sometimes she twirled a tress of hair around a manicured finger. Occasionally a sly smile played at the corner of her glossy lips. But not often.

"That's Francine," said Jackie. She lit a cigarette from a large marble lighter on the mantelpiece, then stood with her back to Lois surveying the photographs.

"My daughter," said Jackie. With a flounce she flung herself into an armchair and took a drag on her cigarette. There were several minutes of silence. Lois cracked icecubes in her teeth and tried to think of something to say. Francine gazed down at them with a hundred sulky stares.

*

Lois spent that evening snooping around Strathmoore. Inspecting bookshelves in the living room, laden with leather-bound classics. Flicking through photograph albums filled with family groups lined up in front of barbecues and birthday cakes. Maggie beamed throughout in an extensive range of knitwear. Lois herself appeared briefly as a toddler, clutching a blue plastic bucket. Another picture showed her a few years later sitting in a paddling pool. Then another, which gave her a sorry pang – wearing a red print dress and holding Rover as a puppy, during what must have been her last visit to Strathmoore.

She lay on the living room floor for a long time, listening to the silence of the house and the creakings and tiny noises beneath the silence. After a while the ticking of the carriage clock on the mantelpiece became very apparent. It was more a crunching sound than a tick, like faraway footsteps walking through fallen leaves. Lois took the clock into the kitchen, wrapped it in a pile of teatowels and placed it in a cupboard beside an empty food processor box.

A door off the front lobby led into Maggie and Roy's bedroom. A mirrored wardrobe lined one wall. Lois slid back its doors and rifled through hangers of Maggie's clothes. Among the elastic-fronted slacks and M&S skirts she found a halter-neck evening dress in slippery turquoise viscose. With a small thrill, she took off her clothes and pulled it on. It was cut on the bias, making Lois want to sashay seductively and sprawl film-star fashion across the satin bedspread. In the drawers of the dressing table, she found make-up that Maggie had left behind. With a slick of green shimmer eyeshadow, bronze blusher and cerise lipstick her features took on the exaggerated expression of a ballroom dancer.

Under the bed lurked the powder puff slippers and a dark mound of old porn mags. Lois peeked through them surreptitiously as if Roy or Maggie were about to burst through the door. She shied away from the thought of Roy gazing at these girls with their glistening bodies and glossy lips stretched into joyless smiles.

*

The next few days were very hot. Lois walked around the empty streets of the village feeling dazed and blank, past the green with benches that nobody sat on, the red telephone box, the shop which sold out-of-date groceries and the church with the orange sign outside which read, "HE'S ALIVE - THIS FRIDAY AT 8PM."

At the southern edge of the village a concrete path led down through a subway to the beach. Several afternoons, Lois sat on the pebbles looking at the sea while Rover ran in circles and played chicken with the water's edge.

The silence of the days was unnerving. Lois kept the radio on when she was in the bungalow. Lying in the garden, she could often see Jackie through the hedge, sunbathing in a stringy white bikini, turning herself every twenty minutes to get an even tan. So far there had been no sign of Francine.

Early each evening, Jackie's husband came home and wandered

around the garden, smoking a cigar and looking at the herbaceous borders. From what Lois could see of him through the hedge, he was a heavily-built man with a red face. She guessed his name was Keith because at six o'clock Jackie would shout, "Keith – dinner," from inside the house.

One afternoon, Lois made a Margarita and took it into the garden with a copy of The Carpetbaggers by Harold Robbins that she had found on the shelf in the back bedroom. The air was humid and the sound of buzzing insects mingled with the distant hum of an electric lawnmower. Lois lay face down in the middle of the lawn. At quarter to six, she woke with a jolt, realising she had fallen asleep on the corner of her book. Sitting up and rubbing the red triangle imprinted on her cheek, she saw Keith through the hedge, puffing on a panetella and staring at her with a slight smile. Lois glared, stood up stiffly and stalked into Strathmoore without looking back. A stealthy peek through the kitchen window, and she could see him still standing there, blowing smoke through his nose. With a smirk, he waggled his fingers at her and flicked his cigar butt into a clump of aubretia before wandering into Rexequus. Lois kicked the bin, sending the swing top into Rover's food bowl and scattering clumps of uneaten Winalot across the lino.

*

The following day, Lois put on her swimsuit under her clothes and went to the Lido, leaving Rover snuffling among the shady parts of the garden.

Like a stranded ocean liner, the Lido curved in a crisp white semi-circle around a small swimming pool, a stone's throw from the sea. A solitary attendant was mopping down the paving between the empty sunloungers and loudly whistling "Nessun Dorma". He wore a yellow sweatshirt with LIDO STAFF written across the back in red letters.

In her swimsuit, Lois stretched out on a sunlounger and opened The Carpetbaggers at the dog-eared page.

A young woman and a little girl arrived and started splashing around with an inflatable diplodocus. The attendant wandered around doing unnecessary jobs, then did them again, whistling continuously. Lois eased herself into the pool, swam a few lengths of breaststroke, then lay back on the water moving her arms slightly to keep afloat. The underwater sounds echoed in her ears. The sky had a purplish haze and the air was very still. After quarter of an hour, Lois pulled herself out and saw that somebody else had arrived. She was lying on a sunlounger in a metallic blue bikini, listening to a Walkman. Her face was lifted to the sun and her long blonde hair splayed around her shoulders. Eyes closed, she lay tapping one finger to a faint tinny beat. Lois stood dripping by the pool and stared. Francine remained lost in music. Back on her lounger, Lois tried to lose herself again in the world of Harold Robbins but every few minutes she found herself looking up to see what Francine was doing. At four o'clock Francine rose, walked to the pool's edge and stood staring into the rippling turquoise. The attendant stopped whistling but continued to stack green foam floats without looking up. Francine walked along the spring-board and dived, barely a splash breaking the water. Surfacing with a sharp flick of her head she swam up and down in a sharp front crawl. Then, in one smooth movement, she was out and sauntering back to her sunlounger leaving a neat trail of highly arched footprints. Lois sensed a frisson passing between Francine and the attendant.

By five o'clock only she and Francine were left. The attendant began folding up the empty sunloungers.

"Closing in five minutes," he said as he passed Lois.

"OK," said Lois but didn't move. She glanced over at Francine who still had her eyes closed and was lying with one arm trailing to the ground.

"CLOSING TIME," shouted the attendant, five minutes later.

Lois made her way into the changing room. Francine remained motionless.

The attendant followed Lois out to the gate of the Lido and locked it behind her. She could hear whistled strains of "The Star-Spangled Banner" as he walked away.

She walked back through tea-time smells wafting from the houses but, as usual, the streets were empty. Turning into Glyndebourne Avenue, she saw Jackie in the front garden of Rexequus. She slowed her pace, hoping Jackie would have gone inside by the time she reached Strathmoore but it became obvious that Jackie was waiting for her.

"Hello," said Jackie with a social smile, as Lois approached. She held a garden strimmer and seemed to be tidying the borders of the lawn.

"Hello," said Lois.

"How are you?" said Jackie with unconvincing bonhomie.

"Fine," said Lois. After a pause she added, "How are you?"

"I'm fine."

Lois noticed Jackie was wearing a black bra under her white sleeveless top. Jackie coughed delicately and then, taking a packet of Consulate from her back pocket and lighting one, lapsed into her usual off-hand mode.

"Would you like to come for dinner tomorrow? Supper, I mean?"

"OK," said Lois.

"OK. Eight o'clock then. Tomorrow. Super." The word "super" sounded odd, as if Jackie didn't usually use it.

"Thank you very much," said Lois, regaining control of normal etiquette, "I'll see you at eight."

Jackie nodded and turned on the strimmer.

*

Lois went to the Lido again the next day. As before, Francine padded in at three o'clock and lay sunbathing all afternoon, except for a few effortless lengths up and down the pool. From the controlled precision of her movements, Lois knew Francine was aware of being watched, although her smooth oval face remained calm and oblivious to everyone. When she padded silently to the side of the pool and executed her perfect dive, the other swimmers looked up and the sunbathers raised their eyes from their magazines. The attendant whistled "La Marseillaise" very loudly and wound up lengths of pool dividers with studied absorption.

As the sun began to dip over the sea, Lois gathered up her belongings and left. As before, Francine lay motionless, glowing gently in the evening sun.

*

"Gosh, don't you look smart," said Jackie, as she opened the front door of Rexequus. Lois suddenly felt ridiculous in Maggie's turquoise dress but took comfort in the fact that Jackie was equally overdressed in a black evening gown with a scattering of rhinestones across the breasts. A purple quartz pendant on a gold chain nestled in her tanned cleavage.

"Lois – meet Keith. Keith, this is Lois, Maggie's niece," said Jackie, leading Lois into the living room.

"I know," said Keith, who was sitting in an armchair swirling a glass of whisky. Jackie disappeared into the kitchen with a cigarette clenched between her lips.

"Drink?" said Keith, heaving himself up from the chair.

"A martini please," said Lois. Keith sloshed gin and vermouth into a martini glass and threw one olive into his mouth and one into the drink.

"Gorgeous, isn't she?" he said, nodding at the photographs of Francine and passing Lois a brimming glass. "Absolutely gorgeous... every man's dream."

Keith gazed at the photographs on the walls with a placid, drunken smile, then threw himself back into the armchair. Lois positioned herself on the arm of the sofa.

"Hello Daddy." They turned to find Francine in the doorway wearing a long silver dress.

"Baby!" cried Keith, "Come and give Daddy a kiss."

Francine sashayed over to her father as if on a catwalk. With the overstated poise of a bad actress she bent down and kissed him on the mouth then arranged herself primly on his left knee.

"And how's my little girl?"

"I'm fine," said Francine.

"Meet Lois," said Keith. Francine glanced briefly at Lois and said nothing.

Afterwards Lois wondered how she had managed to endure the evening. It had felt like an eternity of embarrassment. Jackie had sat in silence with a small preoccupied smile, as if she was watching the proceedings from a distance and was mildly amused. Occasionally she directed an irrelevant question towards Lois, the kind which only afforded a single word answer.

Throughout the meal Keith tried desperately to strike up conversation with Francine. She answered in monosyllables and slowly ate her food with a single fork. The way she spoke was strangely bland, like the voice-over to an advert for moisturising cream. Sometimes she smiled weakly at her father's doomed conversational gambits but mostly her face remained aloof as if her thoughts were elsewhere. For all the attention she paid to them, Lois and Jackie might as well have been sitting in a different room.

After picking vaguely with a teaspoon at her crême caramel, Francine suddenly stood up and announced she was going to bed.

"I'm very tired too," said Lois.

"Oh no," said Keith, sounding crestfallen and eyeing her through a cloud of cigar smoke.

"It's been very nice but I really must go." Lois stood up.

"I expect you need your beauty sleep, don't you?" said Jackie.

"I do," said Lois.

"Let me see you to the door." Keith followed her through the living room into the hall.

"Thank you very much for having me."

"It's been a pleasure. I hope to see you again soon." He held the front door open with exaggerated chivalry. Lois walked down the drive with her bank hunched and her mouth pursed. She felt nasty inside; a crawling sensation that made her clench her fists. A quick glance over her shoulder and she saw he was still standing in the doorway, silhouetted against the light with a glass of wine in one hand. He nodded slightly but did not close the door.

*

Lois woke up the next day to the rancid slobber of Rover's tongue. The night before she had sunk into an uneasy sleep, such as she had not had for months. She was relieved to find life seemed comfortably normal in daylight. In the kitchen the sun shone brightly through the Venetian blinds and she considered breakfast in the garden. A glimpse of Keith, through the hedge, wearing Bermuda shorts and holding a hosepipe made her abandon this idea.

The food supply was running low and, as instructed in Maggie's letter, she found the green foldaway shopping bike in the garage and cycled along the seafront towards the big shops at the Marina. Rover galloped along beside her, unusually vivacious, in the shadow of the bike.

Sunlight bouncing off the chalk cliffs and the white concrete path made everything seem flat and unreal. The tide had slipped out, revealing long stretches of purple-brown seaweed. A few solitary sunbathers lay on the patches of shingle among the seaweed and a man paced the beach with a metal detector. Further along, Lois passed a boatyard full of rusty cranes and empty conveyor belts, stopped mid-flow and conveying nothing. Coils of barbed wire lined the fence of the boatyard and black-boxed surveillance cameras stood at each corner.

Along the fence, in white spray paint, ran the words, "All life comes from the sea...All our rubbish goes back into it." Black spray painted letters retorted, "Fuck off you hippy".

Beyond the boatyard, the marina became a miniature mock-Miami waterfront. There were neat apartment blocks built on small jetties of tarmac with white motor yachts moored in between. The place was empty. Even the beer-garden of The Master Mariner was deserted.

In contrast, the shopping centre at the marina seethed with people. Kids shrieked and wiped snotty noses on their mothers' sleeves. Fat women with breasts and bellies straining against over-washed T-shirts waited for taxis, surrounded by bulging carrier bags. Girls in platform shoes with white streaky bacon legs smoked and paraded past shaven-headed boys. Lois walked through the automatic doors of Asda accompanied by her miniaturised image on a security screen.She pushed her trolley through the aisles, overhelmed by sheer choice. Her only shopping experience recently had been the occasional purchase of a ginster's cornish pasty at the village newsagent.

After loading up the bike's basket with groceries, she unleashed Rover from the bicycle racks and set off back along the cliff path, wobbling with the extra weight. She cycled slowly past the apartment blocks reading the names of the boats; Maybelline, Seaspray, Spanish Lady, Divina, Infinity... As she passed Infinity she ground to a halt at the sight of Francine.

Standing on the polished wooden deck, wearing a white dress was Francine. Her back was arched against the rail of the boat, her long hair trailed over the side and her teeth were bared in a glamour girl smile. She stood in this position for a long time, until her smile turned into a grimace. She relaxed for a split second and ran into the cabin. After a short while she reappeared and quickly struck another pose, leaning out to sea with her head turned back to the unseen photographer in the cabin. One thin dress strap fell off her shoulder.

Lois stood and watched Francine smiling, preening and pouting at the photographer. Between each pose she stopped and disappeared into the cabin. Sometimes she repeated actions over and over again – a coquettish turn which made her hair swing around her shoulders or a rolling-hipped swagger with her head thrown back in a silent ecstatic laugh.

Lois shifted along the path and peered into the boat. The cabin was empty, apart from a camera on a tripod pointing out to the deck. There was not photographer.

Francine, absorbed in the careful construction of her own image, looked up. For the first time her face lost its cool, blank gaze as she saw Lois looking down. Lois turned away and cycled on, following Rover who was far ahead, scampering wildly back to the village.

Rosie Rogers

Bound

Prologue

Not long before he left, I tore apart my Fisher Price television. I had to know how it worked. I had to know its innermost secrets. I knew this would be the death of it; that it would no longer play *row row row your boat gently down the stream* and that I would regret what I'd done. But in that moment I needed to open it up, expose its workings, understand its trickery. The illusion no longer convinced me. I was seven, too old for such toys. The once invisible mechanism which turned the picture around was a simple device. The image of a boy rowing merrily down the stream was revealed to be a series of pictures on a roll of thinly coated paper. I broke the bright yellow knob which worked the music box. An angry string of discordant notes railed from the plastic mess, in its final attempt at the trusted tune. Now that the televison was broken it was utterly useless to me. The pleasure of destroying it was too short-lived to compensate for its absence amongst my other toys. I immediately wanted it back. I could never go back to my life before the television was broken. I hated myself for what I had done to that toy.

Chapter one

My family and I lived in Ireland, in Dublin, in Firhouse. A Suburb. We were the only family on the Close which didn't have nets. Instead we had gaping squares that you could see right through. Which was dangerous because Mum liked to walk around in the nude. Our front garden was wild in comparison to the neighbours'. We had rough long grass, with daisies and poppies growing between the driveway and the lawn. We had a cat called Claws and one called Genevieve who had been in the family since Sandy was born. Which made her ninety eight in cat years. She had moved five times in all. This one to Ireland had been the last and, said Mum, the most traumatic. On the morning of her death, I came downstairs to the hushed loud whispers of my family all huddled around her stiff and vacant body.

"Don't come too close, Jose," warned my Dad.

"In fact, everyone out of here, I'll deal with this," and he rolled up his sleeves and pulled a plastic bag from under the sink. I stood rooted to my spot in the doorway, needing to see what death really looked like, yet terrified that it would give me nightmares forever after. And then mum in her brightly coloured kaftan whisked me and my brothers into the front room. Away from death. Genevieve's death coincided with the Pope's tour of Ireland, so we buried her in the back garden under a rose-bush and the Pope's white and gold flag. I wasn't as afraid of her death once she was buried. Claws tried to take Genevieve's place, but Claws was a new addition to the family. He had been given to us by some neigbours on the Close, his presence around the house made Genevieve's ghost all the more real. Claws did things Genevieve wouldn't dream of doing. Like pooing on my dad's record collection and in the airing cupboard. Once, Liam found one of Claws' surprises under Sandys bed. Sandy, who was in the bed at the time, said to him, inun early morning moan, "Just throw the bleeder out."

Liam diligently tracked Claws down and flung him from the top floor bedroom window. Claws tumbled out and flew past my Mum, who was standing at the kitchen sink at the time. She screamed. Sandy leapt out of bed. "Liam, you dork, I didn't mean *literally* throw him out the window." Claws landed on his feet and strolled off with his tail in the air. I think he knew he we didn't like him, but he didn't care, he wasn't looking for friends.

I was five when we moved to Ireland. Before that, we lived in a house called *Great Kettlem* in a place called Norfolk. The world was flat and wet and full of secrets that only I knew.

We had badger dens and strawberries and clear blue pools of water which me and my friend Tiffany would dip our feet into in the summer. At the bottom of our garden was a dyke that had tadpoles in it, and those furry brown cigars that grow high out of the water. And behind that was a field of cows that mooed at me every morning and all afternoon. I had a goat called Doris who I had to leave behind when we moved. I had lived in *Great Kettlem* since I was a little baby. We had monkey puzzle trees in the front garden and I even had my own sandpit. In our new house in Dublin I would dream of Norfolk and my cosy pink bedroom and wish that we could go back there.

Soon enough, I was saying things in that slightly startled throaty Dublin accent... *ah pleeeaze lemego trickortreetin'*. My brothers laughed at me, called me Dub. I liked the idea that I had a different way of speaking from the rest of my family. I wanted to be like everyone else in the neighbourhood. Have a normal Mum who had nice neat hair, who didn't make a fuss in public and say things like: *You've never heard of Earl Grey... oh dear.* Sandy was eight years older than me and Liam was six years older. My brothers were always and never there. They shared a bedroom and collected racing car cards. Sandy had a poster of the Police over his bed and Liam had Evil Kineval leaping over twenty one red double-deckers. They were always only on the edges of my world. I have no memory of me and Sandy ever playing together. Liam and me played together only sometimes, in extreme circumstances like if he was sick or very very bored. When Liam was at home because he had tonsilitis he reluctantly allowed me to play soldiers with him. I had to be the germans which meant I had no good warfare. So Laim spent the entire afternoon shooting matchsticks at my germans til I was down to one compared to his batallion of a hundred. *You need skill and strategy* he told me at the end of my defeat.

Dad decided we should move to Ireland because he wanted to make it big in the *Music Biz* and also because he wanted to *get back to his roots.* His Dad was from Naas. Grandpa Guinness we called him, because he always had a bottle of black stuff warming by the fire for. when he came in from work. Grandpa Guinness left Ireland when he was a little boy because of his brother Jack, who had ERA connections. Jack was a rebel fighter, my dad would tell us. Grandpa's mum had run away to England with her three sons, to escape the men that wanted to kill Jack. She came to London. She had red hair and a wooden leg. She lost her real one to a trolley bus by Lamertons in Ealing Broadway. I never met her but she lived on in Liam whose deep red hair was a wonder to us all. Grandpa was quiet and meek. He did paintings of landscapes. Nan would say *oh shutuppat* whenever he, spoke so I imagine he just thought it easier not saying much. My Dad called himself a Republican, he was passionate about Irish independence. He had a strange and steady look in his eye when he talked about the Troubles. There's a photograph in the family album: Sandy and Liam stood on either side of a big stone monument to the IRA. They wear matching check shirts and hold their head in the same pulled back, held high way. Little chests puffed up and hands flat against their sides, pointing to the ground. Their faces not smiling or sad. After Dad left Mum wrote on the back *do we have to join the IRA, dad*?

I made good friends in Firhouse. There was Aileen across the road who I liked but she smelt a bit of old wee. The twins next door, Monia and

Maureen, who were a bit weird because they were twins, and Barry on the other side who was sometimes my boyfriend. My best friend was Cathy who lived next door and was the twins' eldest sister. But actually she was adopted. She was older than me, and seemed more like a woman. She had long golden hair and a sad pointy face lavished with freckles. She was kind and funny and dangerous, like she had bigger fish to fry. We spent all our days outside, knocking on doors hoping to catch If someone before or after tea, or waiting to be knocked for. We played elaborate games of dare and risk, staged magnificent shows using sheets, dressing up clothes and equipment borrowed from the grown-up world. And on the days we were stumped for ideas we played *Chips* or *Charlie's Angels*. Once Cathy had the idea that we should go on a day-trip. Get together a gang of us on bikes and see how far we could go. The gang grew in size until on the day even my brothers and their friends were involved. Big racers, choppers and little bikes with stabilisers all pedalling furiously out beyond the boundaries of Firhouse. We went through -other neighbourhoods just like ours but flashier, with palm trees in the front lawns. Cathy and I. had a dangerous unsaid plan that we may not come back, ever. That we might join the gypsies and spend all day at the merry's instead of going to school. My supplies were two digestives, smuggled from the Jubilee Biscuit Tin behind my mum's back, wrapped up in a kitchen towel and placed into the back pocket of my Triumph Twenty.

When my Dad left it didn't come as a surprise to me. There was nothing to surprise me because I didn't see him go anywhere. He just wasn't around anymore, Now you see him, now you don't. Nobody appeared too concerned. His leaving was pieced together from a collection of things I'd heard and imagined. I think if I'd have known he was going I might have been able to stop him. I was seven and a half He sent a letter to me, full of news. It spoke of weather, migrating geese, dogs and farm labour. *Darling Josie*, it went. I had known that eventually he would have to go. I was ready for that: Men go away. Maybe they come back, maybe they don't. They break your heart. His letter smoothed over my questions and uncertain feelings. He printed his writing so that I could read it easily. It was balanced and bright, Kerry was beautiful, a litter of pups was born to Lily. He dug turf all day with Paddy, my Godfather. It was hard work. The little people played their usual mischievous tricks. His letter wanted me to understand he had to do this for the sake of everyone. I think he wanted me to understand things from his point of view. So I did, even though my head was full of cloud and questions I couldn't ask. I said to him it's *okay daddy I understand*. Even though I wanted to ask him why he left without saying goodbye. I wanted him to know that I could be whatever he wanted me to be. That I was waiting patiently for him to return. I imagined him, a cowboy doing his stint in the wilderness. Being brave, being cruel and mean but kind, like Clint Eastwood, He knew his little princess would understand, he could always count on me. At the end of the letter he said, be a good girl for your mother and signed it D with a kiss.

"Why has he gone away?" I remember asking my Mum.

"Because he wants to write a book," was one of the reasons she gave.

"When is he coming home?"'

"When his book is finished."

That day, the day his letter came, I said I couldn't go to school, I felt too sick. Mum believed me and instead of school we went to Greystones and I played in the sea and tossed big pieces of sea-weed in the air.

Nobody ever said the words,, "Dad has gone". As though saying it for sure would make it true and not maybe just a bad dream. He had vanished, could no longer be heard rustling his newspaper between coughs which said, *Ahem, I am the Man of the house*. He was no longer there on the edge of my vision, rolling bogeys over *his* ashtray by *his* armchair which mum told him off for with a flick of *her* tea-towel. The bathroom was no longer dominated by tobacco, cricket commentary and the hour warm toilet seat. At night he never appeared as a silhouette in the doorway, caught through the chink of my eye-lids. Everyone took up a place in this headless family, smoothly, as if they had been rehearsing his departure for years. Sandy and Liam pooled Action man skills in an attempt to make up for his lack. They helped with all the organising, lifting, fetching and ferrying involved in the big move from Ireland back to England. They too had each received a letter from him. Couched less in protective sentiment, addressed in joint up writing. Sandy, my eldest brother was at thirteen to become the Man of the house, was trusted to *take care of your mother*, to oversee the smooth running of the move, to take up from where Dad left off. He was told to keep up with his guitar lessons and to look forward to sharing a pint with his old man soon. Liam,was to keep up with his Rugby, be a good son and brother, and above all else to work hard. There was no apology or acknowledgement, nor even a hint of why this was happening. Just a list of instructions and a D for Distant at the end of each letter.

Mum had been visiting the Nuns more frequently in the months before Dad left. Now that he had gone she was visiting Sister Theresa every day. Mum and Sister Theresa shared the same age of forty, were both Librans, and although Sister Theresa didn't believe in such things, Mum considered them to have shared past lives. The order of Nuns was Cannelite, which, (most significantly to me), meant they couldn't go out and were kept behind bars all day. My mum and I would sit in the room which was for visitors only and wait for the Nuns to appear behind the cold white bars. Everything took forever, the waiting in the room, the waiting whilst Sister Theresa talked in whispers with my Mum, offering her guidance, giving her blessings. Waiting whilst a whole Rosary was prayed upon together and then waiting to see if one of the nuns would pass a Wagon Wheel through the bars like they had once before. I was bored beyond belief, staring at the same old picture of Our Lady levitating above a collection of clouds and seraphims. Wondering if it was true that the Nuns were all bald, wondering if they ever sneaked out for midnight feasts or trips to the cinema.

"Don't they ever go out, Mummy?"

"No, never", she said, snapping shut with the fact.

"So how do they get their shopping?" Delighted to keep it up.

"They get it delivered once a week," she said with a sigh.

Fair enough, I thought. Yet it still didn't sit happy in me. They must be so sad and bored. I felt sorry for them.

"But *why* do they *have* to be behind bars?"

"They don't *have* to, it's a choice they make, to show their devotion to God," she said, happy to strike upon a spiritual note.

This explanation was completely ridiculous, it didn't mean anything at all. There was so much going on out here in the real world. Did God who made all things bright and beautiful really want us to sit in a cold stone building for the rest of our lives? *Behind bars? With no going to the movies or ice~cream or seaside.*

My mum would end these kind of conversations with,

'I wanted to be a Nun once,"

and then a twist of the knife into the wound *he'd* dealt her.,
"But I married your father instead."

Soon we would have to go back to England. Mum had to be with
her own family, she needed her own mother and the sound advice of
her father. Her marriage had failed. The daughter they had lost to the
teddy boy across the road was coming home. Without the strong and
capable steering of a man, our family ship was headed for disaster.
Mum said that men were the providers. "What am I to do, I haven't
worked for fifteen years," she would wail. She complained because
feminism had by-passed her, her hair was too curly to be a hippy, and
she was too busy playing wife and mother for free-love or bra-burning.
Besides she was a fifties bird. She liked being at home, she liked not
having to work.that was why she got married in the first place, so she
could have babies and bake bread. I heard her saying to Sister Theresa
one day,

"He was a teddy boy when I married him, then he was into the
Beatles, next thing is the Sex Pistols and now he's drinking with the
Dubliners in some Shebeen in Ballinskelligs.

Meanwhile his wife and children have been cast adrift because *he
now* fancies himself as the next William Butler Yeats. Pillock."

Sister Theresa always said the same sort of thing,

"Now my child, pray to god for guidance he will show you the way."

I did a lot of praying with my mum. After we had made the beds
together in the morning, folding the corners under neat and tight, like
she had done when she was a nurse, we would kneel beside each other
and pray with our elbows on the smoothed bedspread. We would do
the rosary together. My beads were small pink plastic rose-buds and
hers were heavy and shiny black, they clacked loud between her hands.
After what seemed like a lifetime of hail-mary's we'd have a little chat.
She'd remind me of how she had sung in a skiffle band, that Dick
Green was the man she should have married, and that in her youth she
was known as the Liz Taylor of West London.

I began to learn a lot about my parents marriage. About the affairs
he had, (Sue Oakes was the main *other woman*), the bad things he had
done and the story of how they had fallen in love as teenagers. When
they got married it had all seemed so perfect. Dad was climbing the
ladder as an exec. The houses kept getting bigger. Then punk came

along and he decided to *jack it all in*. Dad's plans to set up his own record label didn't work. The *Noise Unlimited* headed paper and cards were still piled up in the spare room, used only for drawing paper and playing offices. Mum said that Dad had been drinking too much and was under the bad influence of Jim O'Rourke. *Thick as thieves, those two*. Jimbo was a DJ, he was at my Holy communion' giving out signed photographs to anyone who stood still long enough. But my friends thought he was weird because they'd never even heard of him before. Jimbo was as thin as a pipe-cleaner, had a ginger afro and wore dark velvet suits with a matching waistcoat and a frilly shirt. He always stood with his back arched as though about to do the limbo, his snake hips jutting out at right angles. He had a voice which sounded like he had too many Rich Teas with nothing to wash them down. As though speaking was an uncool thing to do. He ended everything he said with *maaan*. And he smoked like a chimney. I didn't like him. Not since the time he had got me into trouble.

He came round the house one Saturday morning. Me and Dad were in the kitchen making egg and chips. When my dad made chips it was a big deal, he had to get them just right, not to fat nor too thin, and it was the same with the eggs, not too hard nor too soft.

"Hey Jimbo."

"Playing the family man dismornin' Mart".

"Yeah could say that, Jim... how's business?"

"Good man, real goooooood, and you?"

"Hot and cold but never warm Jim, ah y'know. Hey Fancy a spot of brunch? Join me and Josie here."

''Ah no Mart, gotta keep trim, I'll have a cuppa thou, milk tree shoogs ta"

Jimbo sat down next to me at the kitchen table,

"Hey kid give us five."

I met his hand with mine,though it felt like a dried up leaf.

"Got a band you might want to hear, Jimbo,"said Dad.

"Oh yeah, bang um on den, no rest for the wicked, no time like da present, hey kid." This Jimbo directs at me with a wink of his ginger-lashed eye.

"Yeah, Babs and I saw them last week at the Castle, tell me what you think."

The tape player churned out a punk band called the Subhumans.

"From Limerick," shouts Dad over the noise. The rash of sound destroyed the rare lovely feeling of my Dad in the kitchen; clattering amongst drawers and cupboards asking me where everything was kept. Jimbo and my Dad were deep in thought, tapping spoons, bouncing ankles to the music. Eventually Dad presented me with the egg and chips. Jimbo had his full attention now. I slowly ate through the chips, dipping them into the glossy yolks. I was very full up, thinking I couldn't eat another chip and yet my plate seemed untouched. I was afraid because with my Dad around you always had to *watch the elbows, eat it all up, knife and fork together when finished and please may you leave.* Slowly I started to throw the chips under the table. Gradually the willow pattern. on my plate came through. Jimbo was sat opposite me, the sun lighting up his ginger afro like a halo.

"I've finished," I said to my Dad.

"I don't think she has, Mart", said Jimbo.

My heart sunk.

"Under the table, Mart." His eyes flicking from my Dad's to mine to the evidence of my deceit. My Dad was silent, he gave me a look which always destroyed me, a look of total disappointment. "Get the dustpan and brush, Jodie, clean it up and then go to your room."

"But Dad"

"Just do it, Jodie".

So when Dad went, Jimbo went too, and like Mum said, *What you gain on the swings you loose on the roundabouts.* Mum got a lot of headaches with the auction that went wrong and the removal men and the bills that needed paying. She wore her dark glasses a lot and had a lot of tissues to get through with the blowing of her nose and the crying she was doing all day. She said that Sandy was a treasure to her and that she wouldn't know what to do without him and she kept squeezing me hard a lot and saying things like, *Whatever happens the good Lord will see us through.* The day came when we had to leave Firhouse and head back to England. I was so excited that it felt to me like Christmas eve I dreamt of Buckingham Palace and red double deckers and having my pink bedroom back again. I said goodbye to all my friends on the Close and I didn't mind because I thought I'd come back and see them all the time anyway. Cathy said that she would write to me in London and that she would plot to come and live with me one day. She said that really we were sisters and that we had to stay in touch no matter what. She had big tears in her eyes as she stood at her front door. I didn't feel that way though because I was the one going away and it was too exciting to be sad. Sandy put Claws in Genevieve's cat basket and took him off to the convent. He came back swinging the basket high in the air and catching it as he walked.

'The nuns were delighted to have Claws, though they wanted to change his name to Barnaby for some reason," he shouted to Mum upstairs.

"Poor nuns, after all they've done for us all we can offer them is a cat that's going to reek havoc and poo all over their pristine convent,"said Mum as she came down the steps with a jungle of pot plants.

Liam, Sandy and me thought this was hilarious. Liam put a T-shirt on his head and did an impression of Sister Theresa, stroking the head off Claws.

"Oooh what a lovely new pet, those Convey's are so kind to think of us, aren't they, sisters?"

Then Sandy joined in and did his best buck toothed face,

"Yes sister, ooooh what fun we shall have, will I get a ball of wool for the dote?"

"Do sister, oh yes do sister," I said cross-eyed.

Then to top it, Liam came up with another boggle-eyed, buck toothed face,

"Um Sister I was dusting father O'Leary's confession box earlier and I came across a little mess which I thought leaked from the rear passage of the new cat we've been given"

We all burst out laughing.

"Liam, stop that," said mum trying to keep a straight face.

As we were leaving Firhouse all packed into the silver volkswagon, Syd the dog who was Liam's best friend was up on his back legs licking Liam's face and trying to get into the back scat with him. Liam had rescued Syd from the gypsies who had beaten him and starved him.

He was a nuisance because he did naughty things, like the time he just came out of the kitchen with the whole Sunday roast between his jaws. But Liam loved him and they were always together and Syd did have a sweet pleading face that you couldn't help but feel for.

"Please lets bring him, mum."

'No Liam we cannot and that's final.'

Mum started up the engine, "We'll get you another dog in London, once we're settled."

Liam was crying now and Syd was whining,

"I 'm sorry Syd," Liam blubbered out the window.

We moved off out of the driveway and Mum tooted to everyone that had come out to wave us goodbye. Syd followed us all the way out of the Close and down the main road. Liam was balling his eyes out and waving to Syd out the back window. Syd just kept on running and yapping and looking like his heart was breaking in two and his big pitiful eyes couldn't believe what they were seeing and Liam was looking exactly the same. Eventually we turned a corner and Syd didn't come back into view and we, knew that we would never see him again. And I felt so sorry for Liam that I offered him all my red opal fruits to cheer him up but he refused them.

That night we stayed in a hotel called the Sheraton that Mum said was very posh. "Top notch," said Sandy. It felt like we were on holiday. I even had a bunk-bed to myself In the morning we had breakfast that a maid brought to the room on a trolley. All the food was hidden under big silvery domes that showed up your faces in them, where normally there would have been the Queen or someone like that. We left the hotel without paying. Mum just held her head high, saying *Come along darlings* in her jolly voice and smiling warmly to the doorman with the top hat who held the door open for her. We followed behind, praying that we wouldn't be caught. Once in the car we were giggling and buzzing with the thrill of what we'd got away with. As we came near to the sea Mum suddenly let out an,

"Oh my God."

"What Mum, what is it," said Liam.

"Don't tell us, you've left something behind," said Sandy.

"Our Lady of Walsingham, she's still on the bed side table in the hotel."

"Oh Mum," we all groaned. Mum always, whenever we went away, left something behind and Dad would always have to turn the car around and collect whatever she'd forgotten.

She swerved the car round in the middle of the road,

"We'll miss the ferry now," said Sandy.

"And we' I'L go to Jail," said Liam.

This was too much for me so I started to cry.

"Don't be ridiculous. Now Sandy, I've still got the key to the room, just flash up there, grab

Our Lady and if anyone asks just say you're on an errand for your mother."

We drove back to the hotel and Sandy went right past that same doorman. We waited in the car fully expecting to see Sandy being carried out of the hotel by two big policemen. He came out, with the little statue held like a trophy above, his head.

"Thank the good Lord," sighed Mum.

We made it to the ferry just in time and Mum said that it was thanks to Our Lady of Walsingham, who was now stuck on the dashboard for safe-keeping.

Chapter two

Two years later and he is walking into the tearoom in Bentalls. Hair dark and wild, he's wearing his Aran jumper and those big old wellies that are mud caked and properly a part of him now. He stands there, awkward, beside a trolley of cakes with doiley trimmings. He is back home. I know that I will never let him go again, that I will do all in my power to keep him.

"Daddy... Daddy..."

The words stand up brittle and hot in my throat. I run to him like I have been held captive by my Mum, by department stores and tea and scones. He lifts me up, hugs me.

'My little pigeon," he says.

I feel myself being woken from a dream with his voice, becoming the Josie I was before.

"Haven't you grown?"

I didn't want to grow, to change, to become something I wasn't before he left.

"But still my little bird".

And I am comforted. Glow in the glory of belonging to him. I fling my arms around his neck. He smells of the sea, of earth, of distance. I see Mum dab away a mascared tear from behind her sunglasses. I nestle on his chest, marvel at the rise and fall of the breath I had tried to forget. Hear him speak without knowing what he says. I concentrate on willing Mum to stop her tears, they threaten him, could make him leave again. He is volatile like a wild animal. He knows I understand this. His eyes are far away, he is hedged in by this small female world, he belongs out there with fields and ocean.

He has the soup of the day, mushroom, with triangles of bread and butter that droop between his newly hardened thumb and forefinger. I wonder what to say, what words will possess enough magic to make him stay and never want to go away again. We sit there, a pretend family, my mother smoking Silk Cut, him Benson and Hedges. Like they always did. The brands they smoked were who they once were : Mum was purple and she had a pale yellow ashtray, Dad was golden brown and he had a deep red ashtray, same heavy bubble glass design but different colours, Each ashtray was beside their velvet armchairs, hers pink his brown. I think how normal they appear, how easy it would be for them to go back to the way it was. He looks at his watch and suddenly he has to go. My stomach drops like I'm in an elevator and I curl inside. I expect it now. Know that he leaves, that is what he has to do. I am powerless, I cannot keep him, no matter how hard I try.

"Oh Daddy, can't you stay, please," I am whining, making it harder for him.

"Afraid not, sweetheart." Reasonable and light, his words fix me, a knot ties up my throat.

"Come and stay for the weekend, we can go and see the dinosaurs and the steam engines in the museums, we can get the tube, would you like that?"

"Yes," I say, through a sulk, "Where do you live then?"

"Oh in a very lovely place right next to all the museums, you'll see. Now give your old Dad a kiss goodbye and promise to be a good girl." His sea-stiffened hair turns the corner into haberdashery and I watch him vanish behind rolls of gingham material. He has gone again. I am back in the small red velvet seat next to my mum.

"Mum where does Daddy live now?"

My Mum says flippantly, happily, like its as natural as the curl in her hair, "With some new woman or other let's choose a cake each, we deserve it."

We moved to a half-way house on the Western Avenue. The house was sandwiched between the Western Avenue to the front and a graveyard to the back. The summer was spent in this limbo land, waiting for the full house to come from the council. A man came to inspect the house after Mum has complained of the noise, the lack of furniture and the rats, in the back garden. He looked at the camphor chest, engraved and ornate and the Bhudda lamp with his wise chuckle, holding aloft a plush red shade.

"Mrs Convey, you can't be that badly off with furniture like this."

"These, young man, are family heirlooms from India are all I have left after fifteen
years of marriage".
"I bet they'd fetch a few bob though."
"Sell them? "I was *born* in India, you know."
"Well, I'm sorry, Mrs Convey, but this is a half way house, temporary housing is just that.
When your permanent house comes through you can apply for a grant to get the necessities."

I went to sleep with the traffic humming in the window panes, headlights combing the room, searching me out. We had no nets and no curtains now. But what really set us apart was the lack of double-glazing. Everyone had to have double glazing because of the roaring of the traffic. But not us. My fear of banshees had gone, and the monsters I used to see dancing on my bedroom wall at night went too. I was grown up enough to know it was just the shadow of the tree in the wind. I no longer feared the dark because it was never true darkness on the Western Avenue, never enough to make you see things that were really frightening. When the traffic died down to the stray small hour cars, the orange street light continued to glow outside my window. I dreamt of lamp-posts marching along, and sirens and cars and horns filling the air. And when I woke up it didn't seem any different and I was shocked because at first I didn't know where I was, and then I remembered. He had left. My mum painted the gate, the front door and the fence a bright glossy yellow. Buttercup yellow, says the tin. Where she had painted was jagged all around the edges when 'you were up close. The house looks like it was putting on a brave face, considering. I never saw the rats, only heard Mum moan about her lot in life, and how the rats were the final straw. When the exterminators were called I was terrified, what would they look like? Darth Vadar, I imagined. He'd have some stormtroopers for back-up and he'd kill the rats with his light sabre. On the day I was disappointed by the small balding man who pulled up in his council van. When he laid poison down in the garden I heard him saying to my Mum.
"Now Mrs. Convey, don't let your children eat the poison."
She laughed merrily, "I shall try not to, dear."

That summer was long and hot. The garden was scorched and bald and the air slumped with exhaust fumes and week-old rubbish. Me and my sometimes best friend, Mandy, sung songs and danced on the old kitchen table in the back garden. After we'd spent an entire day practising our moves we would line up chairs and charge whoever 10 pence to watch the show. It begun with us doing a frenzied rendition of *Shuttupppa' your face* and then Bucks Fizz's, *You gotta speed it up*. And it always ended with me and Mandy telling jokes that had no punch line, or did but we'd forgotten it in the excitement of getting to it. Or singing songs which were made up on the spot because we had ran out of ones we knew. The show went on for too long, trying the patience of the audience, which in truth only ever consisted of mine and Mandy's mum, but felt to us like a filled to capacity Carnegie Hall. It invariably ended in *a scene*, squabbling over whose turn it was next, or one of our Mums insisting that we stop and get down off the table, *Immediately*. It was nearly dark and I would be turning cartwheels, high with adrenalin. Being indoors, bathing and getting ready for bed seemed so small and irrelevant in the light of our imminent world fame. Such stupid rules surrounded me, it was easy to see through Mum's ways. Easy to break rules and *give her lip*, as she said. I would never say things I said to mum, to my dad, no way. Without my Dad around she had no power. Like she was a phoney mum, still trying to sound like the real thing but just not quite right because she had no Dad there to back her up. I soared with the freedom of this new life but I would have gladly swopped it for my old one.

Sandy hadn't been going to school, he'd put on his uniform and go out the back door as if walking towards the station, then he'd fall away from me and Liam and head off in his own direction. He'd take off his tie and put it in his pocket, then he'd undo his shirt and pull out a cigarette from inside his blazer. And he'd saunter off, exaggerating his disappointment with the world, puffing smoke rings and occasionally flicking his flop of dark hair to gauge his position on the pavement. I thought Sandy was weird. He was deeply absorbed by everything I found boring. Girlfriends, music, fags. I wondered what the fascination was, when sweets and toys and games were so much more fun. When the summer holidays came he spent the best part of the day in bed. Around midday the strumming of chords would fill his room, and he would *surface* as my mum put it. Occasionally he would brush past me on the landing, huffing around my glitter and glue creations, barely even opening his eyes.

Mandy had said to me one day, "I've got a secret."

"What?" I said, feigning disinterest.

"Swear on your Mother's life you won't tell."

"I Swear," I said dismissively.

Then judging Mandy's look, added

passionately, "Cross-my-heart-hope-to-die-stick-a-needle-in-my-eye."

This was enough for Mandy.

"Your brother plays tennis with my Mum when he bunks off."

My initial thought was *so what*, but then I saw that playing tennis in this instance was a very grave thing to do with Mandy's mum.

"My Dad would kill your brother if he knew".

I thought about this. I didn't like my brother that much, but I liked Mandy's Dad even less. He was called Owain which I thought was a stupid name. He was big and Welsh, wore a donkey jacket and always had a Lurcher called Spear by his side. He had long grey hair, a huge nose and small mean eyes. His voice boomed insults, remarks and sneers. Spear had huge balls which he'd lick openly in public, and Owain would revel in this. I pitied Mandy having such a horrible father. *Vulgar*, my mother called him.

`Vulgar and crude but a big softie really, our Owain," she'd say.

I didn't want Owain to have a vendetta against my brother. I was willing to be loyal to Sandy, stick up for him in the face of this death threat. I was in a position of power. I had important information and if Sandy was willing to comply with my requests, in exchange, I would offer him a warning of the danger he was in.

I confronted him as he was coming out of the bathroom. Probably he'd been squeezing his blackheads.

"Hello Sandy I've got something you might like to know," I stood in the doorway, tossing the orange light cord back and forth.

"I doubt it," he said, all moody, as usual.

"You wouldn't say that if you knew what I knew."

"Oh what, hurry up I'm going out."

"Ooh -anyone for tennis?" I mimicked, flinging the light cord into the air.

"What are you talking about now?"

"I know where you go when you bunk off."

"Really. Very interesting."

"Yes it is, especially when Owain is going to kill you if he finds out."

"Finds out what exactly?"

"That you play tennis with Janice."

"I see. So playing tennis is illegal, now, is it?"

"No but" Now I was stumped. I hadn't expected it to go like this. I was going to blackmail him and he was going to give me money to stop Mandy and me from splitting on him. The tennis he played with Mandy's mum was wrong, but I didn't know why. He knew I knew this but he also knew I couldn't say it.

Owain knows I play tennis with Janice. Encourages it, in fact," he said as if to settle any confusion for me.

"Well you truant and I'm going to tell mum," was all I could come up with. I knew it was feeble.

"Go on then". And he rolled his eyes at the insignificance of me, his baby sister, and turned his back in disgust, as though this short exchange had already impinged too much on his life.

Chapter three

Christmas was on its way and we were still living in the half-way house. The rats had been exterminated but the main problem was the cold. We had been given some money from the council to buy a cooker, some heaters and some furniture. Mum said that we were living like, gypsies, on hand outs and charity. She would bemoan all her lovely antique furniture she had sold for a song at the auction in Dublin and her anger towards Dad would grow in detail and hue. The injustice of what he had done to her became more articulate and honed with the realisation that he wasn't coming back and that we were not going to be saved. He was, *swanning around with all the druggies and liggers he calls friends whilst his family are here in this rat-infested pit, shivering with the cold and the damp.* Dad, who left us when my mum was fat and forty, *to cavort around like Peter Pan.*

Although Mum had shook her fist at God, *he must be a man as a woman wouldn't be so cruel,* our luck turned for Christmas. MY Mum's friend Lou had a friend who was in need of a house-sitter. Lou wanted to help in anyway she could, she told her friend about my Mum's unfortunate demise. The woman, called Sue was pleased to let my

Mum and us live in her house for three weeks. All we had to do was water her plants and feed the cats. It was a Victorian house on a tree-lined street in Brentford. Sue was going with her two sons to Thailand. The house was lovely, big, cosy. All patchwork and real fires. Three whole weeks away from the Western Avenue. As if to complete my new found heaven, my Dad came to stay for Christmas. We could be a happy family again. I was ecstatic. If only Liam weren't such a beast, so wanting to ruin it all. He said he didn't want to be under the same roof as Dad, that he would run away from home if he came to stay.

"I hate him", he said to mum.

"Whatever he's done he's your father, Liam".

I hated *him* for making such threats. How could he hate Dad so much? Didn't he see all the good things about him? In the end Dad did come and Liam's protest was kept to long silences.

That was the Christmas John Lennon died. I can remember the shock on Mum's and Dad's faces as the news flashed onto the telly and then the silence that fell across the room. Like a member of our family had died. Liam was ambivalent and cool. But Sandy was shocked, he sat staring at the screen with his jaw hung in disbelief Still nobody spoke and the silence thrilled me. I was sitting on the floor watching my parents and brothers for signs, an indication of what this meant. I knew John Lennon was a Beatle but the one I liked was Paul McCartney and he was still alive so I didn't much care. Eventually words began to hit the air, like pellets. A Genius. A legend. Some psycho. Poor Yoko.

"A working class hero is something to be", mused my Dad.

'I'll light a candle", said Mum.

For the first time in my life I saw tears slide into my Dad's eyes and a couple of drops roll down his cheek. I was allowed to stay up late that night, *because it's not every day John Lennon dies.* My Dad found a copy of *Sargent Pepper* amongst the record collection that belonged to the house. We all listened to the lyrics, joined in with the choruses. Even Liam had warmed up a little, began to laugh at my Dad's tuneless notes. *Sargent Pepper* came out the year that Sandy was born. It was Sandy's album. Mine was *Ziggy Stardust* and Liam's was *Waiting for the Sun* by the *Doors.* When Sandy was a little baby he had been played the album by my Dad. *That's where he gets his talent for music.* I stayed up watching and listening to my mum and dad talking about the Beatles, about each other. About when they first saw them in a club in

Shepherds Bush. Later on Sandy got his guitar out and we sung more Beatles songs. When he strummed the chords of Lady Madonna, mum sang it with all her heart.

"You always had a good voice, Babs" said my Dad.

He was skinning up on the back of the *Sargent Pepper* album. Empty wine glasses sat on the coffee table. If this is what death was all about I wanted it to happen more often so that my Mum and Dad could be happy like this forever.

Father Christmas, even though I didn't really believe in him, found his way to the borrowed room that I slept in that Christmas eve. He brought me just want I wanted. What I had wanted for every Christmas since I was six and now I was eight. Three whole years waiting for a *Girls World*. The last Christmas Santa, second to God in his perfection, got it wrong. He had brought me a *Girls World fashion wheel*, which is so obviously inferior to the real *Girls World*. Christmas morning came and I shot to the end of my bed like a paratrooper. The box was there. It was so big that I knew what it had to be. I knew that this time he'd got it right. Liam and Sandy came into my room, laughing at me as I frantically tore off the layers of paper. Finally I held aloft the beautiful Blonde head as though a trophy had been presented to me. All day long I pulled and wound back up the golden tress of hair which poured from the crown of her head. I painted her eyes blue and her lips pink, rubbed it carefully off and started the routine all over again. I curled, brushed and plaited her hair and was mesmerised by how beautiful and perfect she really was. On Boxing day Dad took me to see Flash Gordon at the cinema. The best bit for me was nothing to do with the film but the bus ride there and back. It was the everydayness of him being there, sat next to me at the front of the top deck. Like he was always there. Like he had never left us. Like he was still my dad and I was still his daughter and we did these ordinary things together all the time. Like every other family in the world must do. But he was leaving again all too quickly, and soon the wonderland of pretending we were a family in a cosy well-stocked home was blown apart. His tan leather holdall stood by the door. All the equipment of his life, his toothbrush and razor and aftershave had remained in his wash-bag, ready for his next exit. I wondered how long it would be till my Mum and Dad decided to live together again. It never occurred to me that this new life was permanent.

My memory is like a reel of worn and tattered film, jumping and blacking out, scorches disrupting its surface. My mother is screaming, crying, raging abuse at my Nana, my Dad's Mum. My mum is walking around Nana's house pulling pictures of me and Liam and Sandy off the wall, leaving big white blank squares. *You will not see your grandchildren ever again do you understand ever again you twisted old cow.* She spits with these words. Nana is hushed into a stage whisper *get out of this house you evil woman. Get out of this house.* I have never seen my Nana look like this, she is crossing herself with each swear word that hits her ears. She is shocked and I am embarrassed by the bad language my mum is using.

"Always there for your precious little son, blind. to the hell he's put us through. You old Bitch."

"Don't say that, Mum."

My Nana looks at me. "Don't worry dear," she says.

I love my Nana, don't want to never see her again. Mum takes me by the hand and I feel myself to be light and afraid.

Jump-cut.

I have a plastic shopping bag, there are two books inside and my mother says that I will have to leave them in the road because we cannot carry them all day.

"Come on let's go to Dayville's for an ice~cream. We deserve a treat after all that commotion."

I don't.want to leave my books which are full of amazing facts and information and beautiful drawings which I had plans to copy and paint.

Jump-cut.

It is warm and lovely and there is blossom on the pavement. My mother says to me that my Dad has a new girlfriend and that her name is Mary. And that is why she is a little upset, she dabs away tears with her lacy hanky. I cry too because I cannot think of anything worse than Mum being so upset. And I hug her and say don't worry and she smells lovely. Of clean curly hair and Anais Anias. My heart is heavy and beating fast, because how can my daddy have another girlfriend? How can he love anyone else? I need him so much and I am licking my mint-choc-chip slowly into a point. The taste mingles with My spit and swallowed tears and it is hard to like ice-cream when I feel so full of gulped back sadness.

When I meet my Dad at the weekend he says that he wants me to meet a very good friend of his, that he is sure we will get on famously. I know he means Mary. He says, *The two main women in my life.* And I think what about Mum? But I don't say anything. Mary is beautiful she has long dark curly hair and she is young, much younger than Mum. She has a beautiful smile and she wears really trendy clothes, Pink stripey peddle-pushers and a denim jacket and gorgeous pink shoes like the ones I've seen in the shops. When she laughs it's really loud and hard. She laughs a lot. At things my Dad says, and he laughs at things she says. She calls him Mart and he calls her Mare. When Mary crosses the road she does it before the green man appears and he says *good old Mare, more streetwise than the average Londoner.* She lives in the centre of London where it's all red buses and black taxis, in a big flat with high ceilings and two balconies. There is a garden which Mary has the key to and which all the grand houses back onto. Mary opens a special gate so that I can go and play in there, and I sit in the garden and make a daisy chain and I wave up at Mary and my Dad and they wave down at me. I feel like a goldfish in a bowl. We go shopping together for dinner. We get three steaks from a butcher shop. My Dad shows me how to do the steak. He washes it under the tap and blood swirls around the plug-hole.

"It's disgusting," I say

"Don't be silly." he says.

I feel upset because he thinks I'm silly now. He pounds the steak with a wooden mallet. And I think he is angry with me. Mary is busy with the vegetables. That is how it was before he left, Mum did the vegetables and Dad did the meat. I lay the table with Mary helping me, and we sit down in the front room to cat. I don't want to eat my steak even though Dad says my one is well done. I feel queasy and afraid of disappointing him. Mary winks at me and takes my plate away whilst he's in the kitchen fetching more wine. Mary and my Dad smoke joints together and they laugh a lot. I wonder what to do with myself, wish now that I was back at home with my mum. I play with my rubicks cube, pretend that I know exactly what I'm doing. I feel bad being with them when I know my Mum is so miserable. I put the cube away, it's boring. Mary lets me play with her set of scales and the little brass weights that nestle in a black velvet case. I find different things to weigh, a sugar cube, a box of matches. I am so bored with it after a while that I say I feel tired and want to go to sleep, even though I'm not.

They make up a bed for me on the settee. I get into my pyjamas and go to brush my teeth in the bathroom, I see that my Dad has placed all his things around the sink and on the shelves. His shaving brush which I haven't seen since Ireland sits happily in the dip of the sink, and his tin of badges which I used to play with, is now placed on the shelf above the bath. The duvet smells strange and different. I close my eyes but am miles away from sleep. Everything smells crumbly and old. I see things on the ceiling and hear noises creak around the building. Mary and my Dad are laughing and playing music in her bedroom their happiness slips under the door and through the walls, it hits me like a hard whack in my chest. I hear the wind moaning down the chimney. I imagine the Banshee has come, that she is sitting on the roof because someone has died. I want to go and see my Dad, tell him I'm afraid but I know I cannot, that his arms are around Mary's now and that he wouldn't want to be bothered by me.

Dan Hill

Buzzer, Click, Panic

"Why don't you come and see me," said my mum's boyfriend, his voice nasty and throatish. " Tomorrow morning, for example."

I was leaving the kitchen, a little thief in the cathedral of the domestic, armed with tea and a pile of cinnamon toast. My mum and her boyfriend were on their way in from the pub. I was defenceless because I had no military training and I only had one shoe on. Also, I could not talk properly because of the long dead roll-up, hanging from my lips.

"Here," he said, taking a fat flashy pen from his inside pocket. He scribbled on a card. "336a Victory Tower. You know where that is?"

I nodded and took the card with an available finger. It was a cheapo business card advertising a second hand computer business. On the back, in Malc's hasty scrawl, was the address.

"Any time between ten and one. See you," he said as I sloped off. "Night," I heard my mum call out as I was at the top of the stairs.

All I had for noise in my room was a radio because my sister had stolen my stereo. It was playing a local station phone-in programme, which I listened to when I was lonely. My sister had taken my stereo when I was out claiming I owed her 1,650 quid. My room had a snooker table, big desk and a tv which I watched a lot even though I felt a certain guilt about watching it all the time. My jaw hurt and I wondered if someone had smacked me in the mouth at the party I'd been to two days ago when I woke up with no memories and my shoe laces tied together.

After I'd eaten the toast, made with the white bread I love, I fastidiously washed my hands. I emptied my ash tray into the bin by the door and rolled a fresh cigarette. I liked the warmth on the back of my throat, kind of a comfort.

If you must know, I also had a small passport photo of Ruth.

I was trying to write a short story because I had no better way of killing off this lonely time. It was about the Saxons. I dug out a children's history book, the only kind I carry, to check up on some details. The Saxons occupied the stretch of coastline from Holland to Denmark. There were three main tribes: The Angles, Jutes and Saxons. When the Saxons landed in Sussex in 449 they put every Briton to death, and when they did up London in 527 they didn't bother waiting for the High Court to settle arising property disputes. The main character in my story was a young Saxon boy who was in love with a slightly older fraulein from the village. He was heroic and regularly put enemies to the sword.

Reading shit which seemed edifying. Justifying my absence of life. I was still reading this when I heard the clunk clunk drag of the milkman and his van going about their nightly business. I preferred the night. In the day, the soles of my shoes always seemed to be coming away.

I decided to make more toast and tea. Quietness was paramount here because the sight of my mum or Malc in their pyjamas was abhorrent to me. Thus, if I disturbed them, it would be direct reciprocity.

In the silence of the kitchen, the cat was, as usual, outside the window. A scraggy figure now was our cat. I let him in and gave him a saucer of low fat milk which he had a couple of catty slurps of before taking up on the sofa. I found yesterday's newspaper, which I took upstairs and read, until I fell asleep, the hostile light outside my thin red curtains like a battle field or an ocean death.

"There's someone on the phone for you."

I dragged my sleepy carcass around beneath the warm underfolds of my duvet. There was no point asking who was calling because my mum wouldn't know.

"This is Sandra..from LotaPics."

I had been interviewed by this fudge-brained slag a week ago for a job behind the counter at her one-hour film processing emporium. Well obviously it wasn't hers, but I had detected a sort of maternal proprietorship. I wasn't going to get the job.

"In the end it was between you and one other persod' she droned. "In the end we've decided to give it to them but I really enjoyed meeting you and if it doesn't work out we've got your number."

"Oh, I'm sure it will," I said, gracious in defeat. Oh what a world of profit and delight. It was twelve o'clock. High Noon. I decided to go and see Malc. "Are you going to go and see Malc?' my mother said. "Why?' I said, pouring misty water over coffee granules. "Because he knows lots of people. He can. probably find you a job."

"Yeah."

There's no need to be like that about it. You should accept help when you need it. Malcom said last night how he thought you were an intelligent young man. He can probably find you a job. You do want a job?"

"Of course."

"Well then?"

"I'm going," I said.

"You're an intelligent young man," said Malcom and I was trying to listen.

The address he had given me was high up in a block of flats. From outside in the car park I could see it was near to some other flats I used to serve with a paper round. Malc's block was set well off the road.

The door was opened by a tall woman with long dark hair and electric green eyes. She had led me in and then disappeared. Malcom's curious abode held out against natural light. Heavy velvet curtains attended to that. There were numerous side lights and standing lamps, and on a bureau in-line with Malc's head was a red lava lamp, bubbling up and down in it's larvary patterns. While Malc talked elliptically about money and power and people I thought only of Ruth.

Kidster, of all people, had known her. We were sitting on the grassy playing fields, in the bright sunlight of our second September at college. I knew who she was.

"Hello Julian," she said, sitting beside us. "Are you coming tonight?"

"Yes," said Kidster, trying pathetically to light a hand rolled cigarette. "How about you?" she said to me - her first words ever – with a directness that distracted me.

"Uh..yes..are you?"

"Well I should hope so," she said enigmatically. Our first conversation.

As the cameras rolled, Malc played his role to the hilt. He told me what people – smart people did to stay ahead, to make a bit of money, to get a slice of the cake, to be players. He asked me if I liked girls, but I wasn't concentrating. The girl with the electric green eyes came back in and I saw that she wasn't much older than me, maybe in her mid-twenties. Malc asked me if I liked Charlie. I told him yes. I wasn't convinced. Neither was he. He let it pass. He told me not to tell my mum. This filming was boring and I wasn't concentrating, but I hoped my performance would just seem studied, distant, intense.

I took O'Brien with me to that re-union bash.

I heard the director say that they were going to do Charlie's puking shot, but I wasn't in it. This was going to be an unpleasant scene I could tell. I could hear her retching, off camera.

"Alright old man?" he said, looking carefully at his cigarette. "It's just the perfect length, don't you think?"

In the pub he continued on his favourite theme:

"Sarah smokes her cigarettes right down to the filter, I mean right down. It sounds odd, but the way she does it, it's sexy. Holds the stub away from her and delicately kisses at it."

When O'Brien and I arrived, people were already congregating outside in the night air. In the main hall was a solitary dry ice machine. We joined Kidster et al.

"Hello chaps," said Kidster, fruit that he was.

"Hello Kidster," said O'Brien.

We talked aimlessly for a while. False starts. I went back into the main hall where people were jigging about. I was not very enthusiastic about dancing, except maybe in the summer when I drank rum or broke up little capsules and poured the bitter, powdery contents into my mouth. I saw Ruth dancing among the growing crowd. my infatuation allowed me to stand and watch her, disassociated from reality, lost in an aesthete's trance of my own devising, eyes heavy with unrequited romance, when she turned and smiled at me.

Back in the flat Charlie was being subjected to pea and chicken soup special effects. They had her puking on to a sheer transparency, shot from underneath. POV toilet.

I rejoined O'Brien.

"About bloody time. Where you have been? Kidster's been making a total cunt of himself. Have you noticed how he can't smoke?"

Later, we sat outside with others, on coats layered out across the playing fields. There was the moon and the orange effervescence from the streets.

When we returned to the party I rejoined Kidster who was too distracted by his dwarfish attempts to pull a chunky blonde with a stud in her nose to pay me any attention.

Katey Brown asked me: "Who's your friend?"

"A friend from my old school," I said, running my fingers through my hair for no particular reason. "Would you like a drink?"

I aimed for where O'Brien and I had stashed our supplies.

I saw Ruth standing there. This was a sort of bar. A line of desks and some responsible students dispensing wine from the box. I moved towards her. She turned and moved towards me, smiling. She had a quizzical look in her eyes. I noticed a tiny gap between her front teeth. I tried to kiss her on the lips, telling her I loved her. She doubled back away from me. I had her pressed, ridiculously and painfully doubled over backwards against the tables.

A great gasp as the pantomime villain, draped in black cape and hat makes his first theatrical, dastardly move? Kidster remained engrossed in Project Fatty; O'Brien was giving an impromptu demonstration on how to light a cigarette properly with a swan vesta; no one else reacted.

"I think you've had a bit too much to drink, Will," I heard her say.

Eyes elsewhere, hand over his mouth, Malc said he wanted me to put cards in phone boxes. They were, you know, advertising prostitutes.

When I started placing the cards I wasn't embarrassed or even afraid. I passed the people waiting at the cash point, the people going into the fast food restaurant, the husband slapping his wife's face in the doorway of the trendy clothes shop, the yapping foreigners, talking in their tongues musical and mysterious, and I found the phone booths and went in. And I grew to know and to enjoy the body-heated smells of central phone booths.

I went to see Kidster at home. We sat round the large black table in his parent's house. Whenever I ate delicacies on toast I imagined myself a European (French, say, as opposed to Bulgarian or Albanian) with a big-shirted untucked belly and slimy pink lips, gorging myself on the unusual and unpleasant tastes. This lumpy black stuff was made primarily of olives, but the anchovies gave it it's echo of the sea. Just as the wine contained the silenced shrieks of the mittel-European peasantry being driven mercilessly from their family lands.

"How's it going, then?" Kidster launched in, hauling me breathless to the surface of my reveries.

"Okay. How are you?" I answered.

"Pretty cool, I suppose. You look poncey."

"Thanks."

Lately I had been thoroughly enjoying the inchoate conceptualising associated with the insane. I would come to the phonebooths, go in, and blithely take out the different cards which I had secreted about my body. It was a funny thing, placing those little pink cards, badly cut, in the metal strip-lines of anonymous call-boxes.

I found it undemanding, although somewhat shameful. I was wearing a shabby old suit I had been bought from the Salvation Army shop, and although the trousers tailored to a type of flare, I accepted the ensemble as raffishly smart. My hair, should your interest extend that far, was tight and curly and grew skywards.

The good thing about the suit to which Kidster was alluding was that it had a variety of cardsized pockets so that I was quickly able to develop a routine that was simple to execute physically, and wholly mentally liberating. The enjoyment of mindless routine, I had picked up during my McDonald's apprenticeship. There, everything was done in a particular way and in a particular order, and the timing, as you can imagine, was also precise. They had a word for it that I forget now.

Inside my left side pocket I carried, in yellow and pink, 'Young 18 year-olds'. A description, I assumed, of psychological rather than chronological immaturity. In my other pocket, which was unsafe for money due to the holes, I carried a range of domination titles. And in my breast pocket I had the cards with the pictures that I imagined looked like Ruth. What I mean is that in those black marker sketches of stomach and of breast there appeared a recognizable similarity.

Nobody ever noticed what I was doing. Once, I remember, I picked up a receiver and I imagined it to be still vibrating with the mouths and lips of last nights desperate customers. I looked around, but the people outside were all too busy to notice me. I placed my cards and thought only of getting away. As I was about to leave, a girl approached the booth. Her hair was brown and shoulder length, badly conditioned and lank. She had full lips and a bruised face. I sucked against my lower lip as I tucked the last card into place.

"What are you doing?" she asked me.

I looked at her. Under the bruising she was really pretty, but also really fucked up. I mean, you know what I mean? I handed her a card.

"Can I keep that?" she asked.

"Of course."

Another time when I came out of a phonecard-only booth, an old gypsy tried to sell me worthless vegetation wrapped in tin-foil.

Kidster was now tinkering with dried banana skins and a bong. He

53

started telling me about Aft. Kidster was as thick as pig shit, but he had somehow pulled the wool over the eyes of the idiots responsible for assessing examination essays. Who these people were that they could applaud the work of the arch imbecile Kidster will forever remain a mystery to me.

Aside from the actual card-placing operation, the rest of my job was reassuringly vague and sans structure. According to the directions I had been given, I was simply to wander around, wearing a suit, and place the cards in whichever phoneboxes I came across.

For some reason that has been lost to history, I was minded to relate to Kidster my adventures of yesterday. I had been putting them in a phonebox quite high up a long terraced hill. It was a chilly morning, and the sun was still low over the houses. From behind me came the voices of children, and I realised then that the box I was about to enter was outside a primary school.. I can tell you, doing what I was doing to the accompaniment of playground noises was depressing, and I scurried away feeling like a pervert. I found a post-office and bought ten Benson & Hedges. There was a girl in front of me with a stud in her nose and cropped blonde hair.

When I was younger, I would fall in. love almost every day. With a girl who smiled at me on the bus, with a girl buying a newspaper, with a sweet looking girl dispensing boiled cabbage at lunch-time. Every time I went out, to a party or to a pub, love's small sharp arrows would pierce my heart from all directions. Nowadays, my daily encounters produce nothing but a feeling of sheepish, onanistic, voyeurism. I came out of the newsagents and there was a bus pulling up at the stop. I got on and rode into the countryside, where I got off and wandered around, clambering over a few gates and smoking a few of the Benson & Hedges.

It grew much colder out here amid the trees and fields and stuff, and I realised I was lost. I had the strength and defiance of youth, and also the hopeless abandon of a rudderless ship.

I reported back to Malc. As you may remember, the flat was entirely shrouded from natural light by heavy velvet curtains. This morning it was even darker than usual and the song 'Only the Lonely' was playing.

"How's the filming going?" asked Malc.

"Okay," I said. "How come the lights are ofM

"Darkness worry you, Charlie?' he leered across at the dead looking girl. "Worry you, does it son?"

"No." I shrugged. "Can I have my money?"

He counted it out theatrically in five pound notes.

"Thanks." I said, my voice leaden with contempt.

"Give your mum a kiss from me."

Kidster's parents owned a very small house in the countryside which I had persuaded him to move us into. There was one functional light-bulb remaining in the breakfast room, which now shone in permanent electric twilight. The low level of light made reading difficult. I gave in to my baser urges and de-camped next door to watch tv. My left leg, for reasons known only to itself, had ceased to function of late, leaving me to heave myself around, and, ocassionally only to collapse.

In the corner of the room there was an old rocking horse, and on the top of the bureau was a fading picture of Ruth.

On tv there were people dancing. The music was diabolical, barbaric in its insistent rhythm and lack of melody, and to my eyes the dancers were all young, would-be prostitutes. I sat idiotically frozen and toyed with the idea of masturbation.

I heard the clumsy tread of Kidster in the hall. He was returning from one of his I. socials'. Drunk as the lord he undoubtedly considered himself, after fifteen bottles of some fashionable ale, he would go round to the back of the social hall to paw the motorbike that my now engaged sister had thoughtfully lent him and "Gee up!" apparently. It was only a matter of time before this thinly veiled suicide plan would succeed.

His footsteps died away in the direction of the staircase. I glanced up at the frame that housed the image of Ruth. Kidster, whom I personally had rescued from his life of lonely urban onanism, now drank and acted up where he could, and peppered his dreary personal correspondence with cloying descriptions of the countryside, whilst ceaselessly grumbling about it in real life.

I thought about the last time I had seen Ruth. We had argued and spent the night laying on opposite sides of the bed committing the gravest of lover's sins: conscious appraisal. The dinner had been her idea. I waxed lyrical about what could be achieved and why this and that were so important, and about personal responsibility, and about Christianity and sacrifice. The booze was coursing through my mind, disabling the sensors which dealt with sensitivity and decorum. I ranted on and on and, presumably, on.

"Please shut up," said Ruth. Fin de table.

We were at the house of Kidster's friend. I knew he knew Ruth so I could forgive a lot, which was necessary when he started getting his Trivial Pursuit box out.

Kidster had memorized all the answers at some point but I put up a good show from guess work and general knowledge. Kidster's friend gaped in awe at Kidster, perhaps not fully realising that it was Kidster's powers of memory rather than his knowledge that was on display. Then we smoked a couple of joints, and, apropos nothing, he produced a passport photo of Ruth.

I was so pleased at this diversion that I didn't question why he had it. And how could he have known my feelings. I certainly hadn't told anyone. This was a secret love. A love from afar.

"Ruth gave me this. I said 'Oh, thanks Ruth,'" he said sarcastically.

"Why did she give it to you?" I asked, hoping my voice did not betray my longing.

"I don't know. That's just what I'm saying, she just gave it to me after her campaign."

He struck me as vaguely asexual. "Here," he said thrusting it into my hand. I stared at that photo for a long time.

I would never have communicated with Ruth again if I had not gone to a night-club late in December. I was not so drunk this time, was with a group of friends, and most of the people there were from college anyway.

I had mock exams after Christmas but I knew these would be a disaster whatever. It was late in the evening, and I saw her. True to form I did not act immediately but went to the bar. This was the sort of club where most people, including impoverished students, sported their most fashionable clothes and paid a high price for the alcohol on offer. Conscious that I wasn't exactly the most fashionably dressed male in the club this evening (or any evening) I wondered if now was indeed the time. My time. But given the circumstances ... well, it could hardly be more ridiculous than last time.

When I approached her she immediately smiled, ironically. "Hello" she said. "How are you?"

"Good." I said. "How's university?"

"Brilliant! I'm having a fantastic time."

"That's great?' I shouted as a bass line shook the floor between us. "See you" she said, and smiled as she rejoined her friends.

Over Christmas, I considered the issue. On the one hand, I had made a disastrously bad impression. On the other hand, I was more infatuated than at any prior time in my life. And besides, if she still smiled so sweetly at me, albeit with a look of quizzical mirth, she must surely hold a more favourable opinion of me than I imagined I merited. On this particular count I was, in fact, quite wrong.

"Hello, it's me." I said. I kissed the receiver.

"Oh, hello. Who is this?"

"Me."

Pause

"Aha."

"Look, I want to make up for that awful evening at the reunion. I mean, it was really nice to see you the other night. Will you come out with me for a drink?"

Pause.

"Oh. Will."

"Any night. How about if I come and pick you up at eight on Friday?' "Ahh ..." then suddenly, "Okay."

"Great." I put the phone down quickly before this could change. She didn't have my number and now, come hell or biblical armageddon, I would be there at eight o'clock sharp. I held my breath for a moment, then let my, success wash over me.

The appointed day arrived. I played it cool around the house. I wouldn't be rushed. I readied myself I set out at a quarter past seven. The house, which I had never before visited was a ten minute walk away.

She was waiting for me, and as we walked down the road, our conversation seemed unforced and plentiful as the central issue – namely why she and I were actually going out- was carefully skirted. She wore jeans and a jean jacket, but the central fact that it was Friday, that it was 8 o'clock, and that we were together, remained in my favour.

There were several possible routes to our destination – a pub which I had selected as being grown-up and reasonably neutral. The least likely route was to cut across the town cemetery. I had never taken this particular road before, but it seemed to me that such an expedition could only add an element of adventure to the night's proceedings. My cousin had been telling me much about how he regularly used to scare his dates with fangs manufactured out of bread rolls or orange peels, and how, in his day, a good fright was just as likely to precipitate some lips and limb action as a pricey dinner. The cemetery, at least, was not boring, and thus likely to generate a lasting impression for Ruth to take back with her to university.

The place was a sprawl of landscaped terrain, large enough to cater for centuries worth of burials. There were willow trees and groves. There were inclines and vistas. There were huge gravestones, fashioned from the ramparts of fallen churches and the masonry of forgotten mansions. And there were little plots, with their humble plaques, engraved brass on small black wood blocks. There were flower beds and high walls. There was shorn grass and gravelled pathways. There was suspense and love and horror – all good high emotion type things; there was beauty and universality. And best of all as far as I was concerned, it all came free.

I had been going out with her for exactly eight days before she surprised me in the pub, where we were doing a Sunday evening quiz with some friends of hers, and Kidster.

Towards the end of the evening, she turned to me and said:

"So, are we going to do the rude thing tonight?"

She did seem to be more cordial in her relations with other men when we went out, but I reasoned this a girlish strategy to incite my jealousy. A strategy distinguished by its success, as on several occasions I challenged her. I became rather obsessive about infidelity and great love. I embraced the theme in art wherever I could find it. Martin Scorsese's Raging Bull is, of course, the ultimate wallow in this sort of exaggerated, insane jealousy. You know, we broke up.

When I arrived at university I was greeted by a strapping youth who shook my hand firmly and led me and my attendant parents briskly to my room. It was a standard room in halls on the ground floor. There were only men on the ground floor for safety reasons. This was admirable. We men, together, guarding the fairer sex who lived above in sure knowledge of their protection.

One was quickly abandoned to one's own devices, after being informed about the freshers beerbeano in the college bar later that evening.

I de-boxed and plugged in my brand new kettle and made a cup of tea. I felt immediately at home. My mother was sensitive to the fact that I wanted them to leave as quickly as possible. Understandably. One wants to design one"s own image at university and not have it thrust upon them by a garrulous and lingering father.

My dad, feeling miffed by my seeming ingratitude, demurred and accepted that I was not about conduct a complete tour of campus for his benefit, nor go round introducing myself and him at the same time to my new neighbours.

Radio One blared loudly from my next door neighbour's room. He had his door wide open, but had not himself been in evidence as we had come in. To save time later, I took an immediate dislike to him.

After the tea, I decided to do a bit of unpacking before taking the plunge and going into the communal kitchen at the end of the corridor. The room was impressive in its economy of space. Secreted cupboard space under a seat and under the bed, a deep wardrobe with an internal 'organiser' and a full length mirror inside one of the doors.

I had travelled fairly lightly. I unpacked clothes, ghetto blaster, alarm clock, and my few books including a large new dictionary. It was a factor of my university career that I bought as few books as possible. I sat on the bed and smoked a cigarette, ashtray thoughtfully provided by the university, in quiet meditation.

"Are you 'doing' English?" said the girl next to me.
"Yes."
"Me too."

We left registration together and walked over to the relevant building, an original red-brick erection. She wore a fawn suede mini-skirt and black boots. As we walked

I wore a friendly smile, which outward sign of sanity was nought but a clever disguise I had wrought to mask the criminal lasciviousness which brimmed under the surface.

That day was bright. Ah, those days were bright, and the class itself was comprised mainly of girls who had presumably been detailed together as a sort of pornographic elite. It was a torture sitting there, but a torture of a peculiarly exquisite kind.

I had heard nothing from Ruth.

How one was supposed to maintain the slightest academic interest in literature when the context of that daily project was a confrontation with what seemed the very lifestuff of existence itself is rather a tricky one to understand. Could any rational academic educationalist have honestly supposed that the way to focus the young male attention on the later poetry of Thomas Hardy was to surround it's field of vision, central and peripheral, with a previously unimagined ensemble of girls? Of course, as the intelligent liberal. in you demands, that is a very questionable sentiment, but as an eighteen year old boy who had not that long ago been reporting to the prefect's study dressed in military corps uniform for minor drill, or vigorously resisting a 'kebabing' in the 'horsebox', I freely confess that it didn't help focus my attention on the later poetry of Thomas Hardy. Indeed, that man's profound sentiments pertaining to his sadly lamented late wife were wasted on this heathen youth.

Only when we got to the door of the classroom did I formally introduce myself to her. "By the way," I said, "my name's Will."

"Charlotte," she said, as if a girl's name were the most ordinary thing in the world, "pleased to meet you."

Andy Briscoe

from

Meeting Lucio

sex *n* **1** the state of being either male or female. **2** either of the two categories, male or female, into which organisms are divided. **3** sexual intercourse. **4** feelings or behaviour connected with having sex or the desire to have sex. [Latin *sexus*]

'Our real lives are the lives we do not lead.'
Oscar Wilde

Gun

'In the car motherfucker!'

Faces peer through the deli window, then duck behind canned vegetables and dried pasta.

'Move it, shit-face!'

Blinds of the apartment block on 58th flick open, concerned but not enough to take on a gun, fingers flick blinds closed.

'NOW!'

The whore with the headphones leans against the newspaper box. Leopard print jacket teased by the wind, flaunting bosoms inside the metallic catsuit as she mans her boudoir (the ATM booth). She turns Lauryn Hill to full volume.

'You deaf shit-face? Get the fuck in the car.'

Unwashed hair glows beneath a twenty-four seven neon. Clothes in the Adidas bag squashed between Mark's legs as the man aims the gun at his forehead. It glistens, that gun, the buffed exterior catches the reds and whites of the Budweiser sign hanging in the window behind. Mark isn't sure whether to run or simply stand still, his hands thrust into the air. He's just seen a man wearing a blue suit shot in the head. Images of the way the man's head exploded replay, stealing ability to fight as he's grabbed by the shoulders, his toes like powerballs bouncing from sidewalk to sidewalk to sidewalk to kerb.... no further! He doesn't want to get into the Pontiac. He screams: 'No. No. No. *PLEASE NO!*' His body seems to fold like an old tissue poked into a tight jean pocket.

Inside the car smells of mud, he notices, nose pressed against the carpet by a foot on the back of his head. Musty like the greengrocers on Lewes Road his mum sent him to every Sunday for a sack of Maris Pipers, two swede and a cabbage. Tears wet the side of his face. Or is it sweat? He can't tell. Salty.

Something jams into the back of his head. He thinks it's the gun because the man is saying: 'I *could* shoot you, motherfucker. Shoot you. Blow your fucking brains away! Pull the trigger and watch you bleed.'

New York... Pictures Perfect

Icy blues and passion pinks flash the NYPD as the 100ft Coca-Cola bottle opens itself, drains the colour then glitters with scorching reds. Fenced in by miles of cement. Cattle guided through the parallel streets of Manhattan. Shops. Boutiques. Trailers and dirty fingernails handing out hot-dogs, corn-dogs, NY dogs, pretzels, *souvlakia*, kebabs. 7up to wash down the slime. A greaseproof napkin to skid around the remains.

People. Raceless, from the dirt and grime clinging to their skin, an impermeable layer. Pushing government provided wheelbarrows from garbage can to garbage can where they riffle and pull out bits of old paper and aluminium cans and scraps of food which they sniff and bite, then toss in for later. And a woman standing there, head to foot in black plastic, the same stuff that lines the bins, standing there clapping and cheering as the three guys outside the Marriott Marquis scream abuse at the guy walking past.

'And there's a faggot. They're all faggots! They fuck animals, like that Richard Gere! He fucks donkeys! And the white man rules! And he's a fucking pervert!' More laughter.

I slip into Borders, people all around me with books and magazines and pretzels wrapped in paper napkins. Munching while they browse. Greasy fingers slipping over shiny pages, talking to friends with full mouths and boisterous laughs and crazy hairstyles and loud clothes. That's why I came here, to see this. To mingle with the people who don't conform to the regimental lifestyle that sticks out like starched collars back home. A land where people in lifts look at their feet. No food or drink in Debenhams, thank you. A boisterous laugh is unacceptable. Turner Featherstone, you're really here! A place where people seem to not care how chewed food looks to the person opposite or how loud they laugh. Easy coming, easy going, and this is how I expected it to be. Big hair, big earrings, big personalities. I love it.

There are credentials needed, though. There are people who aren't accepted within the circle. And I wonder if I'm up to scratch as a man slumped in a bench beside the condiments is asked to leave. His khaki trousers bunched up behind his knees exposing weathered white-flaky shins (like the false teeth slipping onto his bottom lip). Chin in his chest so grey roots fabricate the dull orange of his hair. The vacant seat is sprayed with antibacterial. The remnants of the undesirable wiped away with an I heart NY tea-cloth to maintain the pristine New Yorker lifestyle I came to be a part of

I walk back to Times Square and gaze up with amazement at the video-looping screens showing Santa ho-ho-ho-ing with a sackful of goodies, just below an outsized beaker of cup-anoodles steaming as though there are really noodles in there. Perhaps there are. And I could be anyone here, but it feels like I'm nobody. I haven't a stage to stand on, a microphone to scream statements into and be noticed. I could only be someone if I had something to say, something to scream. But I'm fenced by steaming adverts and monstrous buildings.

Someone shoves a flyer in my hand and orders me to have a good time.

'Lip-smacking, heart-pumping, boob-bouncing babes dancing - Totally NUDE! Lap dancing: The Best Way to Relax in New York!'

'I've got to get my luggage first.'

'You Australian?'

'English.'

'*England*? With the queen and all that shit? Well maybe some pussy will do you good.'

A warm donut-y smell wafts for a second. I realise my hunger, and I tell myself I'm going to find that smell and buy whatever it is and eat until I'm sick. A man with greasy hair, looking uncannily like Fred West, pushes a stainless steel carriage of hot nuts, and I decide to pass on the thought.

Another woman makes a bee-line to my open hands and shoves in a piece of paper that says I'm going straight to hell when the day of rapture occurs. If I want to be with God I'll have to starve or be decapitated. Either way, I'm going to lose, acquire leprosy and burn in Hell. Because I don't believe in God. I don't believe in anything I can't see.

I find it intimidating, dissolve into the words, because it really is as though I'm not here when I read. Leaning against the window of the Warner Brothers shop, Taz glaring over my shoulder like some watchful guardian ready to devour anyone who dares interrupt my religious thirty seconds.

'Believe in what you read.' A man's voice

Not sure who. The legs look the same from this angle. Another flyer is thrust into my face, and Taz didn't even growl for me. Maybe he thinks a suit for twenty dollars is quite an awful thought.

I could learn to love this, the hustle and bustle of a city I couldn't imagine. The sirens intermittent like an orchestra of amateurs, slicing through the conversation with ear-splitting volume. And that could be someone getting shot or mugged or raped or injected with HIV. But it doesn't matter, because this place has... something. Being consumed by death doesn't come into thought, because it's a risk you take when you bite The Big Apple. It's almost worth it.

I walk again, cross the street by a billowing manhole, wondering for a second what the steam feels like or smells like, but resist the temptation to sniff as the horn of a yellow cab with a furious Hispanic driver urges me to leg it towards Virgin. Still the people fascinate me, and I want to be like them. Not one person specifically, but a bit of everyone. A bit of the woman in the bin-liner, with the arrogance of the men screaming vulgarities at anyone slightly pasty, and the fanaticism of the woman slapping religious leaflets into unsuspecting hands. (I'd like to have her faith).

I'm shoved towards the Banana Republic by a bloke with a banana sized cigar jutting from his mouth as he screams something in a strange language.

New York: things like that happen all the time. Don't let it get you down. He's walking away now. At least he didn't have a baseball bat.

A woman ahead with leaflets again, smiling. People pushing past her, not even acknowledging her as she waves a leaflet jovially at their faces. I pass, she doesn't attempt to give me one. I notice the heading in tall red letters: 'Stress-free living.'

Another crazy. Maybe I'm noticing too many, because there are normal people milling around too, but they don't seem as prominent as the others. A man in front waving at the sky and mouthing obscenities in a silent fury. Mid-brown hair, I notice as I pass, hanging stiff and matted from a baseball cap.

A man in a doorway waves a cellophane-wrapped umbrella and says two dollars. I just smile.

'Fuck off.'

And I love this place with its people with no pride and no care for tomorrow. It seems time isn't linear to them. Anything could happen.

New York, New York!

I'm safe inside the airport, through the scanners and where those people can't touch me. I'm here to get my cases, to introduce them to a world they've never seen. I realise how secure I am, surrounded with guards packing semi-automatics wearing bullet proof vests. Employed to shoot dead anyone who aims a weapon at me. I feel so much more at ease, wandering through people arriving/leaving/waiting, because it's multi-cultural inside these walls. People employ a higher level of tolerance for foreigners who don't know Rome to be Roman. And I can't wait to get out, to be at risk, to become a potential statistic on the New York state crime report. To take a chance. Security isn't appealing to me, and I leave it behind as doors allow me to exit the artificial temperature and multi-lingual announcements to the throat numbing breeze and American slang.

I'm here. This magical place with buildings and shops and lights and sausages on sticks. So much to see that you forget it's freezing and that man in the doorway is blue, and the bloke looking through the restaurant window is starving to death. That he'll be dead by Thursday. That's how I feel here. Tragedy can wait. *I'm next in line, budge over, you.*

The scum in the street swearing and ready to fuck anyone over for ten dollars. The child calling for his mom because she's been dragged into a car by three men. No-one is listening. No-one cares. There's so much more to life than listening to people who don't matter. Won't matter. I'll wake up tomorrow, they'll all wake up tomorrow and flick through the New York Times, and see the kid who's been hit by a juggernaut, or the bitch with her throat slit and her vagina split. A few seconds of 'thank God it wasn't me, I'll have cheese on my bagel, the juice with the bits in .... oooh, and give me one of those coffees that tastes of warm nuts.'

Missaplication

'So how do you like New York?' Driver.

'Not very much, actually.' Mark.

Laughter.

Mark's tears blurred two smiles into watery colour as a knife sliced a length of rope which tied his hands behind his back.

FUCKING FAG!

He tasted the blood in his mouth as a fist punched his face and his head bounced off the window.

MOTHERFUCKER!

A hand clamped his balls and squeezed so hard that he shit himself They took a corner at fifty - no sixty - and his head smashed against something. Then a flash as the knife, like the teeth of a great white, was pressed against his chest.

*FUCK THE FAGGOT! FUCK THE FAGGOT! **FUCK THE FAGGOT!***

The jaws sliced through his Adidas sweatshirt, then straight through his belt. Straight through, no problem. He mouthed the word no. NO. *Please no*! He needed it to stop. *FEAR!* Uncontrollable like the situation that was happening – which couldn't happen – not to Mark! To *other* people YES.

Jeans and shoes and socks ripped away, boxers too, thrown through an open window through which the breeze goosebumped naked flesh and froze tears as his body was wrenched UP to assume the position.

The knife was swapped for the gun. The driver managed an unnerving toothy grin before turning back to the road after rearranging the rear-view mirror.

Mark saw the sleepy houses, snow patchy on roofs, and wondered if everybody was enjoying their breakfast and coffee and English muffins. He wondered how many people were dressing for work, straightening ties and polishing shoes.

'He shit himself.' Laughter.

The car pulled over to the side of the road.

'There ain't no fucking way I'm fucking it in that state!'

He heard the crumpling of paper, felt it scratching between his buttocks, then tasted it as it smeared his face, the shit like a mask. A deep cleansing mud mask. His face was pressed against the window.

The stink of shit up his nose as it smudged down the glass with his face.

'Don't get excited dude, my *dick* ain't going up that hole.' More laughter.

The gun again, shoved somewhere so uncomfortable he screamed and cried and gulped and breathed all at the same time. A pain so unimaginable, so uncomfortable, then warm as though he was bleeding.

Out. Relief Then hard in the back of his head. A hand grabbed his hair and wrenched him back to face the driver who was leaning over to him.

'What did you hear in Manhattan, shit-face?'

'Nothing!'

'What did you see, shit-face?'

'Some bloke shot in ....'

The gun moved, shoved so hard that he splattered the seat with an enormous fart then pissed over his knees. His head wrenched back again. The driver there. Smiling.

'What the fuck did you see?'

'Nothing.'

'Good boy. And would you recognise me again?'

'I just want to go home, please.'

The driver turned away, accelerated and swerved into the middle of the road. A hand held Mark's head and rubbed it in the piss and shit pooling on the leather seats. A hand grabbed the door handle.

'See ya mother fucker!'

Breathing, sweating.

FRESH.

The road..... hisface.   Flash. Flash.

A billboard with a boat and a sky-blue backdrop.

A tree.

Another tree.   Another.

A kerb.

A screech of tyres.

An exhaust backfiring   distancing.

                               Further.

                                    Further.

                                         Gone.

So Great They Named Me Twice

A man in canary yellow hands me a leaflet after explaining vigorously the way the taxi's run. It's customary to tip. There's a tip chart with suggested rates right in front of your seat there, however, you may waive the custom should:

    a) The car not:

        i) be clean;

        ii) be smoke free;

        iii) be air-conditioned/heated upon request.

    b) The driver not:

        i) be courteous;

        ii) be knowledgeable of main attractions and hotels within New York;

        iii) be able to speak English.

'Have a nice day, sir!'

A boot lid clunks open as an arrogant taxi driver presses a button on his dashboard, leaving me to struggle with the cases before boarding. Fleece blanket there for comfort or to keep whatever might be on me from smearing his polished leather seats. The back of his head seems unapproachable while the photo (together with driver number should a complaint be necessary) smiles at me, with brilliant white teeth and dark eyes. Two-centimetre-bullet-proof perspex segregates the white from the black; the passenger from the driver; the thief from his dosh, a two-by-two hole at the left to poke through the fee and keep out the gun.

'I need to go here,' I say, holding the paper and pointing at the circled ad.

He grunts, which I take as an acknowledgement.

Earther Kit purrs a New York welcoming, advising me to fasten my seat-belt for*rrr* my own safety. *Purrrrrr*. We pull onto the freeway, past the toll gate and into the city - *The* City. Cement spears stab the paint-pallet blues of the Manhattan sky. The lady stands there on her own island, holding a torch and looking at me. *At me!* It feels like that. She knew I was coming, and she held that pose, that welcoming pose, that sexy half-smile to welcome me.

Huge buildings with tiny windows, red brick, stone-grey. Stainless steel! People busy zigzagging roads, horns blaring. A man waiting to cross. Taxi driver waves him on, 'thank you, brother.'

*It's me New York. Here I am. In. YOUR. **FACE**. Let me entertain you. Let me guide you, show you, teach you, blow you, rob you. Let me take you by the hand and show you things you've never seen. And I'm just a place, a great place, so great they named me twice. But you'll never forget the experience I bring. I am. Let me take you by the hand.*

And then we pull up to the centre of chaos, bumper to bumper traffic the length of Great Britain as we edge forward to our destination. Lights bringing the red brick, cement and stainless steel buildings to life. Twinkling like the stars of the planet. And maybe they are. Times Square wishes a Merry Christmas to New York, and a merry Christmas to me.

'Merry Christmas New York! Ho – ho – ho! The temperatures a *cooool* minus five, and Here comes Rudolph! HAPPY CHRISTMAS!!!! And, don't forget, Discover Card is here for you. **Discover Card**.... **Discover Card.... Discover Card** says Merry Christmas New York!'

Tile Birds

I imagine awaiting the Madam in the luxurious reception of the twenty-three apartment complex aptly named the Pleasure Dome. After being shown to a more than comfortable sofa by a Filipino with scarlet lipstick, and handed a glass of water warm and yellowed enough to have been pissed five minutes earlier, I am told the Madam will arrive shortly. Flow through the heavy oak doors wearing a black lace wonderbra and a satin mini-skirt.

Poolside bar and sunbeds; communal hot-tub for exclusivity of the guests, cocktail waiters/waitress, whoever takes your fancy (all Filipino and looking for prospective American husbands). That's what it said in the brochure. Some say the best stress reliever on the East Coast, others say it sprouted from the very pits of Hell like Lucifer's erection. I say I want to meet their marketing manager. I could have spent six months in the Pleasure Dome, but instead opted for a friendly uptown guesthouse. Far enough from the city to enjoy a calm glass of rioja in the evenings, close enough to abuse your liver with shots of tequila and Guinness from the Mexican owned Irish Bar downtown Manhattan.

I have no regrets.

The taxi dropped me outside the guesthouse. The lights gave way to cooing pigeons and an unbelievable quantity of birds perched upon the roof for this time of night. Through the cast iron gates I lugged my cases (I should have got those ones with wheels on special in Salisbury's). Up the stairs to apartment Number One. The bell brought a stench of alcohol together with someone who introduced herself as Helen White, then Nellie White, whatever, Mrs White is an unfortunate name for an albino.

After welcoming me in and offering me a glass of water, warm and yellowed enough to have been pissed five minutes earlier, she introduced me to Snowball. The creature, named after her favourite cocktail, 'isn't allowed out because he's crazy.' It seems Snowball has been crazy ever since Mrs White moved from Utah and her lush garden, in which Snowball had hours of fun chasing butterflies (though he never ate them).

Brushing a feather she'd said was on my backside, lingering more than I felt comfortable with, she showed me into a lounge, wall to wall with artificial flowers and a pungent stench of cat's piss and lavender.

The mauve can of air-freshener by a picture of Mrs White (who insisted I called her Nellie) squeezing the life from a kitten-Snowball sitting above a litter-tray resembling toad-in-the-hole.

'What is it you do again, Mr Featherstone?'

'I freelance.'

'I'm not with you, Finglestone.'

'It's Turner, my name, and I write. Freelance.'

'Metaxa?'

'No, thanks. Long day. Just want to get to bed.'

'Well, Mr Turner, you can certainly have a restful stay here! For a five-dollar surcharge we'll even do your cleaning and a weekly linen change.'

'Great.'

'Jerome, our maintenance man, will be around should you have any problems here at, Heritage.'

'Heritage?'

'This guesthouse. I wanted to call it Hermitage. Didn't notice the M was missing when they did the sign. Bad eyes. I'm an albino. Are you sure you wouldn't like a night-cap, Feath... Fingle.... Turner, you say?'

'Turner Featherstone. And I'm positive, thanks.'

After handing me a key, Mrs White said she'd show me. I said I'd find my own way, but the woman insisted, and I hadn't the energy to maintain the very-pleased-to-meet-you routine while politely assuring her of my capability to follow the deck around to my left to room Number Seven. She left me at the door, flicking the light switch without entering my new home, as if it no longer belonged to her. We said our thank yous, she invited me to lunch tomorrow. I said twelve, she said fine and I was inside, pleasantly surprised by the clean decor. The open plan kitchen/lounge, a desk, a dirty cream sofa. I had a quick slash in the bathroom, admiring the quiet toilet flush, but deciding to dispose of the pink mat set. They were stuck to the floor, and I gave in to passion-pink after five minutes of tugging.

The bedroom. Wooden floor. New York black and whites. Closet space. Side table with lamp and miniature fan heater. Rug and television. Touch-tone telephone – great! Now where's the bed?

Clock, Watching

15:02

Dolores stood looking down at Somerville, waiting for some sort of movement. His eyes were the same, icy blue. Still moist, glistening like the lubricant she had smeared inside herself to accommodate the fifty-year-old's ten inches. She imagined he would have been handsome twenty years ago.

15:25

She prodded his stomach with her finger and watched as the tip disappeared into the belly of the well-fed business man. Somerville had been seeing her for two years. She knew everything that turned him on. She could make him come in five minutes if she wanted. Without touching him he would orgasm at her will. Quite an accomplishment, she thought.

Dolores tried to understand how she was feeling, tried to invoke some sort of affection, but nothing arose. No tears. Emotionless. And if that had been a different client lying there, she wondered if she would feel any differently as she stretched to the glass bowl brimming with marshmallows and poked a pink one into her mouth.

She trailed a gold fingernail over his cheek. A senseless fingernail was all she could bring herself to touch his face with as she wondered about her clients, why they came to delve between the legs of a stranger. Would she if she were them? She wished she'd asked Somerville why he came. What she gave him. The differences between her and his wife, but she always kept a comfortable distance. The last thing she wanted was a friend for life.

15:37

Dolores didn't perceive herself as mitigation for marriage, nor someone with no choice but to fuck for a living. She enjoyed it, she relished the feel of being a whore. The spontaneity of getting up on Monday only to be mock-raped by a businessman/tortured by someone's husband/fumbled with by a virgin/fisted by a stag party. Or more regularly, marching on backs in time with the national anthem wearing a pair of transparent stilettos. The spontaneity meant almost as much as the money.

15:44

This room needs something, she thought, a re-vamp. She could see a dingy red. *Not Little Whorehouse in Texas* red, but dingy. Seedy.

Lamps and a bed made of cast iron.

Maybe even a coat rack. Or ivory. Something neutral, natural. Something easy.

Another marshmallow dusted her lips.

'I gotta do something with you, cutie,' she said.

There were still no signs of movement. She wasn't sure what she was expecting, but she felt obliged to wait, just in case.

16:13

She'd waited over an hour. Listened to it ticking away. Time was up, he wasn't going to move. Something had to be done with him. She couldn't perform to her high standards with the thought of him lying in the next room. Dead. She flipped the bedspread over his body. She was relieved for a second to hide his face, but the blood had soaked through the bedspread and it was worse than seeing him motionless. There was nothing she could do now, she'd have to leave him there. Ian and Jessic were due in thirty minutes and she'd promised them a jacuzzi. She had to get herself together.

A New York Side Walk

Mark had managed to wriggle towards a wall where the wind didn't feel so icy. He couldn't feel the grazes and cuts all over his body. He wondered how long it would be before someone found him. He tried not to think of what might happen if no-one found him.

New York, what a welcoming. He'd hated the atmosphere as soon as he'd departed the Boeing 747. The differences in the way people looked and acted alienated him. The travel agent had made it sound adventurous with pictures of buildings and shops and all-night entertainment at a discounted fare for the young traveller. The hotel wasn't the best money could buy, but with the budget Mark was on, the only option.

'Besides, you'll be in New York. You won't be spending time in a hotel room, I hope!'

Knees in his chest as he tried one more time to wriggle from the rope around his wrists. The cold was through to his bones. His hands ached, his whole body shivered. His mind tortured him with images of open fires and hot coffee. He could almost feel the sensation of clamping cold hands around a mug of anything hot, taking a mouthful and swilling it.

He cried. How long had he been lying there? How long could he lay there? Could he sleep? Would his toes drop off?. Would he freeze to death? Would his skin turn blue and glittery? Would those men return to shoot him in the head and watch him bleed?

The snow was settling on his skin. A while ago it was melting upon impact, but now he was cold enough for it to lay. He imagined a blanket. It wasn't snow, but flannelette. Covering every part of him. Every fold. Every crease.

Quackers

There was a smash. A scraping sound. A noise like a pillowcase being flapped outside my door. A scream, a muffled hand-over-mouth scream. I jumped up, skidding as my dry feet touched the polished floor, but managed to regain my balance and leg it into the lounge towards the front door.

Mrs White stood on the deck, pink rimmed glasses knocked skew-whiff as she slapped a hand over nose and mouth. Something terrible!

It took a Brandy Alexander and a sincere promise before Nellie rethought the threat of eviction. It wasn't that she didn't appreciate the male form naked at six in the morning, it was that introductions were a necessity before that kind of intimacy. Or at least some sort of warning that the intimacy was about to occur.

Leaving Nellie to her breakfast (three vitamin pills with milk and a slice of white bread) I explored the building, which I imagined could be quite lovely if brought up to standard. Cracks in the dirty pebbledash, fingers reaching from the earth to pull down the neglected building. The ground floor, I assumed, was disused. The upper floor was the sixteen apartments which all had an unobstructed view of what Nellie called her aviary. Her only passion. Her true friend (after Snowball). A garden with a ten-by-three-foot ornamental bird table loaded with monkey nuts and a pond large enough to be classed as a puddle, but homely enough for the eight ducks she had skidding upon the frozen surface. Of the ducks, who all had names (though I'm sure when pointing them out she called three Stanley), Casper was the chap who created the hullabaloo this morning. Apparently, Casper, while desperately trying to outrun Snowball, managed to flap up a flight of stairs knocking over a terracotta pot. This consequently sent Snowball back-flipping down four steps and clawing fifteen feet up the elaborate Christmas tree. But not content with the victory, Casper continued to quack and flap his way outside my door.

Walking through the garden, I introduced myself to a strawberry-blond six-footer who was shovelling snow from the pathway and shaking his jelly-hips to something barely audible to me. On the third attempt at trying to overwhelm his personal stereo, he turned.

'Ricky Martin always gives me the Latino-fever, you'll have to excuse me. You must be the English guy.'

'Are you Jerome?'

'No, I'm Mitch.'

'Nice to meet you, Mitch. I assumed, since you were shovelling snow you were ....'

'Jerome is over there,' he said, pointing out a long-haired figure wearing a lumberjacket and jeans who was throwing feed at ducks flapping around his feet. 'Staying for long?' Mitch continued.

'I think so.'

'You look freezing.'

'Not as cold as I was this morning.'

'You want to grab a coffee?"

'Sorry, I've got a lunch date with Mrs White.

'Another time, I guess. So, The Initiation Lunch, lucky boy. I can't imagine why she's never invited me to one of those!'

And then he laughed, but I didn't quite get it, so I smirked before excusing myself and promising to get back to him concerning the coffee.

Nellie had laid the table for twelve, insisting that I should be ten minutes early for an English sherry beforehand. I tried to explain that sherry hadn't been one of my English customs, nor one of anybody I know, but she insisted. Besides, a relaxing glass of sherry would be the perfect opportunity to bring up the fact that my apartment has no bed.

Eleven forty-five. Lingering outside apartment Number One, not willing to seem too eager for the free lunch, I bumped into a lady eating marshmallows and wearing half a cow which laced up the right side of her body, and in the quick glimpse I got it appeared she was wearing no underwear. I smiled, she sank her teeth into a pink marshmallow.

'Hiya, cutie.'

'Hello.'

'Are you looking for me?'

'I don't think so.'

'Are you sure you ain't looking for me, cutie? Most strange men who come here are.'

'My name is Turner. I've just moved in. Number Seven.'

'We're neighbours! I ain't ever had no neighbour looking as *fine* as you!' she said, circling me.

She had strangely stiff hair which curled under around the edges. When she smiled she must have noticed my expression because she promptly pointed out that half a set of teeth complemented the best blow job this side of the river for under twenty bucks.

After inviting me round to Number Eight to Ten for a Harvey Wallbanger, she jotted a time slot on the back of a gold leaf business card, pressed powdery soft lips upon my sweaty brow and wiggled off. DEFINITELY NO KNICKERS.

LUNCH MENU

STARTER

Chicken Salad

Four leaf salad with cherry tomatoes, diced chicken,
tossed in extra virgin olive oil.

MAIN COURSE

Chicken Fried Steak

Breaded ground beef, mash and white gravy with a fried scone dressed
with whipped butter and maple syrup.

DESSERT

Helen's Apple Pie

Apple Pie and vanilla ice-cream.

BEVERAGES

Root Beer: (liquefied Mentadent-P).
Water: Warm and yellowed enough to have been pissed ten minutes
earlier (I must mention the plumbing).

Lunch was filling. Service impeccable. Environment stagnant, but not entirely repulsive once the air circulated and the lungs closed up. Overall scoring..... 10/10 for effort.

The afternoon was completed with Amaretto and Lorna Doone cookies. We sat silently watching the Wheel of Fortune, then Mrs White fingered the remote and Jeopardy livened the mood as she muttered incomprehensible answers and 'I told you so,' every now and then. By the end of the afternoon quiz shows, Mrs White would have been a millionaire she said. Conversation idled. She wiggled uncomfortably close to me after bringing calypso coffee. I sat between the arm of the sofa and a warm thigh.

'You're a good-looking young man, Mr Fingle.'

'It's Turner.'

'Huh?'

'My name is Turner. Mr Featherstone, but Turner is my first name.'

'You'll certainly Turner a lot of heads! You're a good-looking young man, you know. A lovely physique.'

'Um - thanks.'

'I say what I see, no need to thank me. You be careful. People will take advantage of you out there. I know how it can be, but you're safe with me.'

'I'll be careful,' I said. To which a hand on my knee squeezed. A strange look her eye froze beads of sweat on my forehead.

'So, what do you think of me, Turner?'

'You cook a great meal .. ?'

She tipped calypso down her throat before a growling laugh seeming too ferocious to be emitting from such frailty: 'Do you like the more mature woman?'

'I don't have time for any....'

'If you had time?'

'If I had time.... I don't know.'

Her hand began it's ascent, stopping frequently to squeeze. My heart raced. I felt beads of sweat trickling down my back bringing to thought water as my excuse. She returned with the discoloured liquid which I gulped back to prevent further intimate discussion. It was then that Nellie told me her problem.

Snowball's Takeout, Hold The Fries

In the garden, to the left of the ornamental fountain where a stork's beak pin-pointed the moon, I sat beside a bird bath. Camouflaged by crawling ivy and evergreen, I peeped through the leaves, into the windows (like Christmas scenes) where cold flashes of televisions dazzled behind the venetians. And behind one of those windows was a thief. A duck thief, apparently. Nellie, who this time corrected my Nellie to Ellie, had a problem. The ducks she kept were gradually depleting, something which she can't comprehend. She had ten until two weeks ago. And then there were eight.

She enlisted me to solve her little problem, the prize: another lunch (whatever I want) in the flamboyant lounge, with her, for free (not duck, I assume). She'd given me the rundown of the guests:

'Mitch: Number Sixteen. Lovely boy. Helps around Heritage. Works downtown in a bar. Mitch and I were very close a while back, but then he started to work. I guess he hasn't time to come round for coffee anymore. He loves those ducks as much as I do. I'm sure he wouldn't touch them.'

'Ant and Jennifer. Always very pleasant. They're in Number Two, next-door. Out till all hours of the night. I think Jennifer is a bit of a drinker, although I can't see them doing anything with my ducks. If I'm not mistaken, they're both vegetarians. I couldn't do that. I like my meat - but not ducks. I'd never eat anything with feathers. Except chicken, but then that's not really a bird, is it. Turkeys are the same. But I'd never touch anything *else* with feathers.'

'Alison. She's the girl who lives next-door to Denise in Number Fifteen. Sluts. Always together. Too much time partying to touch my Casper.'

'Jerome, Number Thirteen. Maintenance man here. Any problems, Jerome will sort them out for you. Wouldn't touch my ducks. Too busy with other things.'

'Andrea, Number Five. She knows about the ducks going missing. I suppose they all do really, but she knows I know, she helps around Heritage when I'm too ill. I get these off-days, like everyone, I guess. Diet probably, but anyway. The ducks? Oh no, not Andrea.'

'Dolores. Number Eight, Nine and Ten. No doubt you'll meet her. Oh, you've already... met? Yes... a very nice girl, but I don't know too much about her. I like to give the residents their privacy, of course. Lots of male callers. No time for the ducks, I'm sure. You find out what's happening to my ducks and we can spend a lot more time together.'

And that was the extent of the insightful entourage. The ducks were being stolen by a resident, she assumed, only none of the residents were capable of such anarchy. The fact remained. Ellie had been plumping her ducks up with bread for insulation over the winter months, not culinary titillation for a thief, or someone too tired to venture into Chinatown. 'Although the truth might hurt, I'm willing to deal with it,' she'd said.

Armed with a blanket, beef jerky and a flask of hot coffee, I waited until one, maybe two a.m. No sign of Tom or Harry - but Dick made an unannounced appearance.

I began to feel hungry, but not enough to even consider sundried cow. I contemplated raiding the bird table for monkey nuts, passed on the thought and instead opted for getting something to nibble from my apartment. I was halfway up the stairs when I spotted two eyes glowing green behind the replacement terracotta. Snowball. He hissed. I stood blinking furiously for a minute or so (remembering Blue Peter's how to get along with your cat) but to no avail.

Snowball's head followed my every move, ears folded back like a devilcat, fur standing on end, eyes reflecting the light from the illuminated Christmas tree. He had hold of something. A bird? A mouse? A guinea-pig? Undeterred by the low growl, I progressed, sucking air through tight lips and squeaking like a dog toy.

He shuffled to the left, his head sweeping side to side each time he contemplated a dash for freedom. He hissed again before dropping it, jumped on the balcony ledge and took a death defying leap, impaling himself on the stork's skyward beak of the ornamental bird table.

I heard the poor thing yelp in pain, but couldn't take my eyes from what he'd dropped.

'Jesus - bloody.... Oh my... ' was what I think I said while trying to contain the urge to skip around the deck. Perhaps shock is what brought on the excitement, but I'll deny all knowledge of titillation. I'll say I was sympathetic towards whoever suffered.

Snowball had dropped a severed penis.

The First Time

Vivid recollections turned into uncertainty. Senses confused as unfamiliar details blended, became physical. Mixing the past with the present. What happened. with what's happening. Vanilla lingered, strong but without source. A flavour almost as Mark breathed through his mouth and it reminded him of rhubarb and custard. The air swirled around the room, touching his neck and face. Bringing with it the smell of cut, grass and horse manure through the window. The smell of summer.

The temperature was cooler than Mark remembered. The surroundings felt different, not entirely accurate as. though to tell him it was a dream. It wasn't happening.

The bedroom door was slightly open. Through the crack he saw the steam curling from the ensuite like a living being stretching, twisting, shaping in its gaseous form. Beckoning him further inside, carrying with it the artificial aromas of toiletries and designer fragrances. A fizzing in Mark's throat as he peeped through the gap and he couldn't explain why it was making him feel so hot. Further inside, easing the bedroom door open slightly, then allowing his feelings to ravish his morals as he tiptoed quietly, breathlessly inside. Not contemplating repercussions of his actions. Living for the moment. Living for the incredible sensation.

Mark could see their outlines behind the misty shower door. The pounding of the shower stole intimate noise, the steam intimate detail, but he could see their two bodies wrapped around each other. Pressing against each other. It was as though he was watching something else. Two strangers making love. People he didn't know or care for. His feet frozen to the floor. Eyes stinging through the inability to blink, the fear that a split second of blackness may steal something. Cool sweat on his forehead as their bodies became clearer, stepping from behind the shower door, colour once blurred clear, crisp. Water on their skin. A tickling in his throat as he imagined them touching him. Warren's eyes seemed detached from his body as Mark saw he was looking directly at him. Geena looked round. Both of them froze in their intimacy seeing the peeping tom in their bedroom. Watching. Mark didn't attempt to run, or explain his presence, even if he had tried, the words would have been jumbled because the sensations gnawing inside his body were wild. Ravening morals and sense as they ferociously took command of his body and left him standing in full view of them.

It was unrehearsed, raw, unexpected as they stepped from the shower and towelled themselves off. They said nothing. No facial expressions. No words of encouragement as they walked towards Mark. As they touched his face with their hands.

The smell of them so near and Mark recognised them, and he knew those two people. It didn't matter. Nothing mattered but the sex. The feeling. The ecstasy. Eyes closed the situation dissolved. Their faces dissolved, everything but the feel of their hands on his body. The smell of his fleece as it was pulled over his head. Lenor. It reminded him of clean sheets and wet wipes, the ones from KFC. Knees sunk into the mattress, the chill of fresh cotton on his skin. Moulded to his body, hugged him close. And for a moment he was satisfied with the intimacy of a thirteen-point-five tog, as the situation stepped into reality. Hugging it close, the chill felt like cold fingers touching him. Freshly washed hands.

The smell of the pillows puffed into his face. They both had individual scents. Three years of marriage had joined bank accounts, sex lives, aspiration but left their personal scents intact. Behind the artificial Issey Miyake and Imperial Leather, there was something neutral. Indescribable, and he wasn't sure whether he liked it or not. And then all senses but touch blurred for a moment, as he felt two hands on his shoulders, icy. Hard, then warming to his skin temperature as they massaged his neck tenderly. Geena's hands. Two more hands inside the quilt, stroked his skin, kneaded flesh or needed flesh as they worked upwards and around, to his back. Warren. And they felt different. Both of them. Geena's moist and clammy massaged his neck while Warren's talcum-powder dry rubbed his thighs, then the two bodies, the married couple crawled into their marital bed with Mark. Soundlessly. Temperature changed, colder as the quilt was ripped away. Then hot, sticky as two bodies sandwiched Mark's. Breasts pressed against his shoulder blades, chest hair against his face. And it felt like static electricity, or candy floss, or velvet. Touching. Exploring, adjusting. Every inch of skin becoming distinguished, accustomed to the feel of their fingers, their clammy digits smoothing, touching, dimpling.

Mark undressed. Boxers, peeled away, unable to accommodate the swelling. Natural, everything but the artificial smells of aftershave and deodorant and cherry lip balm. Sweat, clean fingers, Imperial Leather.

Coffee breath and shampoo. Organics. But behind that something different.

Hot breath on his face. Lips. Different textures. Greasy lip balm against his mouth as fuller lips moistened his neck. His own tongue slipped over Geena's lips and they felt like plastic, that smooth. Then inside her mouth, polished teeth, squishy tongue slid over wet gums. Then Warren's, he tasted of coffee and bread and something minty.

Onto the floor. No room for such an energetic threesome in the king-size. The flooring was solid as he laid, as all three of them laid. Gradually the laminate took the warmth of sweating bodies, absorbed it as limbs entangled, fingers caressed. Boney fingers dimpled muscle. Tongues, like hot cloths being dragged, fell into folds and creases, moulded to the shape of Mark. Dried on his skin, then taken back inside to moisten, enabling them to slip freely again over his face, ears, neck, thighs. And the change in temperature as the trails of slobber dried on him, something alien for a second, like drying varnish, then nothing. Evaporating. Unable to detect.

Feet, toenails scratched. Soles kneaded genitals that moulded around heels. Sex, poked, opened. Wet, soft, firm. Skin was the sensory element, feeling, crawling, goosebumping at the slightest touch. Moving in waves, together. Three bodies were one as skin peeled away, leaving sweat, a part of themselves smeared over each other like body paint, or oil. Slippery, fingers gliding in spit and sweat and liquid that flowed from all of them as fingers clasped dicks, balls, breasts, vagina. Juicy, everything, like an over ripe peach. Dribbling , oozing. Breath on necks, tongues in mouths, ears.

Between thighs, underarms, around dick, up cunt. At first the scents were distinguishable. Recognisable without seeing faces, but then they mingled. All three aromas, something individual once, then something else. Sweet, acidic, artificial. Neutral. Blending, and Mark could smell himself on their lips, teeth, toes, fingers, faces, cock, cunt. Sex stunk on breath, fingers, faces, necks, thighs. Feet. Soles of feet as they pulled away wet and stinking of the person they'd touched, inserted. Fondled. Overwhelming all other aromas. Only it wasn't as pleasurable as the individual aromas, so noses delved for that one last essence, between thighs, around balls, between breasts, lower back, necks, knees. No boundaries. No boundaries. There were none between them, and nothing was dirty or dirtying as they took time to bring each other to the point when the feeling was like they'd been impaled by something warm that bubbled through their bodies, slowly, gently, from toes to the tops of their skulls. Fizzing inside, like insects. Termites burrowing through crawling flesh. Walls inside Geena squeezed, clenched. Balls tightened and juices were hot, thick, spurted, then cooled, thinned. Dribbled, oozed. Then gone. Dead. Cold and gently rolling from their skin, over contours and twitching muscles. Three scents mixed as they laid there, satisfied, then separated. Cut grass, horse manure. Issey Miyake and Imperial Leather. Coffee breath and cherry lips. Breath stinking. Anonymity fucked away. They knew each other again.

'What were you dreaming about, Mark?'

The room flickers with shadows. The plastic tree contorts into a hideous being which moves and stretches. A vanilla aroma lingers behind pizza as Lucille holds out a plate.

'I can't remember.'

'I've brought you pizza,' she whispers, pulling a chair beside the bed and cutting squares into a slice of Pepperoni Feast with extra mozzarella and anchovies.

Fork after fork Mark is fed, intermittent sips of caffeine-free Pepsi are administered. Chocolate cheesecake mashed and spooned, before Lucille, armed with a bottle of Evian and Colgate, shoves in and out of Mark's mouth with an Oral-B.

'All done,' she says, clearing plates and clinking cutlery before returning with water and three pills.

'May I use the toilet?' Mark asks.

'In the morning.'

'I'm desperate.'

'Take these pills.'

'Please.'

'Lucille says you need rest.'

'I can't hold it until the morning.'

'You'll fucking hold it until I say!'

'I'm going to piss myself here!'

Lucille stands, turns and grabs a bottle of Australian Semillon.

'And why am I fucking tied to the bed?'

Shattering the bottom of the bottle, she spins, lunging towards his neck. With her other hand she clamps his chin and smashes his head three times against the headboard. Mark can't comprehend what's going on as she leans closer to him.

'You'll do as Lucille says, you fuck!'

The acidic stink of bad wine wafts while the glass bottle pricks his throat as smiling she presses harder into the skin until scratches bubble with blood.

'Lucille is a lady! Don't speak to ladies with that tone!'

Steadying him, she crashes the bottle over his head, showering slithers of glass into his face. Unlocking the handcuffs, she clamps one set around his ankles before dragging him from the bed, the glass grating into his back until he thumps on the floor.

He clutches for the chair leg hoping it will anchor him somehow. Lucille notices, drops his feet, snatches the chair and hurls it onto the bed before kicking him in the ribs.

'I'll rip your fucking face apart if you fight with me!'

She drags him into the bathroom and he has no idea of time or destination as she sits him upon the toilet and tells him if he doesn't use it she'll slice off his dick. And he tries, squeezes to a point where he thinks he'll explode. And he'd rather bleed through strain than his dick sliced off, so he squeezes until water splashes with runny shit.

'Are you done? Are you fucking done!'

She snatches him from the toilet and hurls him into the bath where she hoses him down with scalding water until he screams and cries and gulps all at the same time. She calls him a motherfucker, a piece of shit. She dares him to speak to her like that again.

'I bought you a fucking pizza, you inconsiderate arsehole!'

She snatches the spray bleach beside the bath, still directing the shower she squirts, in the eyes, the face, the bloody cuts on his back and his neck and torso, that beautiful flat stomach, hairless, and moving ever so violently.

'Stop!' he cries.

'I haven't fucking started!'

She drops the shower head and it snakes around, spraying steaming water all over the room as she unscrews the spray from the bleach and pours the remaining over his hair. Stilettos clipclop from the bathroom, to the drawer to the left of the hob and she pulls out the revolver. Loaded. Back to the bathroom, where Mark rubs his eyes with fists and jolts each time the scalding spray shoots at him. The water stops. The hissing gives way to drips that echo. She throws a towel at him, but he doesn't realise because all he's saying is: 'my eyes, my fucking eyes!'

'Wipe your *fucking eyes* or I'll gauge them out with my fingernails!'

86

'They sting!'

She leans over to poke the towel at his face and he dabs so it soaks the sweat and bleach and tears streaming down his face before opening his eyes to a blur, gradually focusing from black and red and silver to hair, a black dress. A gun held out straight and pointing at his chest.

Mark wonders how it will feel, a bullet exploding inside his chest. He wonders how it'll look, ankles clamped together, naked and lying in his own blood. His face twists as he lets out a wail, squints and thumps the side of the bath because this isn't fair.

This shouldn't happening.

'I'm sorry. I'll do what you say, just don't shoot me, please!'

'*Don't shoot me please. Please don't shoot me!*'

'I'll do whatever you want.'

'What makes you think I'll settle for anything less?'

'Why am I here?'

'For my pleasure. You're here for me, and if you piss me off, maybe I won't want you anymore...'

'What are you going to do to me?'

'Whatever I want.'

'How long are you going to keep me here?'

'I haven't decided.'

'Why me?'

'You fit the bill.'

'Please, let me go.'

'This is it, Mark. This gun is the only way you'll leave here. Do you still want to leave?'

'This isn't happening. This can't be fucking happening!'

'But it is. Deal with it.'

'My fucking eyes!'

'Shut up.'

'I can't take this!'

'Stand up.'

'I can't!'

'Get out of the tub or you can sleep there tonight.'

He sniffs into the towel covering his body and face. 'My ankles are cuffed together. I can't get out.'

Pressing her palm against that torso, that beautiful flat stomach, moving ever so irregularly, she unclips one handcuff and carries him to bed.

Lying, strapped, gagged and drugged, Mark stares at Lucille as she pours liquid from a brown bottle onto two pads of cotton wool.

'Lift your head,' she says, as she tapes them around his eyes. 'This'll stop them stinging. Just relax.'

Mark flinches each time he feels her touching him, stroking his cheek and his hair. He tries to change the images in his head, to switch off to the fear, but he can't. Her hands are still there, touching him. Lucille's face. The scratches stinging on his back. His eyes. The sound of her palm against unshaven skin. But gradually the sensations lose definition. He feels light headed, and forgets as he falls to sleep.

Lucille pushes her fingers through his thick brown hair. It still smells of bleach, she notices as she buries her nose into his parting and takes in a lungful. Trailing from his chin to his dick, she traces the thread-blue veins. That was good, she thinks. The bathroom. The hot water. The steam. The screaming. The crying was exquisite. She shivers remembering his mouth open wide as he squealed, and how the spit dangled from his chin, like a baby. A big baby. And his body shivering. The way the water caught the light. The way he bunched his fists to rub his eyes.

Ninth Life

Ellie came to me in tears, a quilted gown and flannelette pyjamas. She sat upon my bed slurping Metaxa while telling me about the white sheets, the white cat, her weak pink eyes and the washer-dryer.

I wrapped my arm around the frail Ellie as she glugged five-star Metaxa, before she explained how Snowball must have slipped from his velvet cushion and burrowed into the laundry basket and how she'd been celebrating something she can't remember, and how the sheets had to be washed and dried, ready for Andrea's weekly linen change.

I felt for her as she pressed her face into my chest and blamed herself for the saturated lump she tugged by the sleeve (tail).

'He wouldn't have suffered, as soon as the machine kicked into high spin he'd have been knocked unconscious ......'

She's been crying for half an hour, her face pressed against me as she dribbles spit and mucus into my sweatshirt, but I feel as though I can hold her all night. Sitting here, with the radio humming something, the icy draught blowing through the window vent, the sound of footsteps outside. The smell of Snowball, pissy and wafting up from her pyjamas doesn't seem so repulsive now. And the intimate sniffles of the poor old lady who drinks Metaxa by the gallon, who sent her one and only to a blistering death in the ninety-degree pre-wash. As she slumps further into my chest and the brandy glass slips from her hand, the sniffles turn into breathing, peaceful and dreamy. Unconcerned with life or death, cats and washer-dryers. Her hot breath, moist within the Umbro fabric, and I wish I could join her in oblivious slumber, because I did it. I did it, and I wish to God I hadn't.

His body was like a water bed. Somerville. A man. A person whom people knew and loved. He was somebody's baby. Then a thing, an inconvenience in the whores' work-place. She'd dragged him from the bath prior to my arrival in the black M3 that had a gun in the glove box and a flask of whisky in the door pocket (which I downed while driving through Brooklyn). I'm not sure what possessed me for those few hours. Stoli/marijuana. Coke/Long Island. Even a man with a fertile imagination could have never imagined himself in a position like that.

The streets were desolate. Figures in baseball caps and woollen hats by the two-mile. Neons dead for the night. Sirens silenced. Finally. If there'd have been a road which led back to the world I knew, I'd have driven by. Past the sign, the freedom, towards the conspiracy, because it was exciting. I'm disgusted to think of how it excited me, how ethics and righteousness abandoned me. Dolores worked her magic and turned something dull into fiery excitement. The heart raced, thumped in my chest, my head, my hands. The thought of being part of it thrilled me.

And then the car park across the street from Heritage. Through the gates I walked, to Somerville, a man of fifty-or-so-years, who'd heard 'I love you.' But he was dead. All that remained of the individual, the brain, the persona, the soul - a carcass. A memory.

Excitement gone. Cocktail of spirits and drugs and emotion swirled inside my throat. The room swirled to compensate and the vomit stayed inside.

'You want to see his dick before I dress him?' she laughed.

I couldn't reply, but I saw the bulging of swollen bollocks inside his underpants as gloved hands dressed the body: Green trousers, white shirt, jacket and tie, leaving a figure greyed and still greying dressed to take lunch. To dine in a restaurant. To visit the bank manager. Not dressed for a whore, definitely not dressed to visit a whore.

I snapped on latex gloves. 'Can't be too careful. They can do amazing things with science now,' she said with a dull tone as if the excitement had left her too. She adopted a methodical attitude, shrink-wrapping his body with two jumbo rolls of clingfilm, accepting my limitations and allowing me to sit on the lace bedspread, glugging something clear and potent from a triangular bottle. And all I did was watch, all I could do was witness the way she handled it. The coolness of a woman who could take on the Klingon Empire, wake up in the morning and order a hazelnut coffee. And if I could have placed how I felt then, it couldn't have been one sensation.

Awe/fear/disgust. Anxiety/remorse/uncertainty. Sitting on the bed, looking into the dry eyes, which Dolores said wouldn't close, as a woman I didn't nearly know wrapped a man I'm glad I didn't know.

She said she'd bought the rug five years ago at a market in Greenwich Village. She loved it then, but now it was as dead as the man, then she laughed. It was a strange laugh, like someone had told her not to, and this someone was watching, and she'd forgotten herself for a moment, laughing through her nose. It could have been a sneeze.

All finished. Wrapped and ready to go. She needed help to roll him inside the rug, which I didn't mind, because his face looked monstrous peeping through five layers of clingfilm. The blackness of his nostrils, the blue-grey of his lips. The death-stare distorted even more behind twists and folds of clingy plastic covered at last, until we lifted the weight and his head slipped through the end. *'Hey what are you doing with me this isn't what I wanted! I had a heart attack! Don't treat me like a victim! I don't want this!'*

And I didn't! I couldn't do it, carry him down the stairs, across the road and into the car. I dropped him in the lounge against the sofa or threw him, I can't remember. And the dull thump seemed so loud that everyone in Heritage should have come out to see what was happening, peering through the windows to see Dolores and the man from England with a rug and a dead face saying: *'Help me, this isn't how I wanted it!'*

I cried. I fell to my knees and pressed my hands to my face, hiding my cowardice from the bitch-warrior-woman. And my palms reeked of something sweet/sour/decaying. A personal smell, rotting. Gone off. Clinging to my hands and fingers and beneath my nails. And could I ever wash it away, and would Somerville's stench allow me to wash it away? Or would it flourish, because it wanted to, would it stay with me because *he* wanted to, lingering around my fingers each time I wash my hands/my face/my teeth. Every time I pick my nose/squeeze a spot/ scratch my chin.

I vomited, and it was black-brown. It covered Dolores and her new carpet as it propelled from my mouth as if shooting at the gloved hands that came to hold and comfort me and pat my back and gather my strength to finish what I had become part of, because I drove the car. I helped a crazy fuck who I didn't even know. Didn't even care for. But she held me close anyway. Held my head the way I'm holding Ellie's. Stroked my hair, buried her nose into it and sniffed at the Turner smell (it was still there). She didn't say it was a bad dream. She told me to calm down. She explained she needed my help. She said: 'Help me with the body, wait in the parking lot, and I'll drive the car.' She'd take the rest on herself

I'd never smoked before then. Never felt any kind of inclination before she passed me a fag (English slang for cigarette/American slang for gay) and I dragged until I coughed and coughed and forgot the tears were for Somerville.

I wanted that Marlboro to last forever.

Lifted again. Held my breath. Sucked in quickly through my mouth, and could I taste the stench? His feet down on the ground. Front door open. Coast was clear. Struggled as she bent, grappling with his feet, then onward. Along the deck. Tiptoe please. Quiet. Very quiet. Pass closed blinds. Turner. Ant. Jenny. Ellie. Steps creaked. Too loud. Someone might see. Slower. Remember the creaky steps. That one, miss that one. And that one, step to the left. Totally miss the bottom, that one cracks. Snow crunched. Body heavy, but rigid. Gates left open. Through. Out to where anyone could have walked up and seen.

Strange time to be throwing out a rug?

Cross the road, heavy snow started to fall. A Christmas tree over there, with Santa and Rudolph upon the roof, and the reins glowed with tiny yellow lights. But no-one about. Into the car park. Bleep, bleep (the remote). She dropped the feet. The boot lid popped, the passenger door opened as she climbed in and flipped the back seats down to accommodate six foot. Put the feet inside. Shove. Harder. He wouldn't go in. Shove. Shove harder. Harder! *Fucking get in you bloated bastard! You're dead! What about me? What about my life!* Buckled, the clingfilm snapped as his feet skidded upwards, his head inside. Quickly, close the boot. Close the boot. No-one around. No-one saw.

She said nothing as she opened the drivers' door, and the M3 purred into action. Two red lights glowed. Brighter. Then moved slowly away. White exhausts fumes. Then gone.

The snow was fluffy and brilliant white. I thought of Snowball on his velvet cushion, then eyed the car tracks dirtying the brilliance. The Father Christmas on the roof the other side of the parking lot.

'No presents for you Turner, you've been a bad boy, a very very bad boy.

I thought about home. Nine in the morning there. Within half-an-hour mum would have been waking me up with tea and marmalade on toast. Reminding me to unplug everything before leaving for work, in case of lightning.

'It's always the time ofyearfor lightning, Turny. '

The tree would be up. The porcelain baubles. The kitchen decorated with strips of tinsel, perfectly parallel, lametta glistening.

Dad used to come home for Christmas. Out would come the rolling machine and the ounce of Golden Virginia. (He was only allowed roll-ups in case he dropped one). I'd roll a tin-full of skinny cigarettes, fill the jar with jelly beans and gummy bears. He'd smoke a rollie. Eat a gummy bear. Smoke a rollie. Eat a jelly bean. I'd empty the ashtray.

Check if he needed the toilet. Leave him watching the black and white videos mum kept in the attic. And I'd love those times. Once I'd finished my lunch mum would say: 'Go on, into the lounge so your father can have his Christmas meal.' And I wouldn't mind. It became routine. I ate, then dad. That was how Christmas was. I sat in the lounge picking Quality Street toffee from between my teeth until I became sick of the secrecy concerning the dining habits of my handicapped father and peered around the door: Dad in his wheelchair, napkin around his neck while mum fed him squares of turkey and stuffing and roast potato and ham with a Postman Pat baby spoon. And mum shouted: 'GET OUT! GET OUT' The first and last time she'd ever shouted, because she loved dad. She understood him. She knew he hated me seeing him that way. I'd lifted him onto the toilet. I'd flushed the chain and pulled his pants up. But feeding him squares of food from a Postman Pat baby spoon, who could take that at nineteen? How could a son respect a father after that?

I loved him. So much. And I knew about him, the way he was. I knew mum fed him, and I *could* take it. He was the one who couldn't. Pride wasn't a muscle diseased by Multiple Sclerosis as he screamed obscenities. He nudged the bowl full of traditional lunch after being witnessed eating the untraditional way. The bowl smashed. And so did the Featherstone Christmas.

Albany Nursing Home became the setting for the ensuing Christmases. Spent at the home where semi-circled armchairs hugged the television. Grey-haired ladies with sunken chests and pink cardigans held hands as false toothed smiles beamed towards the strapping young lad with gift-wrapped gelatine confectionery who came to spend Christmas with daddy. Men in grey jackets and brown trousers played cards for matchsticks across the room by the french doors which opened onto a crazy paved patio with three wooden benches. The Blue Lady stared suspiciously from above the fireplace at the strapping young lad who destroyed his father, as the nurse guided me through to room thirty-two.

Dad's hair was weighted and wet like someone had swirled over a bald head with a silver metallic pen. A person I couldn't recognise stared unblinkingly at the paisley wallpaper, sunken and grey, juddering like some old fool at fifty-five. They said it was the pneumonia killing him, devouring him like an anaconda. And then on that public holiday, that joyous occasion when we remember others, a sound like a dog growling into a teapot. He died right there stinking of piss and shit and vomit and stale, Golden Virginia.

It was something I couldn't comprehend. He was dead. I thought he'd always be there, like some fairground freak. *'Come see the Smoking Juddering Man who won't speak, can't wash or do anything for himself. We set him to the left of the cage, see him judder to the right! Roll up, roll up, see the Spastic Man smoke a roll up!'*

The year after he died mum laid the table. A seat for dad, only not a Postman Pat bowl and baby spoon set, but bone china, three forks, two knives and a spoon for the flaming plum pud.

I hadn't noticed the temperature until Dolores' heat pressed against my cheek. The gloves had been disposed of somewhere between Heritage and the body. The leopard print jacket buttoned to her chin with collar folded up and red wig speckled with snow as she gripped arms of the shivering fool. Lifted, linked and escorted back to the scene of the crime where in silence we sipped espresso until the navy injected with white brought sun and birds and sleep and a dream I can't remember.

I woke alone, fully dressed and covered with three blankets lying on the bed where I'd witnessed the wrapping. I could still smell him.

Dolores could have been somewhere in the apartment, but I didn't look. Left without saying goodbye, or where's the coffee. Or did it *really* happen?

My apartment, where I threw my clothes into my wheel-less suitcases, I went to the drawer for my passport. In its place was a photo of me gripping an Indian rug, the greyed face of Somerville that expression I thought I'd never see again, said cheese to the lens.

Suzanne Conway

Poems and Prose

Baklava

At Spurn we sat in the car
rocking with the wind,
watching sand swirl above the ground.

We combed the beach looking for glass,
our clothes flapping like kites,
under a light-striped sky.

We skimmed stones,
counted skips,
wrestled in the wind.

*   *   *

Homebound, you sing the wrong notes,
I smile in the pauses:
You're like a song I always dance to.

Lying in front of the fire
sipping muscat, nibbling baklava,
darkness slides across our faces,

a couple of stargazers,
flushed and warm,
letting each other's hands slip free.

Birthmark

Boxes in the hallway.
Your back to me making tea -
as if this is a time for tea.

I forget myself,
almost trace the Africa-shaped birthmark
on the back of your neck,

the purple map
that betrayed our journey,
made me dream of places unseen,

while you were happy mapless.
Your teaspoon tinkles like a bell,
you're lost in a swirl.

I take your stirring hand -
try to say something, anything.
A man outside our window

clanks in the darkness, fumbling,
changing a tyre by moonlight.
Our faces reflect in the glass,

that's all we're doing,
fumbling for a change in the dark.

Gradients

A man trekking up the main road
drenched through with wind and hail –
Christmas day, and we're driving home
for your medication.

We invent lives for him –
yours uncompromising as the elements,
mine more accommodating:
'He's on his way to his mother's,
he's carless, not friendless.'

Momentarily, I slip into a dream,
lost in the wipers' pattern and the sound of the rain.
The wind catches the under shaft of the car,
lifts, the steering falls away, we flip,
glide on a golden carpet
through a forest of gods and darkness.

In caverns coloured lights illuminate our faces.
We come to an opening, and I find myself
with a fractured mouth,
kneeling at a dried up waterfall,
holding a trembling spoonful of water,
begging you to drink.

Your cough wakes me –
here comes the gobbet of blood
on the handkerchief. Blindly,
I skid onto the side of the road,
massage your ribs.

I catch the back of his red jacket
in my rear view mirror,
stooping into the gradient,
tense with cold.

Driftwood

She believes fervently that God gathers the hesitant souls of the dead on Sundays, that the backlog from the week dance on earth to comfort those left living. Tonight is her last night with her husband, for despite the funeral not being until Wednesday, she knows Sunday is the day when God counts his earthly losses. She is adamant she wants to spend the night alone with him.

She hasn't bathed for weeks, frightened of losing their last embrace, the smell of his old skin grown tired of this world. She imagines him still beneath her nails, and to prevent her own new odour she sprays scent over her clothes when no one's watching, later transferring it onto those she hugs. She plans to wash on the day of his funeral, but until then she wants to live with him on her skin. She plans to wash away her past and to be reborn, she imagines, like a butterfly breaking out of its chrysalis, though she knows too that this is too simplistic, too distant a desire.

Standing beside the open grave, I whisper, "You can be a wild woman now", and she laughs at the possibilities of the life ahead of her – at the thought of wearing slippers in the rain; at a life carefree and without orders; at not having to spend all of her pension on cheap food. When he died her cupboards were stacked full of tins because of his insistence that she buy everything on their shopping list whether they needed it or not, as though the food were rations for a bitter winter when they would be unable to leave the house.

*

Alfred was seventy-five, with a grey moustache untidy at the edges, and bushy eyebrows. He invariably wore a dark green V-neck with the emblem of two crossed golf clubs on his left breast, never having played golf but wanting others to think of him as the kind of man who did. He bought some clubs and they went rusty in the garage. His one true enthusiasm was puzzles, any kind of puzzles. The idea of conquering them excited him. He'd consider crossword clues while strolling to the shop to collect his morning paper, and sometimes he'd stay up late into the night, convinced that a solution was within his grasp.

He liked the idea of the outdoors, but that was as far as it went: "I had enough of all that during the war, out in all bloody weathers whether you liked it or not. Well, I bloody didn't like it." After a life in the Forces he had forgotten how to be a civilian. He barked orders at her and she imagined herself saluting him to let him know how she felt. He had always wanted children but had spent his years looking after those who belonged to other men, continually looking over his shoulder for their shadows.

*

She pretends to be interested in everything you're interested in. I mention that I'm doing a counselling course and she says, "You know, I've always fancied going counselling", as if we might be going cycling together. "She probably thought you said canvassing," my husband says.

She's one of those people who laughs easily. She has shoulder-length curly hair that varies from purple to auburn to brown depending on how successful her dyeing session is. 'Colouring,' she calls it. "Never say dye. That's part of the fun, not knowing what you're going to look like. And the best bit is that at my age you don't care. It's such a relief to shed all that vanity."

"As long as you're not grey, right?"

She spends hours sitting by the river sketching, rustling in her carrier bag for a pad and pencil. I've watched her from a distance and seen how she wanders about trying to get the perfectly proportioned view, how she raises her finger to get the precise measure and line of a solitary tree. She finds inspiration in the dappled yellow and green leaves, in the varying shades of red and brown. She collects things, slipping fragments of nature into her turquoise mac and carrying them home. Today she's pacing up and down, looking at her feet, enjoying the dry crunching of leaves. It's a calm day, yet she's dressed to brace herself against the wind, and in the background ducks are clapping, gliding against the tide and leaving triangles in their wakes.

*

It's Halloween, Alfred's birthday. We drive to the beach and spend our time in the grey noise between stations, avoiding love songs. Looking away from me, she says, "I think part of me needs to sleep this journey."

We're going to their courting place, where their fifty years began, and though she's trying to hide it, I hear the absence in her voice. She's wearing his herringbone overcoat, bought from Oxfam, and I'm in layers as thick as a duvet.

At Spurn-Point we sit in the car and rock with the wind, watching the sea curl back on itself. Opening the car door is like being under water, the pressure's so great, but she climbs out the driver's side. We brave the sand storm and I am nervous for her, for her frailty in the wind. I needn't be; at sixty-nine she's steadier on her feet than I am.

"It's amazing how you never get tired of looking at the sea", she says, then catching me by surprise, quietly adds, "That's what I feel like, a piece of driftwood, rising and falling on the surface of something." I notice her eyes are half-dreaming, half-blinking, and she looks as if she's about to fall into a deep sleep. Then something in the wind catches her and she grabs my hand and drags me knee deep into the water. She doubles over laughing as she splashes me. I chase her and we run back up the beach to find somewhere sheltered to collapse and relax.

*

I remember visiting them as a child. On the way I played in the back of the car, excited at the journey, unaware that I would cry all the way home, not knowing that Alfred would stroke my hair as if he loved me, and then present me with his precious, semi-precious crystals. I trembled as I held those rocks nestled in their velvet-clad box. "Open if, he said, and in that same instant his shadow fell across my face. I raised the lid, but clumsily, and an emerald betrayed my touch, fell and bounced onto the rug at our feet. I shuddered as his shadow enveloped me and his prickly face grazed my cheek.

As I rushed out of that room, I caught my foot and fell, and as I fumbled on the floor his hand grabbed my throat, and lifted me clean off the ground. I coughed and frowned. A child dungarees, he could have picked me up by my pockets.

*

The Chinese believe grief lives in the shoulder blades, in our lost and vestigal wings, which is why mourners tend to stoop. When I tell her this she flaps her arms and runs in circles on the sand. It is now that I notice how proud she stands, and I recall how she sticks her chest out at men. The sky is dark, but in the distance the horizon is striped with a pink and dying light.

It is only now that I remember the sandstone pebbles I collected with her. Half a dozen wet stones that seemed to have the last true sun of the summer in them. "They're all right until you get them home", she said. Undeterred, I slid them into my pocket and fingered them as we walked. Now I retrace my steps in memory, fearful that when I handed her my scarf and coat, I handed her the pebbles too, and she, not liking them much, dropped them one by one. Frantic to find them, I search all our bags. Surprised by my urgency, by my need to possess something, she touches my arm, taps her temple and whispers, "They're in here".

*

Some people in shock lose their sense of taste or smell. For her nothing tastes the same. "I got so used to eating cheap rubbish, maybe my taste buds don't recognise good food." I take her out for a meal, to an Italian, where we spend most of our time laughing. She recounts how she finally ventured into Safeway so excited at the prospect of exchanging tins, for cress, corn on the cob and everything else she had been denied, that she walked the length of the high street to her bus stop without noticing the wire basket was still on her arm. "I was so embarrassed I left it on the nearest bin."

Sipping liqueurs, she said, 'You know, that's what I like about being with you, I can be alone and you don't mind. I can get lost in the grain of this table or a candle, and when I look up you're not waiting.'

*

On the night of his funeral, we found ourselves on the beach, perched on a groyne in silence.

'He used to hit me you know, if I made a mistake on the shopping list or overboiled the sprouts. I'd have walked out on him, but he always said he'd find me'.

The night closed in around us, and as we sat watching the moonlight on the water, neither of us caring how we'd get back, I found myself wondering at the speed with which we all, one way or another, became accustomed to the varying degrees of darkness in which our lives were lived.

Clare Birchall

Winnebago

Emigration. The word made it sound easy. But it was a word without wings. It lied, left you checking out the flights in the *Washington Post* every other day. Made flight a part of your life when mythology told you that this was dangerous: a life obsessed with flight.

The word didn't tell you how English you would feel even though you had never felt English in England. It didn't reveal how you would ham up your role at work and dinner parties, sly witticisms and blunt observations, saying the things others couldn't because their accents wouldn't let them get away with it.

It forgot to say that the telephone would become your best friend, how you couldn't live without it. How words like *duvet* and *Marmite* became almost archaic and obsolete. It did not tell you how your eyes would smart when someone asked innocently at the end of the day, "Are you going home?" How the word 'home' became a simile. How the flat in Arlington was only *like* home.

*

Will had flown to London late Monday night. Lia hadn't wanted to stay behind. She hated Washington, the way you had to watch what you said at dinner parties because you never knew whose father worked for the government. She hated the pride, so second hand: a distance without irony. She often went to George Town to be surrounded by students and avoid fast food restaurants. She would hide in her favourite coffee shop and breathe in the dark aroma of ground beans, glad for a smell that was real. She preferred to be surrounded by these small businesses and shady lanes than go downtown to clean lines and wide streets. Where events were commemorated through form, where every structure meant something rather than did something. She hated the whiteness of it all, as if snow were something you could emulate or wish upon a city.

They had moved there for her.

"For your career," he had said. As if it were something that could be packed in a suitcase and would not crease. She felt flattered that he was prepared to do this for her. To leave his father so soon after his mother had been put in a home, to leave when his parents were so much older than hers. She had been offered a contract at a publishing house that specialised in political poetry. People said it was a step in the right direction.

She had thought that publishing would be the same the world over, but words not only seemed to mean different things in different places, they worked differently. Words let her down over here. Left her high and dry. They didn't quite manage to take her where she wanted to go.

As a child she marvelled at an American camper van her next-door neighbours had imported: a Winnebago. A monstrosity of silver and blue that dominated her dull street. Sometimes, she slept in the van with a friend. But more than these sleepovers – the midnight feasts of raw jelly squares; the miniature kitchenette that had its very own refrigerator to keep ice-pops in – more than this, it had a name she didn't understand. She had assumed that whenever her neighbours went on holiday, they were going to a place called Winnebago. They went for longer and longer holidays. Her Dad said it was because Mr Wilson was retired now and had more time on his hands. But Lia decided it was because Winnebago got further and further away. What kind of place was a place that moved?

Winnebago. To her untravelled ear it sounded exotic and ceremonious. She felt an inexplicable nostalgia every time she set foot in it. She wanted a name that told her where she was going. A name that could guide her.

Of course, now she knew Winnebago was not only a place but a Native American people with their own language and signs, their own lessons in nostalgia.

*

He is her most sobering thought. Her early morning wake-up call. Her way of starting the day, concentrating on the space his body might have occupied. It hadn't always been like that. He used to wake her in other ways.

Back home in England, he had woken her with laughter. Him watching an early morning breakfast show.

She mumbled, "What's so funny?"

"TV'sfunny," he said, lazily running the words together. And she repeated him, a sleepy mantra, and dreamt of acronyms.

He had woken her with chords of a half-written song and she looked up to see his face flushed with concentration. She tried to distract him with naked dances, a playful challenge to make him forget the melody, like a child reciting random numbers when you are trying to memorise an address or date.

She had been woken by him unconsciously clutching her hand. She quietly tried to narrate the nightmare into a different genre, subliminally easing his grip.

She was woken by a name that was not hers, not even if you tried to hear it wrong. A bad note in a familiar piece of music.

*

He had always hated the way she said 'just' as in "I just want you to talk more." As if that were *all* she wanted. The way 'just' coloured her statements in innocence. As if it left him options. He pointed this out once, and she flinched, saying, "I'm just trying to tell you how I feel."

He had accused her of harbouring romantic ideals that he couldn't satisfy. When she said, "But you always *used* to be romantic," he replied, "You can't expect me to live up to myself."

When she wouldn't make love after he called Merchant-Ivory productions "Barbara Cartland for yuppies," he asked her what was wrong.

She said, "I just want a room with a view."

"Jesus, I can't compete with movies," he complained.

"Hey, your ideas of love and stuff are from TV and film too."

"Yeah, but unfortunately," he said, under his breath, "we were watching different shows."

It wasn't that romance was an end in itself. She liked the way it promised things. It gift-wrapped a person you might not otherwise want to get inside.

He had asked her out because she had published a poem in the university magazine entitled *Why Philosophers Make Bad Lovers.* The third stanza rhymed 'Nietzsche' with 'pizza' and he knew he was in love. He had written a reply: *Why Poets Make Fun of Philosophy* and rhymed 'Sylvia Plath' with 'don't make me laugh'. He affectionately called her his poet, pronouncing it *Möet*. After lovemaking, they would ask things like, "What's another word for synonym?" or "What did etymology once mean?"

He told her that this love annihilated all others. That it was the H-bomb of desire. She wasn't sure if she was supposed to seek shelter.

*

He had told her to stay, that she couldn't afford any more time away from work. She had her career to think of. He would be alright, maybe it was better this way, he could settle his father's affairs quicker if she was not there. It would be hypocritical of her to attend the funeral, they had never liked each other.

She knew that wasn't the point, that she was supposed to go for him. To be supportive. And she said this, "I want to support you," not meaning it. She knew he didn't want her to go and she wanted him to say it. What would it take for him to say it?

They had stopped punctuating silence with kisses. There were just silences now. He said goodbye while she was watching TV. She hadn't meant to be sitting there in her pyjamas eating from a tub of ice-cream. In her role as concerned partner, she was supposed to hold him tightly, kiss the loss from him. She couldn't bring herself to touch him. He might have thought she was trying to stake her ground, to leave an abundance of fingerprints. His suspicion was so acute, every gesture had begun to feel insincere. And yet, surely, it was her who had the right to think about trust. Him going back to England.

She remembered the fights and the fragile promises, the way they had reconstructed their future like a matchstick model. Painfully slow. The year together since then had not been easy. If anything, his reassurances had become harder to swallow, even by mistake.

She felt guilty for thinking these things when there was death to think about.

There was so much to do. He had mentally written a list of tasks, and a list of lists to make. But his father's lawyer had taken care of most of the details, and he had already telephoned the people that needed to know. And yet, there must still be so much to do. His father didn't seem to have many friends, although it only really struck him now, thinking about a funeral with nobody there. If there was no one to see him buried, would he really be gone?

The house was not far from Heathrow. It was dark when he arrived, but he could colour in the faint outlines from memory. The year since he had been here was lost to an indelible familiarity. Everything was in its place except his father. He did not know what to do with this absence. It threatened to take him with it. He felt as if he were waiting, for someone to come back, or something to sink in. For himself to catch up with his skin. He lay down upon the sofa and fell asleep to the smell of fresh dust, tucking his knees up to his chest. Dust. The dead skin of his dead father.

He wanted to tie his life up, tight, like laces.

*

At first, Lia did not miss him. She could not have explained it. He just was not there and that was that. It did not seem strange to her that he had not called, not even on the day his father was buried. At nights, she read about grief from books his friends had chosen from the self-help section. They said, *Hug a pillow at night for comfort.* And, *Place all memorabilia in a box.* She dreamt of being smothered by pillows or the lid of a box descending upon her head.

She woke with a hand clutching her heart and recognised the grip as her own. In some ways it was reassuring. She had thought her heart had died and was living on the memory of a pulse. She wondered if anyone has anything interesting to say about the heart.

*

He had not noticed before how the house was made from a slate that could not hold the sun. There was no shine left in it. He remembered his father walking along the wall, one hand trailing over the stone, inspecting it for erosion. His father had been obsessed with the idea that his house was getting smaller, like a coastline. He pictured his father shaking his fist to the sky, angry at the flight path. As if aeroplanes could be frightened off like birds by a scarecrow. When Will thought of his father, he tried to see him with the flicker of cinefilm. Enough frames per second missing to tell you that this was the past. A way to persuade himself that his father was in fact dead. Everyone was always dead when you watched them on cinefilm.

He went to visit his mother. It was a functional place that smelled of urine and lavender. She had already been told that her husband had passed away.

Still, "Is your father alright?" was the first thing she asked Will.

He said, "No," then "Yes." He did not think it was fair to make her a widow every day of the year. She called him by his father's name and

110

he did not correct her. Just smiled and held her cold hand, the finger dented where her wedding ring had been. They had taken it off to ease her arthritis, aid her circulation.

He needed her signature. It was illegible in a way that made it obvious he could not have forged it. Some of the letters faced the wrong way. The ink was hesitant. Each movement of the pen had been thought about and questioned and then questioned again. The name itself seemed doubtful. A spell that failed to conjure her up.

When he left he said, "I love you."

And she said, bemused, "You always say that." As if it were a figure of speech particular to him.

*

She didn't tell any of her colleagues where Will had gone. She didn't mention him and they didn't either. She wasn't even sure if any of them remembered his name. She had occasionally almost forgotten it herself, like an extinct animal or ancient tribe, their names bereft of function, relegated to history or the tip of the tongue. She had tried to forget the name he had whispered that was not hers. Isabel. Somehow, he had been drawn into this forgetting. It was easier that way. It left a comforting space, a lull into which she could fall.

Three weeks after Will had left, Lia was supposed to meet a poet her publishing house had just signed at Dulles Airport. She dressed mechanically and applied make-up in the rush hour hold-ups. She headed straight for Arrivals and stood there with a wilting paper sign. It spelt out the poet's name in unconvincing capitals. She prepared to give him a charming smile. In the office, they called it exercising good poetiquette. People strained their necks to see a loved one among the strangers. Dazed travellers walked hesitantly forward with their trolleys like film stars caught unprepared by paparazzi flashes. They all looked like they had only just woken up and didn't know what day it was. It felt right to stand there, expectantly, as if something might change. As if someone could arrive as well as leave.

The flight was delayed and she decided that she needed a hot drink. She asked if they had any proper tea and the boy quipped "All property is theft."

"I'll just have a latte, smarty." She surprised herself for enjoying this exchange. Pleased to be reminded that language could be played with and still get things done. This was the way she and Will had once communicated.

She sat at a raised, metallic table on an uncomfortable stool and blew on her steaming coffee. By the time she remembered to drink it, it was cold. She was surrounded by the signs of transit. Suitcases, tickets, passports and mild panic. Children were running into each other in their excitement. People drank faster than usual, cursing their burnt tongues. They ate while walking, even if their flights were delayed, understanding somehow that this was no place to stay or enjoy.

She overheard conversations. Mindless, banal. It comforted her to know that people still talked even when they had nothing to say.

"Culture." A southern woman read the back of a yoghurt pot to her companion. "Honey, what is that?"

A man walked past, slapped his buddy on the back and laughed so loud, his laugh had nowhere left to go.

A honeymooning couple asked her to take a photograph. She told them to say cheese and they did, in harmonised pitch. And she wished she could record this rather than their rehearsed smiles.

An airfreight representative sidled up and asked if she had any excess baggage.

*

He had always hated the way she saw patterns in everything. Of how things happen and how they happened once more. He had told her that this was no way to see the world, and she had replied, "You always say that when you're about to do something bad again."

The disconnected phone did not ring to remind him of communication. He removed all the dust sheets from the furniture, telling himself that he would replace them when he left. He wanted to match the house with his memory of it. His father's funeral had been weeks ago now. More of Will's friends had attended than his father's. His mother had been escorted by a carer from the home. She commented on how warm the chapel was. When the vicar said her husband's full name, Will looked over to see if there was any recognition. She only fidgeted with the lace edging of her glove. The surname, hers and his, took up less space than it had done before.

Grief lodged in his throat like a gumball. It bled colours now and again, but did not seem to get smaller.

He began to work on the garden. He told himself that this would help the house to sell. But instead of planting attractive shrubs and flowers, he planted root vegetables and herbs. He spent a lot of time in his father's study, sorting out the paperwork. He almost expected to uncover a dark secret. An unacknowledged child being paid maintenance. A Swiss bank account. An unmarked key. But there were no enigmas here except death itself. Even his personal correspondence was dull and to the point. There were no love letters to speak of, only a picture of his wife with *I'm the girl you left home for* written on the back. He wrote songs about mispronunciation surrounded by his father's leather-bound volumes of the Oxford English Dictionary.

Some days, he wore something from his father's wardrobe. A shirt or a pair of slippers. He liked the fact that they were slightly too large. He didn't want these items to become his, he didn't want the house to be his. He wanted to always feel the jolt of inheritance. To know that these things were his only because of a name. Yet, he felt more settled than ever. He could not imagine wanting to leave.

He knew it was common to imagine seeing the recently deceased. Sometimes it turned out to be someone with a close resemblance, and sometimes it turned out that there was no one there at all. Will didn't see his father on the street, in the garden, or in his dreams. Instead, he saw Isabel. Isabel's dark curls bobbing around a corner. Her smile caught on a turned head while queuing at the bank. The angle of her step, the slow, precise saunter, seen in a woman going into a bookshop. The line of her body, like slim letters written fast without thought. He saw her everywhere and tried to ignore it, tried to accept it as the trickery of a place made more of memories than of life. This was what happened when you kept one eye on the past.

*

One of Lia's clients, an Indian poet, had told her a myth. Saranyú, wife of Viśvavat the Sun, finds that she can no longer bear her husband's brilliant light. Making use of the source of the problem, she creates a double from her shadow to continue her role while she leaves the household.

Sitting in the airport 24 hours after she had first arrived, Lia was cold. She missed being in his orbit. Her Sun and shadow were somewhere else, bickering about breakfast, or catching a matinee. Her shadow didn't share her contours anymore and from this distance, her Sun was just a star you couldn't help looking at when you looked at darkness. What was left was what sat in the airport watching the faces of people who needed to be there. Watching lives waiting to be reunited in the same time zone.

Maybe this was how it happened. Maybe one day you wake up and realise that your life has found a way to exist without you.

There was something strangely comforting about being in a place she didn't have to pretend made sense. Nobody here thought her unease strange. If they had gone to her flat, of course, they would have found such a demeanour unnerving. You could get away with it here. Being uncomfortable. Looking like you were always just about to leave. She had kept one suitcase packed ever since they had arrived. It sat at the back of the large walk-in closet waiting for her trust to finally break.

She looked at the array of destinations listed like horses to bet on. Her credit card dug into the sides of her hand. London Heathrow would never win. The urge to say, "I love you" had been quelled. Her best lines, she guessed, had already been stolen by someone else. Lines like this had outstayed their welcome.

She felt jealous of suitcases all labelled with their destinations, and of the camper vans parked outside arrivals expectantly. The Winnebagos from her childhood, all dressed up with somewhere to go.

At the airport, she was kept company only by her dyslexic heart. It stuttered from not being able to read or write with ease. When she approached the ticket desk and was greeted by the efficient smile of the sales representative, she crumpled to the ground under the weight of his questions: "How can I help you?", "Where do you want to go?" There was no answer, no simple response, except the way in which her body gave in. Someone was cradling her head and asking her if she was alright. What could she say? She wanted to stay neither here nor there forever. Home had flown and was nesting elsewhere. She did not know where to look for it and it could not find the way back. This loyal, but forgetful bird.

*

Isabel. Her name and her body in the same place. An elegant silhouette, she stood in the doorway where he had first seen her, calling for him to walk down the lane and smoke cigarettes. After all the apparitions, he hardly recognised her. He had half-expected to see her for weeks now, and yet, here she was, whole. She still reflected him. Darkly. Like in the skin of an aubergine. He had once promised Lia not to ever say this name again. And in promising had said it. He spoke her name now and had missed the way it felt. How it fizzed on his tongue like sherbet.

Matt Sparkes

Doppelgänger

Okay, this is how it happened. We were kept in the most awful conditions, inhumane conditions. Six of us, in a room no more than four by three, smoking all day and drinking most of the time. We never got to bed before three in the morning, woke up totally fucked to the same thing all over again. The insects, you've never seen anything like them, it was a plague, they were huge. We saw the spiders killing the horseflies and then they dragged us off to listen to the recitations each day. They were fucking with our heads – stuff about mermaids and bee-keeping and family stuff and animal midwifery. We were exposed to this shit every day. They were trying to break us down, it was a nightmare. After a few days they took away our cigarettes.

Like I say, they were just trying to break us down. I said to one of these guys "How much do you get paid for this?" and he said "five hundred" and I thought "You ought to have more respect" but he just said "I take what I can." Why were they doing this? We could hear conversations next door, women talking about poetry and worshipping some Earth mother figure. That was how it was every day. Meanwhile we were drinking and playing cards. By the end someone had got a gun and we were shooting at the insects. They had this cheap wine, charged us £4 a bottle. It was all a big scam. They were smiling at us saying "We hope you're enjoying this."

Eventually they put us all in the back of a van. One by one they took us out, all at different locations. I didn't have a clue where they'd dropped me – it was somewhere in the middle of an airport, I think. Just people walking around with suitcases looking disorientated. I guess they figured I wouldn't stand out too much in a place like that.

For the next couple of hours I was just trying to rationalise things, walking around this place, couldn't make sense of anything. It took me ages to get home but that was where the real fun began. Anything seemed like a difficult complicated decision. I realised I hadn't had to make a single decision all that time and that that had been the point. Those bastards are crafty fuckers, they got me good.

The above comes from a conversation I had with some girls earlier this evening. My world has taken a turn for the worse of late, having become a place of aliases and doppelgängers. I was relieved, therefore, to be in the company of mature women for a change – rather that the sexually retarded fuck-mongols I had spent recent days locked away with. It had been a time of immense frustration, I can tell you. Immense frustration and bad poetry.

In our little corner the numbers dwindled until it was just me, Eve and Claire D, I told her about my doppelgänger, as referred to above. I have a doppelgänger now, you see; a double, someone at work with the same name. I know of his existence but he works on the other side of the building and I haven't sought him out yet. I don't think I ever will. He appeared on the scene while I had a week off and it's freaked me out. If I ignore him he'll disappear like the ghost in my bedroom, that's the current plan. Post is going to get misdirected, things will get difficult. So much disturbing literature has been based around the existence of a double that I can't help but think that things are going to get strange. Claire D. agreed, "Like someone's stolen your identity" she said.

Last night I was visited by my double in a dream. Though his very existence mocks me, he came into my dream with the express intention of mocking me some more. It was a pleasant enough dream until he got involved. I was given blow jobs by four different women in my role as one of the judges at the World Blow Job Championships, had to give marks out of ten. Darting out to get some fags in a break in the proceedings, I got back to find my double with Maria "The Mouth" Chavez (the Brazilian street-child) hanging off his cock. "Hey", I said, "that's my job." He just laughed and gave me a thumbs up. Then his eyes shut and he started shaking. Chavez released his twitching cock, licked her lips, giggled and started again. I went ballistic, ran out into the hotel lobby shouting at any woman who happened to cross my path "Give me a blow job, now." You never get anywhere acting like that, the security people carried me away. "I'm a judge", shouted and I woke up cursing.

I phoned up my double at work today. "Is that the Louis Xiv that works in Claims?' I said.

"No, I work in Admin. You want the other Louis Xiv."

"No, that's me."

"Sorry?"

"I am the Louis Xiv who works in Claims."

"But you just said...."

"My mistake. Can you put me through to Fiona Welch?"

"Yeah, no problem."

Fiona and I are good buddies. I gave her the heavy breathing routine and told her I wanted to fuck her. She told me to get lost. I said "I'm having a competition round my house next week, I'm inviting all the girls, you wanna come?". Fiona said "That's really weird because

118

Louis here was just telling me about this dream he had about a blow job competition." I hung up.

Anyway, the following day this same chap rings me up, says he's got some misdirected post. Where am I? He'll bring it round. I told him and went out for a fag break. No way do I want to meet this guy face to face. I mean, he might look exactly like me, like he did in the dream. I stayed out in the rain, chain-smoked four just to make sure he'd have enough time to deliver the post. By the time I get back there are some letters on my desk and he's gone.

Report on: (Name, age, address and policy number all crossed out)
It was extremely difficult to take a clear and coherent history from this man, as he was almost wholly blind and totally deaf. All contact was made with him through his wife, who could use finger speech, but this was not of a high standard. The majority of the history I obtained directly from his wife, as questions directed to him resulted in a flood of largely incoherent remarks.
He is one of twin boys and appears to have had a normal childhood until the age of 14 he then began to develop increasing deafness. In 19— he started attending a class for the deaf. At this stage he started to use hand signals which he uses to communicate with his wife. On examination, both drums were white and fibrous. He can just distinguish a shout directly into his ear on either side.

His eyesight started to deteriorate in 19—. He has been blind for four years, and has never been out unaccompanied for the last fourteen years. I understand that a rare form of retinitis pigmentosa is associated with nerve deafness. His fundi and discs confirm the diagnosis.

Four years ago in the summer, he became mentally disturbed. He started doing strange things, his wife told me, such as sweeping the chimney in the middle of the night. He went on a hunger strike and took no food or drink for four days. He was seen by Dr. (name crossed out), the psychiatrist, who admitted him to (name crossed out) Hospital as an in-patient. He stayed there for one week. Dr. (name crossed out) considered he was suffering from depression, believing the world was soon to come to an end, hearing voices that told him to prepare for his doom, and seeing crosses. He was treated medically and did not require electroconvulsive therapy. His wife tells me that he says nasty things to her and suggests she has other men in the house and has affairs with them. Two weeks ago she says he expressed a wish to hang or drown himself, and that he gets very depressed. He himself told me that there is a short wave radio situated in the back of his head. He can get two stations on the radio. The right hand side gives him a Red Indian who talks in English and used to tell him to do things, like breaking windows etc., but he has learned to ignore this person. The left side plays music and hymns, and frequently he receives Harry Secombe singing in Welsh. At one stage in the examination, he was receiving these messages continuously.

I made a full examination of him. His blood pressure was raised to 170/100 and he weighed 13 stone, his height being 5' 11 ." Apart from this mild hypertension and the other information I have given in this report, the medical examination showed no other abnormalities.

To summarise: This man suffers from retinitis pigmentosa and is blind and deaf. He is also extremely depressed with marked schizoid manifestations. I am sure that the conditions will not improve and are very likely to get worse. In my opinion, he is totally and permanently disabled as to render it impossible for him to ever resume employment. Signed:.... (signature and date crossed out)

I met Fiona that night in a club in Kingston. "What are you doing here?" she said, "I thought you'd be playing with your train set." "Fuck you" I said, walking past her to the bar. She sidled up beside me as I waited to be served, passed me a cigarette. We lit up. "How can you smoke this shit?" I asked her. She put her hand to her ear and mouthed "What?", I came close to her ear, breathed in her perfumed soul, "How can you smoke this shit?" I shouted. She laughed. "You shine up pretty good anyhow." I'd never seen so much of her legs before. "Gee, thanks!." Her nipples were erect. I asked if she was cold. "Oh, I'm on fire tonight," she said, "I'm on heat."

Later we danced. She started miming lyrics, it was cheese-night. "Motherfucker, gonna fuck your soul, motherfucker, gonna fuck your soul, motherfucker, gonna fuck your soul, motherfucker, gonna fuck your soul, motherfucker, gonna fuck your soul, motherfucker, gonna fuck your soul, 5, 4, 3, 2, 1. 5, 4, 3, 5, 4, 3, 2, 1. 5, 4, 3, 5, 4, 3, 2, 1. 5, 4, 3. Motherfucker, gonna fuck your soul" and I am surprised that Fiona knows the rest of the words and is not ashamed to put on this performance. She even takes the high notes. "Buttfucked to paradise", until it mixes into the next song which she doesn't know all the words to. "Oh, right" I said. She waves her thumb and walks off the floor, I follow her, thinking she is playing games.

In the taxi she palmed me something.
"What is it?"
"Eat it." Without looking I put it in my mouth.

We sat in our goldfish world in her empty room in her silent house, near strangers, knowing nothing of each other than that we enjoyed external appearances. That we had just made love seemed to mean we could discuss things we would otherwise not have brought up. We nodded and yessed each other towards the strangest revelations, the darkest chambers. She induced me into a world where fish flew and birds swam.

"I like books" she said, "They give the impression that life has direction and themes. It's all a lie I know."

"There's no thread in any of this" I said, "just a feeling of falling through space, bumping into things. No cause and effect, no nothing."

She got up to put on a T-shirt. I said no, she said why. I told her I liked her tits. She said if I liked them so much why didn't I kiss them, so I did and tasted her waxy nipples, my hands resting in her hips.

"You don't even know my name," she said, "but I know yours."

I looked up. "You don't know my name either, I lied to you."

"What is your name?"

"Mike."

"Is that the truth?"

"No."

"You're strange" she said.

"That's rich" I thought.

I kissed her breasts and fingered her for what might have been an eternity.

We made love again, lost ourselves.

Later, we sat in the coldness, holding each other's goosepimpled frames, blessing each other with kisses. We fell apart, shivering in the cold. She got under the covers and I closed the windows, sat on a chair and put my feet up.

"What's wrong?"

"Nothing." We just looked at each other. She pulled down the covers, mischievously revealing a breast and smiling. I gave a little laugh.

"You like, amigo?"

"Stop being ridiculous."

She lifted up the covers, displaying her entire body to me. I crossed my arms, furrowed my brow, staring at her pale flesh. She hid herself again.

"You've got an erection", she said.

"Yeah, you can't be that bad after all."

"Don't be wicked."

"How many men have you fucked?"

She shrugged.

"Vaguely?"

"I'm cold" she said, "Come here, fuck me."

The following day I woke up confused. Who was this female thing I'd found? She's lying beside me. I'm on my back looking at the ceiling. She's still asleep, this nameless thing of wonder. I peek under the bedclothes and look at her.

What's up?" she says.

"I was looking at you."

"Oh."

Afterwards, she started to act very strangely, lit a cigarette and paced up and down the room, smoking through a cigarette holder.

"Nothing better to start the day, you know."

"No?"

"No, always makes me feel brand new."

I watched her move back and forth across the room, seemingly preoccupied, as though she was unaware of my presence. Then she stopped.

"Do that again" she said. I beckoned her over. "No, no, over here" she said, extinguishing her cigarette.

The room stank of sex and smoke, made me proud to be alive.

(Address crossed out)

Nov 27/—

Sir,

By this you will note I have got your letter and am upset You has twisted me You has robbed me You has thief me Let me explain Policy no. 1 amount of loan £341. ok Policy no. 2 amount of loan £407. ok

Policy no. 3 amount of loan £417. ok Now Policy no. 1 mature on the 1 october 19— I did not receive one £ off you You had the lot plus the amount of the policy mature sum Notice Policy no. 2 is in force you have this policy in your office ok now Policy no. 3 £417 loan now you take as your charge over £900 plus now I do not have this money for you on no. 1 policy you want £824 plus intres. £93. notice in 19—/— I have paid you over £400 through my Bank notice the money I get off you on these three Policy is far less and look what you have take off me you are a thief Notice on the 1 of october 19— £1165.00 ok You has all the money on Policy no. 1 now on Policy no. 3 you are demanding over £900. Well sir the balance of the money on Policy no. 3 I want you to keep it and stuff your white ass ole with it. You can also stick Policy no. 2 up your fucking ass ole and nose ole You white Bastard is not to be trusted You also got a fucking cheek to asked me for witnesses to sign Sign it your self and spend Policy no. 2-3 on your self and family DO not answer if I am wrong Policy no. 1 Policy no. 3 you take more than £1165 off me However when you have help your self with Black People more let me no in writing how much loan I have left on Policy no. 2 ok However the money you take off me on Policy no. 1 and Policy. no. 3 is more it is too much If however you want all the money I have paid on Policy no. 2 send me a Form and I will signe it all to you I will let you know my next move I cant win But I can escplain to someone and let them know even the newspapers you has twisted me far too much You get the lot of Policy no. 1 now you want ¾ parts of policy no. 3 and I am giving you policy no. 2 and 4 Take the fucking lot ok

Form of authority for payment of surrender value.
Life assured: E Dayes
Policy Number or Numbers: 267542. **Surrender Value:** £1675.00. If however you dont want to pay up you can stick it Signed E Dayes. **Less:-** Society's loan: £824.00, **Interest Thereon:** £93.54, £917.54. **Premiums Outstanding: Late Payment Charge: Clawback:** Twisting Bastards. **Balance Due:** £757.46. *Any further adjustments as a result of overpaid or unpaid premiums will be made at a later date. I/We hereby authorise and request you pay the above mentioned Balance Due by cheque made payable to:- Dear sir this is Mr E Dayes I do not want any witness for my money ok. And send it to:- Mr E Dayes, (address crossed out), in full discharge of your liability under the above numbered policy or policies. **Signatories** (i.e. those persons requested

in the attached letter to sign authority). **Witness** (One witness for each signatory. The witness of this form should have no interest in the Policy and not be related to the signatory or the life assured).

1) E Dayes (signed) Date 27/11/—   1) Name/Signed: E Dayes, Full Address
2) E Dayes (signed) Date 27/11/—   2) Name/Signed: E Dayes, Full Address
3) E Dayes (signed) Date 27/11/—   3) Name/Signed: E Dayes, Full Address

N.B. Please ensure that the policy and any other requested documents are sent in with this form. POLICY IS IN YOUR OFFICE OK MY WAGES OFFICE IS MY WITNESSES THEY KNOW I PAY YOU OVER 5 YEARS EVERY WEEK NONE STOP PAY UP OR STUFF IT ALL Signed Mr E Dayes.

Eugene didn't stand a chance. The police phoned him up saying his car was parked dangerously, Eugene said it had been stolen, the police said why hadn't he reported it as stolen and Eugene said it was only the police saying it was parked dangerously that made him realise it was stolen. So they said why didn't he deny that it was parked dangerously rather than just assume it was stolen. Unable to think of an answer Eugene invited them round to discuss the situation. He reckoned on ten minutes to think of an alibi, but he only got seven before they knocked on his door. He admitted he'd lent his car to his mistress, Fiona, uninsured to drive the vehicle, then he heard the rest of the story – Fiona had parked the car on the corner of my road while she was fucking me behind his back but could he explain the stash of Finnish hardcore and dumdums in the boot? Infidelity breeds contempt and he blamed it all on Fiona. By the time they came round for her I had her doped up and well trained and they already suspected the double-crossing little cunt anyway so he ended up facing the charges. I said to Fiona "You know I'm packing two inches on that bastard" and she made up her mind on the spot; that is the way she is made, she reacts to stimuli, like an animal. Feldman's Cars is the pits, the guy is a dead ringer for Nixon, and he shuts on Saturdays. I picked out a 72 cherry red Capri, bounced one of Eugene's cheques and me and Fiona set off up the Ml to Scotland. That cunt Eugene cut off his earlobes aged 15 because he thought they made him look like an elf, when the police look for more porn and bullets they'll find a gross of Deutsche Madchen and a fully operational WWII flame-thrower, he doesn't stand a chance. As we drove north Fiona got sleepy, a neurotic Lois Lane. She loaded up the Luger with the remaining dumdums. "Where did you get these things, mail order?" I told her they were handcrafted by dwarves for maximum exit wound damage. "Those guys get a bad press" she said, hiding the gun under the carpet. Somewhere in Yorkshire she wanted to see the thing in action, I pulled up the car in the middle of nowhere at about two in the morning and showed her what happens when you shoot a tree with a dum. "Nice exit," she said, "take me to a hotel now." Later I sat in a wickerwork chair smoking as she demonstrated her vibrator collection. The girl had a porn obsession. When we got to the Borders some barman asked if we were on holiday or something. "We're looking for girls with names like fairytale princesses, like Claudia and Flavia." He gave us a strange look and underchanged me. Hard up for cash and down on our luck we turned to the ads in newsagents' windows. Amongst the televisions, massages, black beauties and nannies I found what we were looking for: "Make money, no catches, no modelling, P.K. Bockmaster, 23 Blaydon Drive." Not falling for the no catches line and not having any better offers me and Fiona found ourselves outside the semi-detached empire of our benefactor-to-be. Upon entry he proved to be a man of genuine calibre. The Bockmaster's deal was as follows, sperm for money. Go upstairs and produce as much as you can, everything laid on. Come down, he measures it, pays you by volume, you go home. Scientific research, he says. The guy was clearly a ½ carat pervert. "How much are you paying?" Fiona says. £10 a cubic centimetre. I looked at her. "Twelve" she said, "this guy's a pure bred Aryan." Bockmaster gets out the Leibenfels charts and the cranial measuring gear and eventually concedes the point. "I want high grade stuff from you boy." This guy's idea of everything being laid on was two copies of Amateur Gynaecologist, dick pumps, a big poster of Samantha Janus and some Polaroids he'd taken on a beach, mostly of women covering their breasts and shouting. No one's ever been able to pull me off as fast as Fiona. She's a twenty-two year old divorcee and I guess she just has a kind of pride. After three quarters of an hour I presented Bockmaster with the results of our work. He eyed the seed warily and looked me up and down like a pawnbroker. Eventually he parted with the money. Back in the car on the way to our rooms Fiona asked me what I thought Bockmaster wanted with the sperm. "He's rubbing it all over his face right now", I said "Believe me. High zinc content, elixir of youth" she said. "Didn't you see his skin?" I squinted at her. "That wasn't what I meant. Suppose they let Eugene go" she said, "and come after us. You bounced his cheque to buy the car. Feldman'll get involved and they'll trace the car." She was right. We traded the Capri for a pale green 79 Mini Cooper using a false name and cash in hand and moved on to the next town: profit £100. Fiona complained it lacked the glamour element but I waved the money at her as I drove. Next stop "Innerleithen, please drive carefully."

Eleanor Hartland

Vicious Folk

"I am borne like
a ship without a sailor,
as, through the paths of the air,
a stray bird is carried;
chains do not hold me,
a key does not make me fast;
I seek those like myself,
And I am at one with vicious folk."

In the Tavern, Carmina Burana.

Chapter One

Life stinks. I'm sick of it. Sick of war and warring against life: against people, against myself. That is why I am leaving. There is nothing here for me anymore. There is no one left. That is why I am standing on the dock at Texel in the Netherlands, watching the black waters fringed with ice, and the glittering hull of the Amsterdam as she lies low in the ebb tide. She will not sail until morning. By that time I will have hidden myself in the hold and be bound for God knows where. Quite simply I do not care.

I do not want the night watchman to see me so I stand well back in the shadows and listen to him whistle a tuneless song. The air is thin and his lungs scream out for a warm fire, but he has another three hours of his watch before he can go below deck. He makes do with the small flagon of brandy he keeps concealed beneath his coat. When it is finished he will lean up against the gunwale and fall asleep, as he has done the previous four nights. Then I will make my move.

But first I must feed. I know the type of woman I am looking for. I can see her in my mind. I want someone who resembles the ungrateful turncoat I gave my heart to, who chewed it up and spat it out, and then laughed at my fall from grace. If I had listened to my old friend Samuel when he told me to walk away from her then this never would have happened. But I am impulsive; it is in my nature. It is the fact that there is no one to blame other than myself that makes me furious. I hate being wrong. Even more I hate being wronged. But I can stand here and seethe until the sun rises and it will serve no purpose other than to drive the canker deeper into my heart, where it will slowly poison me like hemlock. And despite my love of loathing and hatred at this moment I do not want that. I need to turn my mind to other things. Take out the anger on someone else. The one thing I have always been good at is killing.

As I walk through the slums of Texel I am composed of nothing but shadow. There is nobody around; the streets are silent and the houses dark. I like the quiet; it makes me feel at one with myself. I own the night. It is my domain. If anyone crosses my path now it will be the last thing they do.

In the West Square I find what I am looking for. Two whores standing on opposite sides of a fountain that spouts water from the mouths of three salmon. Tonight I am lucky, these two women are still plying their trade despite the late hour. They know they are not safe being outside at this time of night but it has been a slow evening. It means they will be more eager to please me.

I make no effort to conceal myself and slowly I make my way anti-clockwise around the edge of the square. They watch me cautiously, wary of the way I move. I must be careful not to scare them away. In my present mood it would be all too easy.

I pass one and then the other, and then I start my circle again, moving with less speed this time. As I approach the first whore she steps towards me, placing one colt-like leg slightly forward to flash a worn boot and a measure of pallid leg. If her hair had been slightly less lank, and her eyes had been brown instead of blue and had at least shown a little spirit, perhaps I would have chosen her. I shake my head. She would not be to my taste. I smile as I hear her huff at my back and then her heels tap their way home along the cobbles. She is worrying that she will not bring home enough money and will get a beating. The bruises on her back are only just beginning to heal from the last time.

Now there is only one whore left, and I quickly cut across the square to where she stands. I agree a price and hand her a silver piece before she can have any doubts about me. When I run my fingers across her cheek and down her throat she shivers deliciously beneath my touch. This one even bears some resemblance to that Judas. I know she will taste sweet to my palate.

I can still taste her blood on my lips as I walk past the sleeping night watchman. I lift the latch on the entrance leading to the ship's hold and climb inside. I light the stub of a candle that I brought with me. The resulting glow throws dim shadows against the walls. There is not much room, as they must have finished bringing on her cargo during the day. I let the candle drip onto the top of a heavy oak-bound chest and stand it a pool of its own hardening wax. There are hundreds of crates containing bottles of fine French wines and brandy, barrels of bacon and cheese, and a healthy arsenal of muskets, bayonets, and gunpowder. I find myself a corner well away from the hatchway, where no light can reach me if the hold is opened while we are at sea, and where I will not be seen without careful scrutiny. There are a few pieces of sacking draped over the crates, to keep them dry I presume, so I pull them off and roll them up to make my stay more comfortable. I feel somewhat more relaxed than I did earlier, and as I lie down in the dim light I spend a little while carefully picking out the blood that has dried beneath my fingernails.

One can become a little jaded when ones means of escape returns to port three times because of inclement weather and contrary winds. I spend my nights dwelling on my past misfortunes and listening to the talk of sailors above my head. There are over three hundred men on the ship, three women, and a dog. I know roughly how many men there are because I was bored enough to attempt counting them as they boarded, I know about the women because they are talked about incessantly by the crew, and I know about the dog because I can hear it yapping. Finally, with my patience stretched as far as it will go we depart from the northern end of the Zuyder Zee.

The further away I get from the Netherlands, the better I feel. She is no longer a threat to me. My rage is not so intense now but I still cannot stop hating her. I do not think I ever will. I can do nothing but bide my time in this dark hole and I am slowly starving. Sooner or later I will have to go up on deck and feed, but I am disinclined to do so. The crew is sick. I smelt the taint of plague in their blood long before their physical symptoms began to show. They are scared and are losing faith in their Captain. I know their movements are weak and their thoughts sluggish because sometimes I can barely make out what they are thinking. There is scarcely any talking now and the ship seems to sail silently through the water as if she is not manned. Every now and again

I hear a splash of water as another corpse is thrown into the sea in what passes for burial around here. I am beginning to think that I can use this plague to my advantage. No one will miss one more corpse when there are already dozens piling up on deck. Tomorrow evening I will leave this place.

The air is humid and still. There is a storm coming. The stars are tiny lights in the heavens guiding this silent ship. There are few people about but I am careful not to be seen. I do not want my presence felt. The feeling of tension and fear is thick in the atmosphere, and all I can smell is blood and sickness and sweat. There is a strange, quiet despair among the crew that seeps into my soul. I do not like it here, and must constantly tell myself that I am not a party to their mortal suffering. I can hear coughing and moaning in the sleeping quarters and the ropes and sails creak and groan fitfully as the Amsterdam holds her course for the Indian Ocean. I have never before seen a ship under sail whose crew has been so despondent: so dejected. Even the ship's timbers seem to reflect their melancholia. In the stern two shrouded bodies lie side by side, waiting to be dispatched to the fishes at first light. They cast blue shadows onto the planking and omit the stench of death. I know I am hungry but I do not have an appetite. It is with some revulsion that I creep into the sleeping quarters and it is a long time before I find a man whose body does not carry the stink of disease.

There are whispers of mutiny amongst the crew. As I listen from the ship's hold I can hear hushed voices curse the captain for continuing their ill-fated journey. Last night a sailor crept into my den and stole some muskets. He did not see me, but I was close by. He was a young man with a mind full of doubt, who had been chosen to lead his men, to get the guns and the ammunition. But he had a wife at home and was scared of what would happen to him if he were accused of mutiny. He did not want the honour that had been forced upon him, but equally he did not want the reputation of being a coward. He was a weak man and I tapped into his mind as easily as a weasel cracks open an eggshell. I am keeping his thoughts with me for the next few days and am letting him be my eyes and ears as this mutiny unfolds. The crew's tactics are virtually non-existent and I am wondering if they will have nerves enough to carry out their fragile plans. But watching the development of this little struggle is so refreshing after this many weeks on board, and it helps me keep my mind off unwelcome memories.

The weather has remained humid since last week. The smell of the cheese is beginning to make me nauseous and I am longing to get off this wretched ship. They have thrown the remainder of the corpses overboard now and the odour of death has thankfully sunk to the depths with them. According to the mutterings of the crew they have lost nearly a sixth of their men, and although they continue to get sick, the ferociousness of the disease seems to have abated.

The young mutineer keeps me abreast of the situation above deck. He doesn't know that I can see what he can see and hear everything that he hears. It takes a great deal of concentration to be this subtle. I could turn his brain to soup if I chose to. At this moment he is standing on the poop deck watching rolling clouds of yellow and purple as they swell like bruises on the horizon. I do not need him for me to hear the crackle of thunder that rends the heavens. Lightning forks through the sky, spewing a stench of ozone into the air. His stomach is a knot of nerves and he is worrying about the musket that he has hidden beneath his bunk. He wonders if this storm will bring about the final destruction of the Amsterdam and her crew. Through him I can see the wind whipping the sea into a white foaming mass, and I can feel the ship being tossed like driftwood caught in a weir. I can hear a hundred and one different voices clamouring, barking orders, praying to God, and somewhere amongst them I can hear that damned dog yapping. The young man is running across the deck to help lower the mainsail. I have trouble keeping up with him; it is harder when they are moving. His mind is fixed on his job now as he fights to keep the sail from ripping. Through his eyes I can see the faces of the crew around him, their skin glistening wet from the spray and the rain. The brine washes away the smell of the blood in their veins but the scene still remains invigorating. Waves pour over the decks washing away men and supplies; sucking them into a churning mass grave of brown water. There are ropes slashing at the sailor's heads, whipping at their ankles. A nearby brazier has fallen onto its side sending hot coals spinning across the boards, spitting steam as water strikes them. Men are panicking, shouting. I can no longer find a hold on my young mutineer. In the ensuing mayhem he is lost.

In the hold crates are being thrown from their stacks, barrels rolling under my feet. I have to give up searching for him in order to steady myself. I cannot afford to be harmed now in case the ship goes down,

I would need all my wits about me to escape the waves. For a moment I am disorientated. Being able to see the events unfolding above deck, and almost stand in the shoes of the young sailor gave me more confidence. I could see where I was going, so to speak. Now that I am myself again I am once more entombed within this dark hole. I shut off the sounds from above, blocking out the cries and screams and shouts. Now I can hear the booming of waves against the Amsterdam's hull. There is an eerie echoing, thundering that can only be waves hitting the shore. We are close to the coastline, closer than a ship this size should be. The waves are pounding, slamming into the hull. The sound is deafening. I need to be outside the ship's hold until this passes. I crawl silently and stealthily through the hatch, unnoticed by anyone. I risk the remaining daylight but it is so overcast now that it scarcely burns my skin. Men are rushing backwards and forwards, lashing timbers and hauling ropes and sails. The waves rush up the sides of the ship and are dashed to spray over the decks. My clothes are soaked in minutes. Icy water runs down my neck and the sting of salt is in my eyes and nostrils. There is panic in the air and I have to tell myself to stay calm. I have never been a good sailor. I have never felt at home on the sea. I cannot use any of my usual tricks. I have no time. And even if I had, in this much disruption the chance of my being able to concentrate is virtually none. Instead I must use my wits and suffer this mortal form my spirit is locked into. I look around. There is nowhere for me to hide. These barrels that I am crouched behind are not good cover and are in peril of being washed overboard at any moment. And if I should go with them...

Then without warning, I am thrown from my precarious place, as there is a splintering and screaming of timbers. The ship lurches to starboard, thrown perilously onto one side as the hull scrapes across the rocky teeth of the coastline. Two more men are thrown into the sea, disappearing without a sound. The barrels tilt, tip, and roll across the deck. But I am quick. I land on my feet like a cat. Despite the slippery planking I duck and run towards the quarterdeck. There is a doorway leading into the belly of the Amsterdam, into the sleeping quarters. Water is rushing down the steps in miniature torrents, and the wood is stained dark where the sea has soaked into the grain. There is no one here as I hurry through the narrow corridors, banging my shoulders as the ship flounders in the surf. There are doors on either side, closed, revealing nothing. Several that I try to open, I find locked. I turn a

133

corner, happening on another row of doors. This time I am in the officers quarters. All the doors along here open. The cabins are small, two bunks on one side of the room, and two on the other. There is a bare table against one wall and a few pieces of clothing rolled neatly and placed on a trunk at the base of one of the bunks. An officer's coat is hanging on the back of the door. That is all the decoration the room allows, but it is still a welcome respite from the vicious weather. At least here it is dry. The ship has righted herself again and she does not seem to be going down in the water. But I have no real way of knowing for sure as I have seen ships sink before and they can take hours. It is a long, slow and painful death, and now that I am in the belly of the ship I would not know until she started to overturn. I am only slightly better off than when I was inside the hold, and I am beginning to think that being here is not such a good idea. I can still hear the storm outside although it has abated, and the shouting of sailors and officers is subdued so I can choose to listen if I want. I sit down on the bunk and search for my young mutineer. I find him easily.

It seems the panic has lessened. The word flying around the ship is that the Amsterdam has lost her rudder. The officers have told everyone they can still sail and will continue on to Batavia to deliver their cargo. This has not been met with approval, and some of the men have gathered together and are talking to the young sailor. They are pushing for mutiny. I can see their faces through his eyes and I can tell they are equally scared, but self-preservation has taken control of their senses, and the hidden muskets give them the confidence they lack. I think the rebellion will not be long in coming.

But for now I must turn my attention to finding a proper hiding place on this ill-fated vessel. The trouble with a ship is that everyone goes everywhere; every room has a use. I can think of no places but the hold where nobody looks once it is sealed. I am resigned to the fact that I will have to return there and it is not an inspiring thought. My one consolation is that there is much to do on deck and the sailors will be kept busy for some time yet. It will give me time to dry my clothes and get the chill out of my bones, although there is only one true cure for that coldness. I have not fed for a while and my body temperature has dropped. If I do not do something about it I will start to weaken. If that happens I cannot concentrate and in turn that will endanger me. If I stay here there is a good chance that the officers will return. Eventually they will fall asleep, and then I can see to it that they become unknowing donors. The thought sends a shiver of anticipation through my body.

It is pure luck that I stayed here. I have been waiting and listening for two long hours and now the crew have finally mutinied. One man has been shot dead. Now they are ransacking the hold and getting drunk on wine and brandy. I saw all this happen through the eyes of my unwitting sailor. All fear is gone from him now that the officers have surrendered. He has his musket tucked into his belt and a half-empty bottle of wine in his hand. Hearing everything that is going on around him is fine, but my vision is getting a little blurred. It has been longer than I can remember since I suffered the effects of alcohol consumption. I had forgotten what it felt like.

The storm is still blowing and the sky has darkened as if it is night. Many of the sailors have come below deck and I can hear a group of them just along the corridor. They are raucously playing a card game and occasionally I hear the smash of glass as an empty bottle is discarded. This could go on all day. A short while ago the young mutineer passed out drunk and I lost the connection with his mind. It is a shame; I was enjoying the party. Disappointingly it does not appear that anyone will be returning to this cabin now, and the chill in my bones is beginning to irritate me. I can either sit here looking at this wall or go and find myself a victim. The choice is not a difficult one.

On deck everybody is so drunk that I could walk among them and they would clap me on the back and offer me their bottles. I am sorely tempted to see if anyone would notice that I am not a part of this crew. But I keep my head low and creep. I am not good at creeping. I do not enjoy subterfuge of any kind. I have always considered myself an upright kind of man. On the poop deck I find a likely candidate for my attentions. He is on his own, just the way I like them to be. I can see by his manner that he too has partaken in the celebrations, and for a while I watch him teeter alongside the guard-rail, holding on to it tightly with one hand, a nearly empty bottle held loosely in the other. He is singing under his breath, but it is more of a slurring hum than words. Finally he succumbs to his inebriation and collapses, half-conscious, onto the planks. The bottle rolls to where I stand and stops when it hits my boot. As I step towards him I gently kick it aside.

I feel better now. Glowing with the warmth of life. I did not kill him, but he will sleep for a while and no doubt wake with a very sore head. His intoxication has seeped into my veins and left me a little light-headed, but deliciously so. I have my vitality back, and my strength, and my incredible hearing and vision that was beginning to dull. I feel like a king again, ready to take on the world. This blood fires my soul. I want to rage war on all humankind, then turn my wrath on my kin. Well, one of them at least. I could pull up this planking that I stand on with my bare hands and hurl it into the churning waves. I could snap men's necks with one hand and enjoy watching their eyes bulge from their sockets as I squeeze the breath from their bodies. I am death unleashed, allowed to walk on mortal plains where there are mortal sacrifices. I am doom, and fate, and loss to whom I choose. To a few, I might give freedom from mortal ills and strife. But it is up to me. In the end it is my decision. That is a privilege given to the strongest.

As a gesture of my defiance against the world I pick up the bottle that I kicked away earlier, and hurl it out to sea. It is swallowed by the murky darkness and the sound of its fall is lost in the crashing surf. This tiny rebellion reminds me of man's attempts to make a place for himself in the world. One voice spoken among millions is drowned out, so the attempt is utterly futile. If I cared more for humanity then I might be subdued by that thought. But the blood is rushing in my veins and I am free to be the master of my own will. There is no reason why I should care.

We have reached land. This has been one of the worst storms I have seen this century. There is no colour to the horizon. The sea is pallid and ashen. Torrential rain makes visibility even harder, and the wind and salt stings my eyes. The Amsterdam sways from side to side, port to starboard, as if she too has partaken of the liquor. In the cabins and the mess I can still hear the sounds of drunken merriment. There are fewer than twenty above deck and it seems as if there is nobody steering the ship. Those sober enough to stand are happy to drain the stores once bound for Batavia bone dry.

About an hour ago I spied land and we have rushed headlong towards it ever since. It is now near enough that I could reach it in an instant if I put my mind to it. I don't know why I still wait here. Perhaps I have half a desire to see what will happen to the crew. Maybe I just want to see this land as it seemingly floats towards us through the rain.

The shoreline is low, and hazy because of the storm. The beach is flat and not the golden colour I have come to associate with foreign climes. It has a black sheen to it as if there is something evil lurking just beneath the sand, waiting to push through. I can make out rocks crawling in long fingers towards the sea, and ridges in the sand that look like veins or tendrils, giving the place a sinister, living air. Beyond the beach the land becomes green. It is not a pleasant shade. It is the colour of rot and mould, and against the horizon it has the appearance of lichen. Washed-up seaweed and stagnating pools of tepid water left on the rock make the air brackish and putrescent. The humidity keeps the air warm but the dampness still seeps into my bones and leaves me cold. It makes me remember how much I hate England.

But here I am. Fate, destiny, bad luck, whatever one calls it, has brought me back to these shores after so long. The ship appears to have beached herself. I think, as she is no longer rolling so much in the water, that she is stuck fast to a sandbank. The waves still crash around her hull and spit spray onto her decks, but at least she doesn't surge and dive as she did before, and for that I am relieved. The tide is on its way out and in a few hours I could probably jump overboard and not get my feet wet. But I cannot wait that long out here on deck, in the open. Members of the ship's crew are beginning to stir, leaving their quarters to see what has happened to their vessel, and they are still roaring drunk. My curiosity as to their fate is rapidly diminishing, and I am a little disappointed that the end of this journey has not been more dramatic. I think now would be a good time to leave the ship. Let them drown their sorrows; be court-marshalled; hanged, or whatever it is that mortal man does to its navy mutineers. I am done with it all. The decision has been made. Without any further delay I summon my will, gather my wits and use the trick that Samuel taught me so long ago. Within moments I am on land. Nobody has seen me leave, and nobody has seen me arrive, I am a stranger to anyone I meet. The driving rain on the coastal road keeps people away and I have to bend into the storm as I walk. My clothes are soaking wet once more and I am beginning to get a little irritated by this constant deluge driving down upon my head. Of all my travels in all these years England has the worst weather. It is no wonder that I left it behind at the turn of the fourteenth century. Even France was never this bad.

I seem to have walked for miles. Thankfully the rain has finally stopped, but the wind is still blowing a gale. The shore along here is one of rocks and stones, and the boats that have been pulled onto the land and upturned look like beached whales. Stray pebbles litter the path I take, and I send them clattering across the road with a sound like scattering bones. I have watched the uneven line of rooftops, black against a deep blue sky, grow closer. A lone seagull dives and wheels above monstrous cliffs, and I can hear its mournful cry from afar as it signals the close of this day. Now the night has fallen like a damp black cloak across my shoulders.

I stopped a traveller on the road a short while back and he told me I was headed for Hastings. The lights I can see, nestled in the base of the cliff, tell me I have nearly reached the town. The first inn I come to will be my refuge for the evening. I am sick of this inclement weather.

The Stag is a rowdy public house, but it has rooms and will accept my money. The cloying stench of wood-smoke and sweat, pipe tobacco and cheap ale spills out through the doorway and onto the street, like the whores and drunken sailors. Inside are the sounds of a fiddle being played and the click of gaming dice. I hear the chug of a cork being pulled from a bottle, the clink of glasses, the indignant cry of a serving wench, the rough laugh of a seaman and the slap that she gives him. The drunkenness is all too similar to that of the Amsterdam in her final hours. I know I will not find rest here but it will at least serve to get me warm and dry.

I find myself a space beside a wood fire and lean against the mantel. There are people rubbing shoulders with me who do not realise what I am, and the sensation of being so close to them brings me alive with excitement. I love it here. Who needs rest when I can drink in this kind of atmosphere? Sailors and merchants; fishermen and craftsmen; whores and mistresses, surround me. There is vibrancy and mystery, life and light. I can still feel the brandy in my veins mixed with another man's blood. There is dancing and gambling and talking and laughing. I can almost feel the potency within myself attracting these mortals and I have no intention of pushing them away. If these women want to flock around me, and swing their hips against mine, put their arms around my waist, then let them. I will be delighted. This is what I am here for. This is what I enjoy.

Maybe it is the aura I project, perhaps it is the fact that I am unusually tall, but whatever it is I attract women. I am blessed with something that all men would have. Who would push away a woman who virtually fell at your feet? Certainly not I. It is with some reluctance that I must choose just one to take to my bed.

This one has red hair and green eyes. Her Irish lilt sings like an old memory to me. She has dimples and a rosy blush of happiness on her cheeks. I am sorely tempted to pick her.

But then there is the tall one. The one with milk white skin. Her hair is as dark as the night sky, and her eyes sparkle like the stars. I like the huskiness of her voice and the feel of her cool skin against me. She has a mannerism not dissimilar to mine, in her poise, her grace, and the elegance of her limbs. I could watch her for hours and drink in her radiance like a thirsting man drinks wine.

But I choose the third because she has the strongest will. She does not have the beauty of the other two, but her eyes have intelligence and her manner is forceful. It would be a privilege to win this one over.

Carefully I tap into her mind. So gently that she does not realise. I do not want to put one with such vitality at risk. Not yet anyway. I will do that when it suits me.

She drapes herself around my waist and I smile at the thoughts that run through her mind. Such ideas from one so young! It will be a pleasure to fulfil them. I smile down at her, and I like the smile she flashes back at me. She is really quite shy, obviously new at this game. At the moment she does not think of it as a profession, it is all new and vibrant and exciting. She is yet to meet a man who will cause her pain. There will be time for that later.

Her breath is sweet and warm when she whispers her name in my ear. It tickles my cheek. Ellen is a name that suits her. She accepts my offer of a drink and I waylay a serving girl. We continue this way for a little while, Ellen seemingly quite happy to spend my money. But what is money to someone who has eternity to accumulate and lose it? I am equally happy to make her last few hours enjoyable.

She is curious to know where I have come from. She doesn't recognise my accent, and why should she when I have picked up intonations from France, Scotland, Ireland, Holland, and most of Europe? I tell her that I am on my way to London. She is not satisfied with that and presses me further. Why am I here? What is my name? Is there someone waiting for me in London? I smile and say little. Instead I call for a fresh drink to replace her empty cup. She accepts and continues her pursuit for information.

"Ellen," I say pulling her aside by her waist and guiding her through the throng, towards the door to my room. "Why do we waste words when there are better games our tongues can play? "

She laughs gaily and swings me round as if to dance. Giddy child. I do not want to dance. My smile is forced.

"Come with me. I can show you a merry dance that will spin you off your feet."

The door shuts quietly behind us. Ellen is breathless. She leans against the door, waiting for me to make the first move. Her mind is full of lustful thoughts. She has never met a man so strange and silent before, and yet she is not scared. Instead she is full of curiosity and excitement. It will not be long before I dispel that innocence. I watch her bosom rise and fall in her lace frilled blue bodice. Her eyes shine in anticipation; her lips, slightly apart, are soft and tempting. I feel a different kind of hunger awake within me.

Ellen bends into my body as gracefully as a reed bows to the wind. With delicate, trembling fingers she unbuttons my shirt. There is a slight fragrance of lavender on her skin and her blood is strong in my nostrils. I press my face into her hair and breathe in her mortality. Her fingers are warm against my arms as she pushes my shirt off my shoulders. The sensation is strange but not unpleasant, and after so many years, I am used to the way mortal skin feels. It is warmer, more pliable, and prone to small blemishes. Mine, on the other hand, is quite cool, smooth, and almost waxy in its texture. Ellen touching me is like feathers brushing against my skin. I can hear the echo of her heart beating in her veins, pulsing through her limbs and down into my fingertips. It is a strong beat. But not so strong that I couldn't bend her to my will, though I think that would be too easy. Nothing is worth doing if it is not worth fighting for.

Her throat is smooth beneath my caress, the steady rhythmic pulse in her neck thumping like a drumbeat: the tolling of time. I rest my hand there for a moment, savouring the sensation that echoes in my own chest. I can almost believe that I have a heartbeat of my own. Then I take away my hand and my body is as silent and still inside as it was before. Samuel was right; we need mortals to remember what it was like to be alive. Without them we forget how to act and feel human. It has always been a forced relationship for me. I do not have enough respect for mortals. They waste their years with petty concerns and then, when the pendulum begins to slow, they rush to say everything they have to say, and do everything they haven't done. I need to be around them, but only when it suits my purpose. Only if it pleases me.

I turn my attentions back on Ellen. She is pinned between the door and me. I press against her, feeling myself grow hard, and she gasps at my arousal. I must admit that I am pleased. It can be difficult, even impossible to achieve, if one has not had enough nourishment. When I unlace her bodice she helps, eager to end this foreplay. I nip her gently on her bare shoulder, listening to her small moans of pleasure. Even now she does not realise the fiery ground she walks upon. I tap into her mind, gently pushing against her will. She looks up at me as if to question this intrusion, and for a moment I think she has felt it. But she smiles and I realise that it is just coincidence.

As I lay her down on the bed I press a thought into her mind.

Give him everything he desires.

I hear the thought echo back and I know that she will succumb to my every whim.

She has really been quite pleasing. Young as she is, she knows a few tricks. I can remember the whores who used to follow our military camps, and they did not have half so much imagination. She lies spent at my side, drifting in and out of sleep, relaxed and content. I will let her lie a little while, but I am not finished with her yet.

"Ellen, wake up." I whisper.

It is just after midnight. I short while ago I heard the toll of a church bell somewhere in the town. But now it is quiet, and the lack of moonlight steals the shadows. I am lying close to her side, my forehead pressed against hers. I can smell the sweet fragrance of her skin in the darkness, and hear her steady breathing in the silence. We have been like this for a while and I have listened to the sounds of laughter and music in the tavern grow quiet. My skin is quite cold now and I shall have to feed soon. It comes upon me so quickly, sometimes without warning. I have never understood why we must be so dependent on such a weak race. When this feeling takes control I can do nothing but sate the animal that wakes inside me. When it has fed, it is subdued, as am I.

Ellen stirs beside me and the scent of her blood rises in the air. Even in the gloom I know she has opened her eyes, I sense her consciousness. I roll over so that I am above her: bearing down on her, and lean on my elbows so as not to crush her fragile form. In the darkness she is insubstantial, immaterial. I cannot see her eyes and so she has no identity, but her scent is so enticing, and I am so hungry.

"Leon?" she murmurs drowsily.

"Ellen, do you know what I am? "

I can feel her interest awaken. The pillow rustles softly as she shakes her head.

"I am hungry."

She giggles.

"Hungry for you, Ellen."

She stretches out and wraps her arms around my shoulders, drawing me closer. She is so young. So powerless. I desire her, thirst after her. I need what is beneath that sweet flesh. My appetite is keen, my passion aroused. She is warm, and sensuous, and mortal. I cannot hold back; this craving is too strong. It is necessary to my well being.

Her struggles are futile, my weight upon her too much. Her blood tastes of honey and elderflowers and burnt guinea fowl. It rekindles memories of the last meal I ate before my death. I let myself be consumed by the images. I ignore the struggles and cries of the young girl beneath me as I am absorbed by the whispers of the past.

I am back on the battlefield in my homeland. I am surrounded by the snap of wind in the canvas; the sting of smoking fires; pungent leather; the metallic tang of armour and perspiration. I can hear the crackle of roasting meat, the stench of oil and fat and salt. The taste of blood is in my mouth, tingling through every part of my body. I can hear the air as it is cut by arrows; the rattle and clatter of steel; the thunder of hooves. Bleeding, burning, screaming, the rending of flesh. The sound of mortal death echoing through my silent clay.

And then Ellen is gone. Flown to wherever the spirit finally rests. The carcass rests on the bed and the animal is sated.

I will leave The Stag this night. Tomorrow they will break down the door and find the body of a murdered whore. It will not be the first time, and I am sure that it will not be the last. They know the risks.

Robin Hill

Road Trip

Prologue

I have stories, I have stories. Terrible stories, make the blood run so cold.

Q - Doctor, doctor, every time I try to think about my recent past, I am struck with terrible heartburn. What is wrong with me?

A – You're a ramblin' drunk, mister, molester of women in dark Downtown night. You know the true meaning of WRONG, the true meaning of meaningless, top down, sucking it like a storm drain drunk. Now get the fuck out of my surgery.

The thing is Woman. Woman the missile exploding in my brain. Woman the red mist over my sweaty midnight sheets. Woman the figure reduced to two dimensions in my memory by cheap time and distance, like shadow puppet prostitutes at night-bleached dusk.

Sell it with chapter headings. That's the best way. Pure chronology, pure direction, although it never played that way to me. It played out unfair and fragmentary, slippery with beer as toxic swollen song titles, fireworks spelling half-glimpsed phrases, strangled words, screams, silences of ears bleeding, ears emptied out with gun shot blasts and stolen moment whispers of lust and love.

Chapter One – The Silver-Tongued Devil

Feature old school Hollywood party, pictures of Orson Welles standing in the exact position you are in to see the picture, lounging out in the Olympic pool behind your back. Party cluttered with innastry types, swanks all talking swanky, all set sharp out from huge view, stunning vista of the San Fernando Valley. House great mansion overlooking Mulholland, stacked with bad taste seventies décor, bad art, shelves loaded with great books and multiple copies of great movies, vintage Cary Grant and holy posters from lobbies of a bygone era.

I'm there and drinking hard, spend first hour in morbid silence soaking up the twelve box of bottles I brought with me, then come round to conversation a whiskey or so later. Meet a delightful redhead from Iowa, pure sweetness, statuesque just like I like them. A sweet dimpled Kim with long hair which she lets me hold, laughs with head back and I have to pull focus to find her ample tits.

I don't remember what we talked about, but I know for certain that I was witty and urbane, didn't talk about work, just old stories, laying on the good stuff, the old stuff, filling her glass and doing impersonations of Robin the good guy, that silver-tongued devil that slips from the shadows, lets them know how much they want him.

Can't remember what I said, but the evening moved in great arching circles of cat and mouse as she followed me and I followed her from spot to spot. Finally, we both settled at the open-patio bar, slumped in whiskey concentration as she wrapped her legs around me under cover of cold and I kissed her long and deep. She moved me hand in hand into dark recesses of the garden where stone statues stood sentinel. What lovers they had seen! What summer night kisses and more had passed under their eyes!

She gave me her number through hot-lipped kisses. We smelled of booze and passion as the night grew weak and weary and the planet tumbled soundlessly through great space.

Chapter Two – The Great Adventure

And so it came to pass that the next day I called young Kim and she enthusiastically came to meet me from work the day after that. We met at a local bar.

Here is my summation written the following day:

"I almost feel a person like other people, a guy with cookie-cut shoulders that doesn't slouch and sweat when the wind carries perfume past him, a Joe B. Regular whose hands hold no terrible secrets and can be opened to any kind of light. I feel an airfix satisfaction, smiling the kind of smile that looks impossible to master when you're running as fast as you can to keep up with the rotation of the Earth. I feel crisp and original. I have turned all the mirrors to the wall.

A five ten strawberry blonde, thirty one in years, with flowing straggly hair that makes her face look small and neat and vibrant. Powerfully built with all the parts carried at the appropriate height by a body firm but unpretentious. If leaning, then leaning to statuesque like a forties movie girl, a Rita Hayworth, a Paulette Goddard. A lover of fine things: old Bogart movies, unsqueaky booze-drinking, kissing on bridges in light rain with shallow breathing and laughter and holding hands while walking and telling long stories that have no point except 'This is me. Here I am, real and in your arms'.

With unblinking wide and watery eyes that seem filled with strength and humour, yet turn oblique, fragile and delicate when flicked off for a moment; darting eyes and fleeting glances that speak of years carelessly lost without memorial and now a need for a few kind words and a moment of romance in the narrow margin left at close of day."

It was that kind of date, nothing like the drunken farrago with the previous Kims. This was the real thing, real romance with Woody Allen magic movie moments; watching the Vietnamese fishermen catch their supper on the end of Santa Monica pier, staring out to the black Pacific eternity night and holding hands and counting the stars as the night rain began to fall and we had to run for cover. We found it in a wide bright doorway where I stood close behind her and she arched her tender neck to find my lips with hers. A long deep kiss that didn't stop when we parted but that continued for the whole next day. I told my friends about it with giggles and said thanks to a future I thought I already knew.

How wrong I was.

Chapter Three – Tumbling through space.

I wake with her scent still on me and carry it to work, oblivious to the over-crowded bus in the bustling city of fifteen million people. I ring her again and arrange to meet two nights later, this time to meet her friends, an informal affair in Manhattan Beach.

I impress myself by nimbly negotiating the geography, the transit system, walking briskly through streets I do not know, finding her house it seems by some natural internal radar. I take a bottle of good wine, turn up a few minutes late, introduce myself with a kiss through one day's stubble. Faint memories of her apartment: old stereo, new teevee, not large, not small bright room with darkened bedroom off to one side, filled with a large bed viewed once in chiaroscuro temptation. She hurries me back out and we move down to the Beach holding hands, down to where her friends are waiting in a low maintenance drinks and burger bar. I unwisely eat a salad and then embark on some fairly serious drinking. It is a difficult situation and it always will be. You must show willing to socialise with her friends, but not ignore her altogether. Mindful of this balance, I spread myself thin and kept the drinks flowing. The evening wore on and I wore down. I became aware, real slow, real gradual, of her friend Denise. Denise who made goo-goos at me from diagonally across the table, who kept tagging my name to the end of all her statements. I was embarrassed and looked away, played tolerant as she gasped and made shrill pronouncements about what I must think of her and so on. It was rude behaviour, drunken behaviour, but I bore it well and squeezed Kim's knee humourosly underneath the table. She smiled faintly, sweetly, a smile that only I was supposed to see.

We moved on, as a group, to another bar and another round of heavy drinks. Then the damage was done. Somebody got the smart idea that they should begin ordering Shark Attacks and never stop. For the record, this is a painter or window-cleaner's bucket half loaded with crushed ice and topped to brimming with random quantities of spirits, generally heavy on the tequila. The bucket is then placed on the centre of the table with half a dozen two foot blood red straws cascading out from it. The process is reminiscent of Mugwump suckling.

Now, you know me. You know that I am an unflinching boozehound. You know that it takes more than a cocktail served in a bucket to make my eyes water, a flashy name to make me blanche. Well, then be sure that when I say these people were psychopathic, suicidal drinkers, I am talking with a reasonable perspective.

From here, the evening can only be broken down into small change:

Searching for the delightful Kim, unsteady on my feet, drink in my hand, like some strong, dark beer, riding the high waves. Sticky mess on my throat, feels like blood but has sugary texture of a rich fruit drink. Find Kim outside smoking a menthol Virginia Slim and talking to a sexless teenager with long blond hair. They are discussing the kid's hemaphroditism. I bust into giggles, grab the he/she's chest and spill my drink onto somebody's shoes.

Back at the Shark Attack, somebody is going through my jacket, finding Chandler novels and Anti-fungal cream.

Suddenly, I'm in some other bar and don't know why. I look for Kim but only find her friend Denise. Denise...how did I get here? What happened to....What ever happened to....?

I'm in the street and lurching, Shakin' Stevens on my toes, Denise's upper arm in my tight left fist. Moving into a back alley, Denise with a too-big chin, and too much frizzy blond hair, sluttish Denise whose hungry lips are suddenly gnawing at my sticky throat. I put my tongue in her mouth and my hand in her pants. She doesn't like the idea so well.

Desperate action is called for. I am having the opposite of the classic out-of body experience. I can see sentient thought has left me and is hovering a way off down the overlit street, hovering in the safety of a crowd of spectators, angry onlookers. I am begging Denise to perform unholy sex acts with me, pulling her frizzy hair down to my unholstered hips. She breaks free and runs off up the street, collapsing in a spectacular heap on the main street of Manhattan Beach. I decide to cut my losses and find Kim. Staggering on through unfamiliar streets, through wreckage, through derelict, empty glasses and red-hued eyes, staggering on by crashed cars and drifting rudderless boats, up San Francisco streets to Brighton.

I am outside Kim's friend's house. Kim's car is there. She must be there. I bang on doors. I bang on doors, confront an ancient Mexican woman who points to a balcony or maybe to the sky. I climb the balcony and pound angry fists on strangers' sleeping doors. Maybe I shout a little.

I am waking up. Several of the people from the bar are standing over me. A friendly Oriental face. Did I try to kiss it? Did my tongue crash into another out-stretched palm? I am placed in a taxi, a million miles from home. Somebody pays the driver fifty bucks. It isn't me. I sink into a back seat of black shiny leather, stare up at the ceiling and out to upside-down pylon tops, lurching oil donkeys, smeared streets burnt to damp red by the blood in my eyes. I close them with a smile. The evening had seemed to go pretty well.

I woke up the next morning with a clear head and a good conscience. That went terribly well. What a sweet girl Kim is. What a wonderful guy I am.......

....handinpants....unholsteredhips.........hold on, what happened last night?

Then, the sudden disintegration of my entire world, the booming recognition of what I had done and what had driven me to such incredible follies. I rang Kim. She wasn't in. I went to the gym for a little penitent racquetball and had a terrific juddering crying jag on the court. The whole day was a trembling lip of precarious tears and unhinged judgement. I wanted vengeance on the blank saboteur who had ruined me, but he had gotten away, run back inside, escaped the moment and the denial and the brisk and the glum and the lynch-mob justice.

I finally spoke to Kim that night. I apologised for having lost track of her. It was quite alright, she said, as everybody was very drunk. You must apologise to your friend Denise for me, I said. No problem, she said, Denise doesn't remember anything about the whole evening. Really, I said, then neither do I. Okay then. Okay then.

I clipped the toenails of the conversation until it was possible to leave it without being rude. Finally, I slammed the phone home and began dancing furiously around my very neat and ordered living room. I got away with it. I GOT AWAY WITH IT.

I got away with it.

The next time I called, she was friendly, friendly but firm.

"It was nothing that you said or did. I mean, you are a blast. We're just very different people. I'm just looking for something else, that's all".

It was nothing that I said or did? Meaning then that it was nothing specific. Meaning that it was a non-specific accumulation of thousands, perhaps millions of tiny negative judgements. Meaning, in fact, that it was Everything that I said, Everything that I did.

I am a blast. A blast. A blast. Speak the word aloud. 'A blast'.
I can take it on the chin, I say.

Chapter Four – New Directions in Terror.

Soon after, Ben Howard hit town, ignored my staring red eyes and said
'Fun Fun Fun, baby, that's what I'm here for, that's what I'm expecting.
Fun.' My heart in my mouth, my teeth brittle with bad living, I nodded
and said a word that I couldn't hear. Later, it transpired that the word
was 'Vegas'.

The first part of the week played out cool and mostly human,
anxiety and dread sublimated into Mr. Entertainment, showing
Howard the new Star Wars, editing rooms of Venice Beach and a
variety of reasonable hang-outs in the Hollywood and surrounding
areas. One good night at Musso and Frank's on Hollywood drinking
gimlets and getting utterly sloshed after four or maybe even three
either way a great embarrassing fun evening of drink and talk and walk
and careless exploration of the big bad city.

But the real thing, the real deal, was hiring the convertible - a life
long dream of course - a life long thing - maybe 'Fear and Loathing'
responsible, maybe movies, maybe bits of everything - who cares in
fact what associations or emulations? The point is it seems right to
travel across a desert in a soft-top to Vegas or to anywhere, but of
course especially to Vegas, where things can go wrong badly and
unnoticed, where I could go savage and teach Howard the meaning of
loss.

So Alex Grey was in town on some extended literary pilgrimage,
traveling half for inspiration and half out of sheer boredom, an escape
from the suffocating nightmare of nine hour days in a grim warehouse
in Eastbourne. He had been making letter threats of this kind for some
time so at the last minute I thought I would invite him along to Vegas,
thinking he might provide me with some contrast to Howard and the
boredom of the road. Meeting him at a Hollywood Italian restaurant,
he seemed a real tourist and a real youngster – under 21 in this Union
and you can't even drink a fucking beer. For just a second, I regretted
having asked him. When he suddenly sprang it that he was bringing a
friend, I was skeptical. When he then went on to explain that his friend
was some girl he hadn't seen in over a year, I was doubly doubtful. Oh
well, I thought, all life is drama. All life is Drama.

Chapter Five – Las Vegas

Juggernauts thunder past on their way northwest on the fifteen to Vegas. Hot desert wind pounding the road, bouncing back up to meet the windshield of the car. The car is a snow white soft top Chrysler with the top down. The car a rented convertible out of LA. The passengers me in the front seat, a couple of others in the backseat, buffeted by 117 degree blasts at eighty miles per hour. Their lips are dry, their faces numb, but they're on for a free ride and say nothing about their terrible suffering. Suckers. This would be Alex and his lady, a short, big-titted something introduced to me as Billie Peacock.

Billie Peacock transpired to be his 22-year old ex-girlfriend, a girl from Hailsham who turned up looking utterly underwhelmed and proceeded to smile politely throughout the journey without saying hardly anything. She had also left her identification badge in my house- the mark of an absolute dumbkopf. Her huge jugs and jodhpur-shaped thighs did, however, exert a certain fascination on this leering old pervert....

It seemed that Alex had invited her along in order to slyly creep into her pants in their hotel room in the dead of night. An admirable objective, finally giving some understandable motivation to his bringing her.

We pulled into Vegas at dusk, holding the roof on by hand after an unsuccessful and abortive attempt to 'convert' while doing eighty on the freeway. It was super-uncool, but added a kind of ironic childish fun to the whole affair, the type of nervous laughter that incidentally bonds people who don't know each other terribly well. We were staying at a low-end hotel on the far end of the Vegas strip, the part that has now been bastardised and turned into a series of grotesque pleasure factories.

First night spent drinking and eating, drinking and eating, then getting the feeling of the place back, letting the nausea seep into the bones, watching the cookie-cutter ghouls and manics pushing their pocket money into the honking tooting slots, standing still for thirty seconds and concentrating on the incredible wall of competing sounds that fills the air with howls of glee and shouts of terrible blasted agony, finding the layers of silence under the noise, the silence of suicides, the silence of freeze frames with static twitching diagonals across frozen fearful faces, the silence that lives in vacuums and unread books and love letters that were torn to shreds before she ever read them.

And then to switch out of that to be back in Vegas, back in real time, back in the great unbelievable lamplight, the black and white rainbows, the murky lighting of a billion burning bulbs. Turning on the spot, head spinning to the chorus of sound and light, pitch black dots bubble in my eyes like a melting photograph. It would be worth screaming if anyone could hear it and if I didn't have a mouth full of pins.

That night emptied out and ended with Ben and I stumbling into a three a.m. strip joint, recommended by a stern Eastern European cabby, who pronounced the best place for us as 'Crazy Whores Too'. So we slope out the back of the Riviera, through the Circus-Circus and find ourselves in a grim RV (recreational vehicle) park and traipse out onto a road called Industrial where we are immediately approached by a man asking if we want hookers. We tell him no thanks so he gives us a hand-written business card with a shrugged 'Later, maybe, huh?'.

Crazy Horse II is a Gentlemen's Club by name but I didn't see a single gentleman in there. It centres around a large raised area on which overly greased women dance mechanically, swing around poles with their pants on and make bold demands for money from anybody who appears to be looking in their general direction. Around this is a series of concentrically arranged soft deep armchairs where the real punters are sitting.

I called over a couple of beers and slouched down into the chair wishing I was in my hotel room and this was my bed, wishing I had a girlfriend, wishing that my life was all different, was better…..drunk….I don't know how, just better. Just Better. By this time, I had a girl on my lap. She was six foot, sleek, black as the night, rotating her ass in a circular motion over my interested cock and balls. I didn't want her there, I wanted her there, I didn't want her there. I told her to leave, I pulled her back, I told her to leave. She pulled down her sports top to reveal plentiful breasts and a long slender neck. I kissed it with trembling fingers. Howard staring at me in wonder as the girl pulled my glasses off and I went underwater.

Resurfacing several minutes later with my wallet out and her asking me if I had any more of a tip for her. $27? Jesus… And then more girls, sitting on my lap, great Amazonian statues, little Asian baubles, tiny blonde Russians, Estonians, Bosnians, college girls from Mississippi, girls who studied law and politics and peace and justice and ended up on my lap in a Vegas titty bar at four a.m. and don't know how. Little Ukrainian Mimi who danced on my lap to songs I hate, telling me how handsome I am, how all the girls must think I'm just fucking fabulous. I told her that all this felt like some dreadful teenage party where you dry-hump some girl with the lights on and know that no matter what happens you are not going to get to fuck her. Mimi laughed and moved away with forty dollars of my money. I looked across at Mr. Howard and was amused to see him staring anxiously out from under a huge pair of tits. The owner was some great skank who was sitting astride him and humping him like she was on an exercise machine of some kind, as though she were only in it for very powerful ankles.

The next morning I woke with a start and the smell of Ukrainian Mimi still stirring in my nostrils. I had a shower and felt giddy with expectation for the brand new day. If you saw Fear and Loathing in Las Vegas, we were staying in the hotel with the revolving bar and the high wire act. That is where we spent much of the day, getting shantied on terrible cheap American beer and slowly revolving. It was about this time that I began to formulate my plan....

I had noticed that morning how when I went into Alex and Billie's room, both the queen-sized beds had been slept in. Absently inquiring what the fuck he was playing at, Alex had told me that nothing had happened. His attempts had failed. I had passed this as idle conversation at the time, but after a certain number of beers, I became aware that I had an ulterior motive of some kind or another. Clearly, there was a spare female at table. I was being especially charming, telling all sorts of interesting details about my recent excursions into strip clubs and the pants of frightened strangers. She was clearly lapping it all up. I now also recalled two other important pieces of physical evidence that I had witnessed earlier in the day. One - The contraceptive pills by her bedside indicting that she was sexually active and quite generous to boot. Two - The dreary post-feminist hag manual on her pillow with which she had evidently waved off the unruly advances of my friend Alex.

With these two pieces of the puzzle in place, it was surely a doddle to perform the old Jedi mind trick. Two ingredients are needed to ensure success in such cases. Firstly, a scalding honesty about one's own shortcomings and neurotic sexual pathology. This makes them feel like you are just one of the girls, a crucial disguise that becomes invaluable later. Secondly, a blisteringly personal psychic attack. This is an essential part of gearing up to bed the average reader of post-feminist books. They have such low self-esteem that a few well-placed and terrible insults drastically reduces their ability to withstand even the most lame drunken pass. In fact, they find it utterly irresistible without ever quite knowing why.

Putting this plan into action, I shouted at her to 'shut up, you great big sow!' in the middle of a crowded casino. She stormed off. Mr. Howard and Mr. Grey were scandalised but I knew it was all over. The coup de grace was my apology. I went down on one knee in a crowded lift, in the customary marriage proposal configuration. I left a dramatic pause and then said, 'I'm sorry. It's just that everything you say fills me with contempt'.

Half an hour later, she was looking over my shoulder, helping me play the fruity and stroking my leg with her surprising tenderness.

She honestly could not help herself.

Anyway, I shall draw a discreet veil over the subsequent frotting. I will just report that I looked up briefly to catch Ben Howard's sunglasses looking surprised in the rear view mirror as the temperature rose across the midday high desert road home. The temperature rose all over, but nowhere more than in the backseat of a snow white Chrysler convertible pushing on through the baking Nevada mountains, just behind the back of a snoring ex-boyfriend.

That's most of the story. The rest included heavy losses at the blackjack table, a hundred and ninety bucks in thirty minutes, Howard's sore losing and subsequent funk, the incessant desert heat, the most fear I have ever experienced on a thrill ride on the needle of the tallest building in Vegas.

Chapter Six – San Francisco

Coming back from Vegas to LA, just for a day, to see Howard off on his plane, then back to planning the next trip, to Frisco, with the same two Englishers as before, Alex Grey the writer friend and the ex-girlfriend of his, the big-titted short something Billie Peacock. Only now with an added layer of sexual frisson and strangled drama as I am moving with forty four save all stealth into her pants with Alex the ex-boyfriend antsy as he sees me laying stern moves on the lady, the lady yielding absolutely, sucking my lower lip with growls and mumbled pleas for sex. Left LA straight from Friday office, drove up the Pacific Coast

Highway, through Malibu and on and up through nothing beach communities that still haven't earned their dot on any map, through valleys and mountains, through seal colonies and writer's colonies, through dense primeval forest and swaying bridges between precarious teetering winding roads, the beautiful Pacific laying out a million blue miles far below the sheer drop canyon cliffs that yapped at our rear wheels.

Stopped at San Simeon and checked out all of the local hotels and motels which are all arranged there in a straight line in apparent ascending price order. Sent Billie into check prices while in the car, I told Alex that I had made his girlfriend and he thanked me for telling but already knew and in total proved to be very big about the whole thing. So then we booked one room between three of us, that being two beds between three, with another small single cot on the floor for young Alex. And of course an evening spent getting smashed on big Bushmills at a bar of Mexicans only and every time Alex left table, the girl is on me desperate and lusty, her heavy arms hanging round me like arms haven't done in a long, long time and at midnight by the ocean she can make me sweat with this overwhelming desire.

And back in the room with a full tumbler of scotch by the bed, we flick the lights off and all lay awake in the darkness in the stillness waiting to see what's up. And shortly in darkness I slide across into her bed and she's reaching out for me before I'm even there and waiting with a hot long kiss and soft smooth breasts and pajamas not sexy but like crazy pajama parties of your thirteen-year-old dream. And then as silent as possible we kiss and hug aware that he's probably listening in eyeball horror from the floor. But we fuck anyway and I come inside her and she gets mad, pushes me off with fingernails whispering 'I don't know you or where you've been' to ruin the moment so I apologise and soon it's funny and sexy again and we're trading kisses great and tiny and listening to our breathing, listening for the sea which we can hear or maybe hallucinate and I drift off happy, knowing Alex is probably still awake five foot away and choking on bile.

And the next morning everybody is just perfect and polite although Alex probably knows everything but doesn't say anything because Jesus how could he? And the sun is bright and the air is thick with salt in San Simeon where William Randolph Hearst built his great castle, towering great, dominating the horizon, using the sky like a painting uses its frame. Hearst Castle the inspiration for the Xanadu of 'Citizen Kane' but I didn't even stop to look, just kept moving north, on towards Big Sur, Big Sur home to Miller and subject to Kerouac, an awesome place cut out of the thundering pine mountains, packed with barefoot Mama Cass ladies and greying hepcats who look like they got beater as every other soul got beaten. Moved through South San Francisco in grey fog dusk, found a one night cheap hotel. I sprang for two rooms and took the lady into mine. My friend looked sideways and twitched minutely. I reminded him that Carolyn Cassady moved from lap to lap and closed the door in his face. Two minutes later I was fucking again, in great hip thrusts, slamming the bed against the wall and him behind that wall listening with a pillow over his head maybe like in a frat movie. And he had to come and knock on the door half way through without announcing himself behind it but just to say "jesus christ you two fucking bastards why rub my face in it what did I ever do to you please knock it off." And I laughed a guilty laugh and went in and apologised and he said, "don't be stupid it's fine I'm biggeren that". And I think maybe I even hugged him and if I didn't I should have done and I'm sorry that I didn't.

San Francisco is an incredible city riding the peaks of the great rolling San Andreas hills, ripples at the edge of America, great solid hills that seem so sure and ancient but are actually trembling champagne glasses waiting for their stems to break. San Francisco, the old Flame of the Barbary Coast, where Alcatraz lays out in the shark infested bay, still spins its sad searchlight, illuminates the nooks and crannies of Fisherman's Wharf with an uneasy pulsing glow. San Francisco, where Haight-Ashbury boomed and Janis Joplin sang sweet sad songs and died stupidly, where millions turned up hopeful with a guitar and finger cymbals and incidentally blew their minds to a soundtrack of protest songs protesting the American womb that churned them out.

San Francisco, home of the original Beat Generation with historic City Lights bookstore on what is now Kerouac Alley and Columbus Avenue where I bought a copy of his Big Sur just for kicks before moving down through the downtown business section, through streets bustling with limbless buskers, mendicants and loons. Talked to an old negro preacher who wore a white hat on grey hair, held a board that said, 'No Unlawful Sex' in huge letters, then listed in tiny print every single possible perversion the human mind could think of, each one preceded by the word 'No'. He was a nice fellow, told me about his calling, how he had sat on that same downtown corner for twenty-five years. The only thing that ever changed was they invented new perversions that he had to find out about and add to his board. Another man shouted at the cable car queue of unsuspecting tourists. A huge negro painted silver, wearing a bakofoil suit like a cheap astronaut, alternately shouting zealous gospel and foul, taunting abuse. 'Fucking faggots renounce. The Bible says Adam and Eve, not Adam and Steve'. Moved on to the Bay, the Golden Gate bridge poking through soft grey fog, the Bay Bridge huge and intimidating, the most incredible structure I have ever seen. Walked backstreets for a few hours, chasing down the real city, found the same chain link liquor store streets that define all poor black areas, then moved back into the city to have more fun. So the weekend folded up neat like a navy cot with booze and sex and random walking tours and driving the long bridges at night with windows down and Blood on the Tracks up loud and stumbling back to our cheap hotel laughing at lamp-posts and walls and cars parked on pavements, high laughter sent drifting up the cable car streets to Nob Hill and beyond. Evenings of bruising honesty, talking cure for all our ills, all the micro-dramas that were playing out. Concocting possible endings for the trip, finding the dramatic structures and working out crazy third acts, unholy, violent and obscene, dueling with drinks and words, the lady moving from lap to lap as we sang our strange and terrible love songs.

And nights the lady Billie spent with me as our romance actually blossomed unexpected until we got into a situation where I just opened my mouth and let the words come out no matter what without a thought or filter and listened to them back and they were beautiful and this went on all the way through our sex which was great by the way and all this talk mounted up and I took to spouting these outrageous things while fucking, tender and obscene and full of love sometimes and other times not but always true and always honest and always beautiful because of this.

In the early Monday morning, woke early at a hungover six thirty, began the long haul back to LA. Took the inland freeway, a six hour drive rather than nine or ten along the coast. I had heard it was quicker because it doesn't pass through valleys or over mountains. This is the understatement of the century. The Five runs dead straight for over three hundred miles through nothing but hot, flat zip, baked rest stops where truckers blister and one horse towns where nothing moves except the hands of the clocks. I am not kidding. Three hundred miles of Californian dusty nothing. Towns like Modesto where a young George Lucas dreamed up Star Wars, the story of a boy on a desert planet saved from a life of boredom by crazy aliens coming from faraway cities like Los Angeles or San Francisco. Towns like Newman which lure drivers from the highway with great signs for food and drink, then prove to be ten miles out, a baking two shed subsistence nothing which sells warm Coke and beef jerky to survive. Towns dwarfed by the big sky, a hundred and eighty degrees in every direction and pure frightening blue in the cloudless ninety five degree heat. And then the sudden ascent through clouded mountains as Los Angeles approaches, condors flying through the traffic, mountain passes that fall away to azure lakes in deep gorges on either side of the road. The freeway rumbles on twenty miles an hour above the limit and then the sudden thrilling descent into Santa Clarita. Santa Clarita the first signs of proper civilization, a town of rollercoasters stitched together into a huge theme park. The great twisting hoops come into focus as the temperature drops by fifteen degrees and LA announces itself peacock proud with all the subtlety of a tossed brick.

The day after that I wrote this: "...And all this whole time, this whole trip reminded me that moments are beautiful if you let them be beautiful, that simple seconds and minutes can be wreathed with smiles and laughter and made to seem like great adventures. It made me realise that all moments are the same, all situations equable, all emotion and experience just raw material from which great pleasure can be derived. Simply, I remember now what happiness is, where it comes from, how thin the ice is between the blazing daytime and the freezing darkness. And I have jumped the barricades, stepped across the line. I am looking forward, not looking back, not staring into the drowning pool of my belly button."

Chapter Seven – San Diego

Feeling that our story was lacking something of a third act (after the Vegas first and the Frisco second acts), Alex, Billie and I decided to try one more trip, this time to the almost randomly chosen destination of San Diego. I say random, but insofar as it's the nearest large city and the only remaining direction not traveled in (splashing off into the Pacific long ruled out as an option), it seemed like the natural and obvious choice.

I had had them staying over at my house for the few preceding days with Zaki tolerant of the intrusion in Andy's absence (scouting in Germany) and also probably feeling nostalgic for her own crazy traveling days with their terrible embarrassing intrusions into the homes of almost strangers. I was feeling indulgent and generous as I threw them my door keys and stumbled out to a ten hour Thursday day at work. Friday I slept in, long morning of sex in tangled sheets, consciously not rubbing the dust from my eyes and ringing in to work with a tiny tremulous voice that said 'I'm not ill, of course, but I'll be happy to stay in bed if you'll be happy to see through this shallow fiction'. The telephone said, 'Sure, I hope you feel better, hee haaw'. That day, I took Billie and Alex up to the La Brea tar pits, host with the most and so on, show them something interesting about this dirty city they were beginning to hate. (I have seen through them that without any money, this city is woe and terror and long unnegotiable boulevards and not much more). But as soon as we arrived outside the tarpits, both of them were bored like resistant children on a trip to the Museum of Schools. They rolled their eyes and said 'but we're thirsty. Why oh why is it so damn hot? And I'm tired and need a drink'. And I was glad to be off the tourguide hook as we ran out of LaBrea park laughing and piggybacking and found the nearest darkened airconditioned cool breeze on our backs bar and sat up for cheap American beers and watched a rerun of a famous fifties baseball game with the ol' Irish barman and suddenly we had fallen through dusty nineties chrome midday west coast LA into fifties oak midnight Hell's Kitchen where St. Patrick was a drunken god with Babe Ruth at right, hitting Olympic lightning bolts out of the park.

And then a slow walking back to base, with fearless silly walks in public spots and photographs of us standing like statues outside cheap coffee diners and gleaming glass banks and kissing and cuddling with

Billie and ex-boyfriend Alex looking on perplexed at first but then finally smiling big-toothed not drunk but amused. And this is the way it went and so much more and just to stop there but actually to say again or suggest again that every moment is not just a moment when garlanded with this crazy type of laughter but instead transformed into a tiny miracle, a tiny adventure, a tiny book.

Next day, we set off late after another great long bed morning. I sprang for a cab to Union Station and got there late too and found we couldn't get a train out till two o' clock when the original plans had said the nine fifty. And then a great long hour and an oh no half wait on the incredible old-fashioned station concourse which is like being in a movie just being there and which has these fantastic tunnels and hallways like artwork from the near death experience and everything seems jeweled and exquisite and born of ancient forms maybe Aztec or something. And so we waited and found everything exciting. Exciting coffee growing cold. Exciting newsstand with drowsy readers thumbing through the New York Times, exciting conversations about everything and nothing at neighbouring tables which I even took the trouble to transcribe with straining ears - two middle age ladies oozing concern for one of their fathers. He's close to death, grandkids working up touch-face codes of communication, they say. He's under-stimulated, lost the joy in his life. Now he's moved up with his grown-up kids, back into their lives and running around like a brave bear in his grandkids pantomime life, coughing agony breaths in the sidelines of bedtime.

Alex and Billie went to buy the tickets and came back glowing and telling excitedly about how the tickets were special today, special cheap at thirteen bucks and not the thirty we had been told. And so eventually, after the waiting and drinking coffee adventure, we found our train, the sturdy San Diegan Southbound which spoke to me of old movies North by Northwest, Twentieth Century, great double decker juggernauts that shudder desert floors and rip the sky, not rumbling dreamily like old cowboy trains but rather soaring fiercely with gleaming chrome like something out of Things to Come.

And on the train I bought bottles of the buffet wine, white local Chardonnay which we shared equally and drank from plastic cups and then rested our heads in the afternoon desert sun and let that sun do its work on our drunk heads, make us go a little crazy. And then running up the train, Billie and I, like it was built just for us to run around in this crazy state, this otherworldly romance. And I made booming declarations to the other passengers and they laughed and didn't look disgusted or upset or annoyed as Billie hung around my neck and spoke the word 'kiss' onto my face with tiny breaths, the lightest kiss of all.

And then the ticket guy came round and told us that we didn't have tickets for San Diego at all and that we actually had to get off at the next stop and rather than it being a drag it was actually hysterically funny and we spontaneously reenacted for him the conversation we had had an hour before when Billie and Alex had come back glowing peacock proud about the cheap tickets they had found. And the ticket man laughed and sold us tickets sly and with a whisper and ended up telling us all about his job and all the elaborate codes of crinkling and tearing tickets and colour codes and pointing out passing restaurants and saying, "that's a great restaurant. Ex-president Richard Nixon loved that damn restaurant", with these great sad gay eyes that had seen a lot of things flash past at eighty miles an hour.

The train pulled into San Diego about five o'clock and we didn't notice for ten minutes where we were because I was telling terrible stories about other times and other people. In fact, that time at college in Nick Hallard's little cell, mad and high at two a.m. and a girl coming in, looking for the Rock Society, a crazy zombie stranger looking for love. And telling (as Billie's eyes widened) how Nick and I played that hand of poker to see who got to fuck her first and how I won with a lucky pair of fours and took her by the hand to my own little cell and then undressed her, angry at first and then filled with the unfathomable universal sadness and animal terror to see great spider webs of scars across her broken body. So I'm at this part of the story and telling about my screaming horror but also my lust for sex and power and Billie leaps up sudden and moves away. I smile and follow and find her upset, not crying but holding head sitting in the middle of stairs and saying 'Why? Why say these things?'. And I can't tell her why except to say that I just had and therefore must have a reason and I tell her also it wasn't spite but just openness and that that is something rare. But doing this and saying this and knowing it's somehow wrong and egotistical, I also see that I have responsibilities and that although I play lonesome hero mysteries in my head (spurs jangling as I flip off the world), in fact I do not want to upset her. We begin to fight but the guard or rather garbage man comes along and tells us to get off the train and laughing again we see that we're in San Diego and have been for a while without knowing it.

San Diego is a beautiful dusky city, ten minutes from Tijuana and the border and therefore a favorite stop-off for holiday-makers as they travel south. The city is criss-crossed with electric tram-trains that run every couple of minutes and only cost a dollar and so we hopped one of these (without even paying a dollar, parasitic tourists) and found our way to the Gaslamp Quarter, an incredible hive of activity, an incredible tight-packed arrangement of clubs and bars and restaurants, even more amazing and crazy and beautiful than the San Francisco Fisherman's Wharf I thought unbeatable. And we trudged about with heavy bags and looked for a place to stay and felt the electric energy white wine high wearing off as our feet grew heavy, our brains animal stupid, heads heavy also and now all of a sudden filled with an original dread, a sense of actuality and inevitability and noticing physical things for the first time in a while like the comedown from bad acid, (grime suddenly appears under your fingernail sweaty hands and shirt untucked with blackheads in the naked lightbulb morning etc.).

But in fact that too was all a joy because it was also just sensation and experience and more important than that it was experience shared and felt simultaneous with the others and therefore beautiful no matter what. And it only took me pointing out how this logic worked (toasting the awkward frigid air, the awful awkward silence) to raise the other two back up and this raised me also and then quickly we were laughing again and finding the city's dead hotels romantic again and saying 'hello' and crazy 'hi' to people in the street and kissing.

And then finally we found our place to stay, an International Hostel with cheap rooms with no bathroom or toilet and a communal kitchen that serves all the travelers and passers-by and even the vagrants that scrape the small change together to get a clean sheet night inside. And having parked our bags we set off into the Gaslamp Quarter night and hit some bars and drank beautiful Mexican beer as the sun went down behind gleaming downtown towers and the streets began to fill with drunken teenagers, homeless hobos, pushbike buggy hustlers and lovers of all kinds. And we ate a great steak dinner, Filet Mignon under a nine foot bronze statue of John Wayne and I bought a great huge plastic gorilla from a beggar and sat this as fourth man at table and shouted 'barman, a drink for my monkey' at the Duke as the patient waiters cleared the plates from underneath our great big glowing smiles. And Billie began to flag and had a headache and I thought that this was probably just exhaustion because the day was already long and full and already seemed like history in a strange way, like the anticipation for the next day was making the present tense feel like a prologue that was dragging on and holding up the action and if that makes any sense then I must be a writer after all.

So we went back to the hostel and ditched the monkey which I realised with horror was in fact filthy with vagrant's chewing gum and not a holy object as I thought. And tried to find a dead bar in this live wire high wave city and finally did, a hotel bar at the Clarion hotel which was filled with old Japanese and sly old Americans toasting their Nancy Reagan wives with Irish whiskey. And we sit in that dead air empty airport atmosphere and I call out and declare that this is 'happening' and believe it too as I'm thinking that with these people reflecting my light and me reflecting theirs maybe everything is and would be happening. And I drink myself drunk with large and wonderful Chivas Regals and nestle down affectionate with Billie on strange high chairs like Blind Date that don't let my feet touch the floor.

And then back at the hotel we take to our night's bed in half-light and baking desert air because the fan don't work. And Billie has a headache and I'm strangely relieved as I'm too beat by the day, too tired, drunk, too weary with the love and guilt and momentum of travel and desire to do anything but lay as a half-moon smile across the bed as outside that great party rumbles across the night, a thousand feet stamping out their defiant rhythms into the tunnels, deep forest oil wells and internal organs of the Earth.

Finally, out into this great heartbreaking mess of life I wander, feeling naked and half-made, out on a three a.m. mission to get water for Billie as I feel bad about not having sprung for a decent place with a bathroom or at least somewhere a girl can get a glass of water. Out in the street, the hustlers are hustling on overdrive, making the day's best money as the streets overflow with dancing light and twinkling eyes and beautiful border women and on the street corner of Fifth and Market an incredible girl is singing ol' Billie Holliday numbers to a grateful crowd and musicians are flocking to join this great jazz jam and I stand and watch and am amazed and wander out further to find an all-night Ralph's and buy water and orange juice and a single red rose and feel damn pleased with the world and the way it's spinning.

The next morning I woke up slowly to find myself speaking

beautiful exquisite improvised love poetry that sounded grand but that I can't remember now (Billie said she wrote it down as I showered so maybe one day I'll find it wasn't so great after all). Alex came in excited and pulled us down the hall to meet old New Jersey workhorse Russ who had made a living selling postal uniforms and was retired and now had strangely offered us a lift to wherever we wanted to go today. And so I began to talk to old man Russ to see what more there was but quickly realised that there wasn't anything but a terrible yawning sadness and loneliness. Whatever personality there had been had been eroded and washed away in the rootless five year search for something since his wife died. Old man Russ who latches onto something I say in passing about having once been a cadet tying complex knots on Monday afternoons and makes this the bank for his river of conversation, telling me with indescribable sad eyes how he never saw service in the war, how the whole shooting match was over before he had the chance to become a hero or a martyr. Old man Russ, driving us way out of the way on a useless driving tour on the winding harbour backroads of San Diego to show me ships he had cased earlier in the lonely day. Old man Russ, the terrific ghost who haunts motels and hostels of the world, searching for his children or himself in rental cars with borrowed dreams, ever farther from his wife and a life he seems embarrassed at having lived. Old man Russ dropped us outside the San Diego Zoo with our thin smiles and we began our day with coffee and giggling about The Tragedy of Old Man Russ, turning his sadness into our happiness, not with a meanness of spirit but by way of giving thanks, reminding ourselves about joy and luck and love and what it would be to be there alone. And so, with renewed knowledge of why we were there and there together, we saw the world famous San Diego Zoo, and spent an extraordinary day reveling in the diversity of life and reveling in each other, talking to the animals and seeing the patterns and great art and ironies of nature, seeing in everything new colour, new meaning and the great loving rubberstamp of GOD. Just kidding.

And then that night out again into the crazy Gaslamp Quarter where we ate beautiful lemon chicken dinner at a huge restaurant that generated a forties noir atmosphere with a cool jazz quartet although the ceilings were too barn high to finish what the band had started. And then downstairs to the empty underground bar to play pool and of course Billie and I formed one team and Alex the other and Billie was affectionate (in fact too affectionate) and kept kissing me and hugging me and stroking my groin through my jeans and I began to wonder if any of this were right. And then in slow motion to me I saw Billie knock a glass of water over and saw it pour onto Alex's resting jacket and then watched as he became actually upset and shook it in her face saying 'Do you know how much this cost? Do you KNOW? A hundred and fifty pounds!!' and I thought he was joking and telling a line from a film like he often is and in fact does too much but then a sudden realisation that he was actually upset. Upset really bad with wounded pride like a person would never be over spilt water and in that moment I saw clearly what I already knew. That I had hurt my friend and that through the show of male ennui over the whole situation he actually felt angry and annoyed and I suddenly felt bad terrible knowing as I did that I had laughed at the competition that existed between us and had won it effortless and immediate. But those things were put away as Billie began to storm towards the door, as the whole thing, the three musketeers and bullshit fell apart in the face of something real, something that was not fun and imagined or literary device but pain in his heart and therefore all our guilty hearts. I chased Billie down and told her that she had to stay. She resisted but I spoke a quick prayer to not break all our hearts and to keep within the tension and see what happened and this she did and soon we were all together again laughing again but a new fragile laughter, a new wiser laughter that knows exactly what it's worth.

Back at the hotel, I said a quick and unemotional goodbye to Alex, knowing that this probably was the last adventure on the road, the third act incomplete or at least ghostly ambiguous and full of tension. I turned my back remembering already with affection these times these holidays like distant memory of childhood, something passed and passing simultaneously.

And in the room, Billie and I made sweet hot love and let it last a while as she made that wrinkle nosed surprised face that I didn't yet tell about but was in fact a major feature of our time together, a sweet face not sexual at all but rather childish and full of pure joy and like I say surprise or disbelief or something, a face that gave me a great big head and made me feel like Don Juan the world's greatest lover and in fact still does because indeed the sex was something very special that wasn't sex at all but seemed like 'making love' in that it changed the world suddenly and dramatically and unpredictably and made me feel holy. And in this sudden holiness I would roll over off of her sweating incredibly and tell my pure thoughts of how I felt great about people and things, about how I saw the great living connection that runs through everything adding new hues, new colour, new love.

Then, like naughty children we snuck out of our room and moved along the sleeping small hour hallways, Billie in nothing at all but a waistlength black plastic coat, me in jeans a shirt and socks and moved downstairs on a crazy mission to have sex somewhere different maybe the kitchen or the poolroom (remember that we are drunk in all of this) and finding that these rooms were locked we just made it on the carpet floor of the corridor laying down around a corner that anyone could turn at any moment. I don't know why we did this exactly by which I mean that it followed on from no logical discussion but was rather a sudden irrational thing which although contrived seemed spontaneous and brilliant and like a beautiful moment we would always share no matter what.

Chapter Eight – Back in the World

The next morning, the Monday, I left at half past five, left Billie sleeping and smelling that secret night smell of women I crept away into the pink light of dawn and walked silent footfalls to the station. My hands trembled as my butterfly heart burst at the indistinct Diego limit, as my smile faded on six fifteen train with characters let me tell you. Woman traveling with her two teenage sons but chose to sit with me, leave them seats and seats away. I offer to move so they can join her she tells me no. I fall asleep she wakes me with startling coughs, tics and sniffles like falling redwoods. I read my book the great now sacred Big Sur bible of shallow moments made profound. She brazenly interrupts with questions or rather aimless statements that could be for me or for herself or maybe just the air. I put down my book look into hollow terrible eyes that say, 'help me I was a prom queen once and now I don't even know how real that was'. That say: 'I was beautiful in a tiny ugly world before and then one day I got the train and never got off and the world got bigger and more beautiful as I grew old and unattractive'.

And these things these thoughts are passing through my mind without direction or intent as we whistled through that ugly blank industrial nothing that fills me with The Dread of South LA. She's wittering on and so I begin to talk back to her, describing the great chaotic sadness that I'm feeling, ascribe it to the view and not to her, describe the sense of time made null and void by seeing these places of work without the people in them. She falls silent and watches the view blur six feet in front of her eyes. I speak again but she is no longer listening. Her eyes stare black nothing turned inward. I step off the train at Union Station as her sons amble over casual and sexy for some liaisons further up the coast too drear to mention here. She snaps back out of herself and smiles me off the train without a word. That was the whole journey back if I avoid telling of the panic ticket buying with one minute to go at San Diego station, the cruel sorry microwave sandwich that stuck white melted cheese to the back of my teeth and left me feeling dismal for four hours and the clock-watching one and a half hour bus ride that bounced me in my seat from Downtown LA to Santa Monica, left crazy jagged word patterns in my notebook, added spider spikes and stalks to my faithfully recorded memory. Arrived only one hour late for work to find that my H-1 work visa application had finally been denied on the grounds that the ridiculous back catalogue of education and practical experience that was stressed in my application is supposedly irrelevant to the job description they have assigned to me. I was, as you might imagine, extremely upset and annoyed by this particular stroke of idiotic lawyering. My so-called expert legal councilor turns out to be an escaped lunatic Mickey Mouse Man with wild hair and Max Schreck teeth and a diploma in Klingon from Toytown Polytechnic and so I'm left jobless and returning soon washed up to Brighton, with wild tales of Hollywood that will come out at parties and when I'm drunk and hanging around outside the dole office wondering how long I can afford my pride. All this and more occupies my mind. These fiendish modern problems that are actually nothing, actually just buffers on a pinball machine. Their soft and rounded rubber edges never graze or change the ball, just set it off in a new direction. These modern problems, like sleep dust to be rubbed away in the bittersweet morning of each new day.

Alan Morrison

Poems

The Last Warmth of Autumn

When the last warmth of autumn's breath
Breathes on the wintry air
You will remember me once again
Though my shadow no longer falls there.

When the last warmth of autumn's breath
Breathes on your restless soul
You will potter through my forgotten things
As memories take their toll.

When the last warmth of autumn's breath
Breathes on your haunted mind
You will no longer be haunted by me
But will leave all thoughts of me behind.

When the last warmth of autumn's breath
Breathes on the wintry air
You will find the place where shadows lie
And your shadow will join mine there.

Gorgon Stone

Looking back I see it as
some Gorgon's cottage for
everything about the place
seemed as breathless as stone;
even the apple tree outside
seemed in its stiff brittleness
like a sculpture frozen to the bone
as if its branches were lifeless limbs
frozen to the bone.

The cottage stone was solid
more than solidness I've known;
rough to the touch,
as age-worn and engrained
as my father's face inside it;
its sturdy frame of lumpy bricks
felt as old and unshiftable
as a great fat oak stump
rooted in the earth –
no storm could ever shake it.

And then there was the lifeless garden,
wild and sprawling,
of a trampled sadness,
untameable and colourless,
as if winter was all it knew of life,
before timelessness set in
to paralyse its weeds
and fade its tumbled green
and turn this tired place into
the still life of a dream.

The Rosary Beads

Dour-faced, stood before us
as our moral tutor
her shadow fell upon us as
she fingered the rosary beads
and made us chant
a Hail Mary for each wooden ball;
our morning instruction
with bottles of milk
at English Martyrs Primary School.

Impressing on our infant minds
guilt, our holy canticle,
without speaking any words
she gave us this instruction;
Question your desires.

My eyes restrained tears.

My thoughts leapt back.

Each bead stuck in my throat
as I broke out in sweat
imagining Hell's fires.

Tales of the Empty Larder

I hate the smell of the stale breath
Of an empty larder only filled
With tins of soup long out of date
And rotting rice where the bags have spilled,
For it reminds me of the days
When our parents both earned paupers' pays.

And to this day I can barely stand
The rumbling sound of an empty stomach
And the smell of hunger-scented breath
For which a full belly is the only tonic-
The famished itch in-between the teeth
To which only food can bring relief.

The sight of an insubstantial meal
Is to me a symbol of poverty,
Though better still is an empty plate;
Cold, damp and dirt, and green-grey tea
Stained from one tea-bag again and again;
And the sickly smell of a singed dog-end.

Should I be thankful for my taste of strife
That ruined my appetite for living well
And diseased my heart with bitterness
And crippled my spirit in its living Hell?
Well I have at least found some dull truth
In the necessity of warmth and a roof.

And I suppose the lessons I have learnt
Have nurtured in me a need to dream;
A need to believe in impossible things –
For you need a God when you can't keep clean;
And you hope, when your faith overspills,
That Socialism will cure most ills.

But oddly it's often the human way
To come to love what you should despise;
Just as, in depression, sadness can comfort
With blessings of tears in hungry eyes,
And so I feel some perverse nostalgia
For those times of hunger-fed neuralgia.

As I've said to my brother, it's strange to think
That amongst the dirt we found ideals,
A sense of justice in second-hand clothes,
And creative ideas in cold soggy meals;
That the glooms of a larder's empty shelves
Was where we first found ourselves.

Overgrown

We moved down here some years ago
escaping brick and mortar lives
but they were all I'd known.
We broke away
from old suburban moulds
to find all overgrown.

No neat lawn there, just tendrils
of tameless, trailing wilds
cramping the light
with thick nettles and brambles.
A dilapidated greenhouse
trembled in the night.

A bare apple tree
wept blossom on the path
and into a filled-in well.
To us the house seemed
beyond repair
in its crumbled garden wall.

Deep in this brittleness
a weather-beaten cottage
of wind-gnarled Cornish stone
glared at us
with deep-set windows –
how could we make this home?

In those cottage glooms
we would later come
to live in disrepair,
to colonise rooms
that had known no sun
and breathe the cold damp air.

A place of folly
we came to see it as
and still do now –
and yet our lease
offers us no permit
to sell this house.

Slaves to a mortgage
in possession of a sunken roof
of wilting slates.
For some change of fortune
the moaning wind
waits and waits.

Few Never Envy

Should I envy others their stress-free,
fully-furnished lives,
their neighbours and their friends,
their husbands and their wives,
their savings, television sets,
cars and portable phones,
their spacious lawns and gardens
and spotless Wimpey homes?

Should those in the same boat as me,
capsized where most still moor,
envy the blissful ignorance
of those who kicked us from the shore?
Well there's no point in throwing stones
at deaf, dumb double-glazing –
leave the semi-detached to their lives
of net-curtains and crazy paving.

All I own is in this shabby room
that's furnished grandma-style;
the carpet is a dirty umber
and the thin beige curtains pile
themselves up like mosquito nets
over the drafty window pane.
A large round table is the centre-piece
Where I eat cold meals and find an aim

embodied in a typewriter.
Smoking soothes me when doubts take their toll.
My only other luxuries are tea,
and sleeping pills when I get my dole
of hardship maintenance that feeds
my lapsed Protestant shame;
thought I was born a Catholic
I am English all the same.

It is hard to be appreciative
of one's true assets when in arrears
and only thoughts of future aims
help one cope.   For fifteen years
I've been without a break.
A holiday or a year of fags?
Well, it's too late for my lungs
and the half-p's in the money bags.

And in this lingering staleness
of a hungry, smoke-filled evening
I sit at my typewriter
to express my every feeling.
I owe the landlord two months' rent;
I owe the bank a hefty sum,
but I feel sure they owe me more
than money can refund.

Dance of the Dragonflies

Around the still lake the dragonflies danced
In a flurry of cobalt and green;
They buzzed their glass wings and blindly they chanced
The skimming of the water sheen.

And one hit the water across which is skidded,
Seemingly out of control.
A pilot was drowned where the lily pads lidded
The mantle which merged with the shoal.

The pilot's son cried as he tried to forget
But leapt up with a new sense of hope
As he spotted a dragonfly, wings stuck with wet,
Drag itself up the bank's sandy slope.

The Water Shallows

When I went padding in the water shallows
There were things that I didn't anticipate
And one was that the ripples would turn to waves
Through which I would have to wade,
And that colourful thoughts would turn dour and black
Till I'd start thinking of turning back.

As I sat sullenly by the water-side
Trying to find an appropriate rhyme
To flow with the motion of my racing mind
Rushing like the shallows that helped me pass the time,
The thoughts that swam in the water shallows
Were chased as fish by the shadows of sparrows.

Brightonians

Hubbard's Brigade stand on the street corner
Clutching their clipboards close to their chests,
And you know that one has a Gorgon's eye:
She's turned to stone the tramp and his meths;
And just round the bend is the Big Issue vendor
Desperate-eyed but unpestered by Them –
He looks to the gape of the Imperial Arcade
As the seagulls circle inland again.

Waiting forever at the old Clock Tower
The boy who's stood up looks down at his watch
As the West Street itinerant asks him for 10 pence
While he shivers and scratched his crotch –
Earlier today he had sat in the park
Slumped on a bench by the coveted bins;
He's watched the young couples kiss on the lawn
As the sun shone on the Pavilions.

Down in the North Laines artists of tomorrow
Flit back and forth on a barren chance
And bohemians ponder their frothy coffees
As, sat outside, they meet with the glance
Of another lost, blinkered disciple
of God-knows-What-Type-of-Religion,
Who shouts himself silly touting his Bible
To the coo and the nod of a pigeon.

Two pensioners eat mushy peas on the Pier
And look through the gaps in the planks to the sea
Where a cornet lies oozing its melted ice cream,
While a widower, sat chin elbowed on knee
In the tits and oak-tiles of the Seven Dials Caf,
Sips at dishwater and dreams of the suburbs
And listens to chatter on the Bingo results
As through doily-curtains a car hits the curbs.

The Deposit Seekers

They've been spending all afternoons
looking in the frosted windows
at the properties they'll never be able to rent.
It doesn't matter how much they save
for a rainy day or drought –
they'll never be on the snug inside
looking out.

Staring at the unobtainable all day
is their non-competitive sport –
it reminds them of when they were children
staring in through their favourite shop window
excited, frustrated and awed,
gazing at the toys their parents
couldn't afford.

And again they're on the outside looking in:
a pastime of nostalgia –
maybe they'd rather return to the safety
of the stuffy back of their parents' car,
reminded by Dad, when a tramp passed by
traipsing the pavement, of how lucky they were:
"There, but for the Grace of God, go I".

Strays

They traipse in and out of the hostel
Like stray dogs dragging their leads –
Eyes like those of hungry hounds
Pining for their feeds

Whether they inject themselves with drugs
Or imbibe their lighter fuel,
I don't care for judging those
Who barely live at all.

Do they deserve just to exist?
To pay forever for the system's sins?
Are we to leave them to their diet
Of meths and rubbish bins?

Well I'm tired of asking questions
For the answers I have heard –
So I'll fall silent like the strays
And not say another word.

Sonja Henrici

Poems

from InnoSense

Pier

On a bench
overlooking the West coast,
a woman comforted
by four furry toys
as if they could keep her afloat
in an emergency:

a white rabbit,
a grey elephant,
a black panda,
a purple cat.

I try not to look
for the child owning toys,
not to notice her shivering,
with only a jumper.

Not to look into her eyes
cast downwards,
in case she recognises me
or my gaze.

I simply walk past,
hooked into your arm,
waiting for the next throw,
the next game, the next ride.
Not worrying, about her,
sitting by herself.

Mango Blues

The accidental mangotree
in my garden sparks
its first fruit, picked,
its skin just soft enough
to leave a fingerprint's impression.

The knife cuts deep into the flesh,
cuts it to the stone.
Juice drips over my hand over my knees
and bleeds onto the ground.

I take the two soft mangobreasts
and twist the halves apart.
I touch and tear – the stone
won't move from its tender bed.

I take the stoneless half,
draw a pattern of cutting lines,
turn the inside out,
cover half my face with mangobreast.

Pieces of fibre,
caught between lips and teeth
flirt with my tongue.
Juice sticks on my cheeks.

I tackle the second half,
twist and tear the stone,
end up cutting lines around it,
to lush in its fruity tease.

At last the stone is left
with scars of flesh and skin -
I throw the remains into the garden
to decompose.

Pusher

Throw a ten pence piece
into push-it-over-the-edge,
and win fifty pence,
throw five ten pence back in again
and lose. Ten pence.

So what? I'm pulled along.
We order fresh doughnuts,
watch them tumble into oil and sugar,
burn our gums on first tasting.
All I am turning over,

cheeks sugared from eating
doughnuts with your furry prizes
in my other arm, is my head -
had I just walked past a photo
in an exhibition of my memory?

Brunswick Square

Here,
the chatter of the old blokes,
scraggy, near the bushes on the green,
sitting around a Thresher's bag.

Propped,
like a piece of wood,
in a broken sash-window,
she'd watch the seasons change.

By the colour of the sea,
the height of the waves,
the slant of the last remaining trees,
the ones that didn't fall in the storm of '87.

She'd smell the summer-barbecue below,
see the couples on their blankets whisper,
a football kicked about – dogs undecided
between sausage and game.

She hears the sewer lid flap –
the transit van's futile preying
for a parking space.
He double parks below.

Moved,
she'd like to follow the pigeons' dive from the sill,
now swarming over the scene.

Instead,
she trails the echo of her landlord's inventory
around her emptied flat.

Guts

Her scales peeled, her body offered
at the hospital altar, slit –
the length of her a degutted fish.

Thrown back into the bloodwater
– her living cells, stitched,
to be scorched from the inside.

Composed she swam a weekly trail
of chemical snags, upriver.
Her scales grew back.

Ink stains ordered for her final scan:
Much clearer than the water
she was made to breathe.

EXT. UNDER A STREETLAMP, LATE

MEDIUM CLOSE UP:
You say
I'm hungry,
and yawn.

MEDIUM CLOSE UP, REVERSE:
I'm hungry, too.
I reply.

MEDIUM SHOT:
We say
Good bye.

CLOSE UP:
and I think,
But I'm feeding on
the love we made,
a few weeks ago.

Nirvana

Louise walked into her living room and switched on Nirvana, the TV, her window to meditation. Today was like any other day, but today would determine the days and months that followed, like only some days do. Jumping ahead of ourselves. She sat down on her sofa, staring – she never just looked, it could not reveal the depth of perception she was seeking. At the same time she was aware that her other senses retreated to the background. She ceased listening to individual sounds as they all assembled to one big soundscape. Couldn't even smell the perfume she made a point of putting on every morning. Her backache went despite her slovenly posture, she forgot how she was sitting. Lost the sense of where her hands were, or her feet, if she was lucky, her whole body. She loved TV.

Her whole flat was painted white, even her TV was white. Visitors sometimes had difficulties distinguishing the floor from in-built wall-cupboards, to ceiling, or couch and laughed at her seventies design. But really she didn't have many friends anyway. The room had one big cinemascope-style window, it had a blue tint, no curtains. Overlooking the river, she loved framing people, cars, boats passing that way. Gazing out of the window was second favourite to watching TV.

Today, which was unusual, she didn't have to pull out the TV from her wall-space where she hid everything, so that one couldn't find anything in the room, as her whole flat was arranged as empty. Even the kettle in her kitchen disappeared after use. But today, the TV stood in the middle of the room, in front of the window – as left from the night before.

Or so she assumed. She was puzzling about this while watching her favourite station, FlexiChannel, the one which did the zapping for you, so she didn't have to use her remote control. Her memory was blank apart from having just walked into this room, her eyes wandering across the white coffee table which she never used because she never drank coffee. Black-white aesthetics made her nervous and often she only drank hot water from white mugs.

There was a book which lay there, open, face down in the spine-ruinous way, which annoyed her completely. Normally she bound books in white protective envelopes, and she would never not use a bookmark. Too lazy to get up from her white leather, she sighed the first words of the day, What's this, Louise? Her white cat, which had been a present by someone who's name she couldn't remember but who had thought she would fit into the flat, jumped from her special spot at the window and sneaked over to Louise's feet, rubbing her head against her ankles. Louise patted her head. When she put her bare feet on the table she discovered that she had painted, black toenails.

I wanted to shout: What, who are you, who did this, where are you? The questions would have echoed in the empty flat: there was no one. The cat hopped onto the couch.

Opening Shot

Forrest Gump, opening shot, a very long take, a solitary feather slowly drifting through the air until it lands in front of Forrest Gump. A little angel feather.

No way, how puffy, what a thought.

Sometimes she hated herself for remembering details such as this, as easily as tabloid headlines. So much brain taken up by random and superficial memories and information logging to entertain you and others. Why do I never remember stupid things like this when it comes to striking a conversation? Socialising, I can't think of anything to say, can't small talk, hate it so much. Get awkward, lose friends, they are plain bored. I would be if I was my friend. I need time, like the feather. One long take. Which director will grant it to me? Reach the ground and base myself, to formulate my ideas. Leave sentences unfinished, floating, hoping to dock onto new things and catch the unsaid. It's all relative, her mother used to say. Eclectic, erratic, that's my life, I suppose, so what?

She remembered she used to have a friend with whom she played 'Associations'. Once a word was given they spilled forth anything they were reminded of. Often an erotic collection, but everything boiled down to sex anyway. Freud would have had a field day, they used to say, looking at each other, but who cares, and continued together, it's all relative anyway, and laughed. Then they looked at each other once more: but who believes in Freud? Laughing again. Fond memories.

They had drifted apart through no fault of anyone, time, lack of correspondence. Louise got up and rummaged through her secret drawer. The first thing to fall into her hands was an old present of Sylvie's: a brightly pink credit-card size plastic card. 'Birth Control Card' it said on the front, and on the back: 'User Instruction: When someone horny comes your way, just put it between your knees. This device is 100% contraceptive, environmentally friendly and reusable.' And so she had, used the card. When Sylvie gave it to her, Louise had willingly signed the card with her childish signature. It actually worked so well it was contra-sexual. It was all up there, of course, mentally. It had all been a seventeenth birthday joke, but Louise cringed.

She found her old address book. Does Sylvie still live where she used to? Found her name. Or maybe she is married and got a different name? A prickle around her heart. I haven't thought about Sylvie in a long time, and felt guilty. Where have I been? Why did we give up? At least we had each other. Didn't realise then how much that was worth. Quibbles about men, not with men, about boys. What's changed for me since? But suddenly she was gone. I was gone. Where did we go? Loved her like a sister, like a mother, like a lover, like a friend. But it wasn't even drifting, no, just sudden silence, distance, nothing to say, bagged and zipped up. No idea why, Louise lied to herself. She stopped thinking about it because she knew she was lying to herself and because she hated selective amnesia in others too. Back to her old diaries flicking past the days where they had been in school together and had seen each other regularly, like only school-kids do when there is a time-table slot in their mother's driving rota.

Infantile, it just became anal, our fights, our conversations, our preoccupation. The best thing, the honest thing was playing Associations, no pretence in that. The rest was fake and the rest was talked behind backs. Louise felt a sudden urge of nausea burning its way up her oesophagus and ran. Over the toilet bowl like in a praying position, holding on to the white cool seat, to confess. Here we go again. When the third big retch only produced bile she pulled herself together, cleaned up and looked into the mirror again. An old face answering, a confrontation, a question-mark-line on her forehead. It's alright, don't panic, it's not all your fault, what do you think? You egoist.

Nagger was back again. She instantly stiffened and worried. Worried as in heart-flapping as in like a fly trapped inside a glass. I can deal with you. Fuck off. The face in the mirror was still old.

He had a big voice. Always nagging, eating her conscience, consciousness, alive and whole, giving in to her self doubt, exaggerating it. Worthless piece, you have nothing to say, who are you. Nagger. Nagger. As she screamed and shouted, he kept repeating, you don't accept yourself, you hate yourself. You're disgusting, fat, ugly. He almost made her faint, almost beat her up. Bastard.

She confronted him, she thought now or never, I'm still strong enough. Who do you think you are? He stood there with his arms provocatively on his hips and legs spread in John Wayne style, casual but superior. And licked his lip. You macho, fuck off, I don't want you around, not you. Not you. Go away. Nagger just stood there, not listening, as if he didn't have any ears at all, mocking her and throwing the same words back at her and they stuck like felt balls on Velcro. Imitating her faint go-aways. Don't be so fucking desperate, Louise, it turns me on. Licking his lip again, tapping one cowboy-booted toe and cracking his knuckles. Don't you dare do that again, echoing and laughing his most vicious laugh she'd ever know. Don't laugh at me. Her childish whiney tone was desperate. He never took pity. Instead he commanded her over with his dirty index finger and she obeyed like a naughty child. Louise, he said in a vicious Jack Nicholson tone and reprimanded, don't be so naughty, Louise, otherwise Uncle Nagger will put you out. Small, so small she felt and shrunk to the size of his finger and he took her into his hand and patted her on the head. In her size, it equalled a beating. That's good, be a nice little girl.

Breasts

Louise looked at her Mum, at Frances, and at Naomi. Overcome by a wave of shame she cast her eyes to the floor of the living-room. Far away, somewhere, she heard Frances' faint voice asking her whether she was embarrassed now, but since she was so obviously embarrassed she wanted to kill Frances for even daring to ask such a stupid question. But what Frances wanted to hear, of course, was a No, so she said No.

Naomi was much more developed, she knew that. Frances continued to state the obvious. Louise wanted to burst out telling her that Naomi had watched her mother and father having sex, too, but that would have been too embarrassing again, she couldn't get it over her lips. So she stood in her white unbuttoned polo-shirt which hung out of her pink shorts, like someone who was waiting for something to happen, wishing for someone to whisk her away, but frozen in time – flushed, after Frances had checked out her budding breasts. She had only asked her Mum whether this would be okay and although Louise was deeply bewildered, Mum had refused to return Louise's accusing gaze saying, begging, no way, NO WAY. But Mum, eager not to appear too uptight about these things, just nodded something like: Sure, whatever, and then Frances had hitched up Louise's shirt and started pressing and squeezing around her tiny nipples, touching her unbrable beasts investigatively, as if she was trying to discover a woman in a twelve year old. Was that all she wanted to find out, whether Naomi was more developed than her? She felt like saying, My Mums breasts are not as big as yours so why should mine be bigger than Naomi's?

I think Frances was breast-feeding at the time so maybe her breast-obsession was forgivable. I should have never come into the living-room and said hello. And mother had stood there, next to Frances with whom she had shared many secrets, if not more, with a perplexed and helpless laugh. A knowing laugh, one between women. Louise wondered whether she'd ever have a friend like Frances.

The dawning of a feeling. A vague mood of embarrassed silence. And fumbling.

Cinderella

What am I doing here? She had entered the pub with an uncertain feeling – she liked the fact that she would be meeting a stranger, on the other hand she felt sad about being so desperate in having to resort to this measure. An ad in a newspaper. "R U lonely, too? What strong ♀ won't make me run away? What strong ♀ wants a strong ♂, to be vulnerable. Replies…" As she walked in, she noticed she was wearing a ball-gown with a huge bum-pillow and an expensive little crown on her head stuck into a perfect hairdo, crowning her ex-centric make-up. Entirely overdressed. Waiting for her prince. But this wasn't a fairy tale although she felt stuck into some kind of film indeed. She realised it wasn't a pub either – it was a café-bar and according to the number of Smokings, a pricey one. Still, she felt overdressed. Where did I get this anyway? No one stared at her, though she had trouble fitting through the aisles with her expansive frock.

Waiting, she ordered some coffee, and waited. A taxi drove up in the front of the mirrored café-windows and a guy with four bodyguards jumped out. A smoking, sun-glasses, and… He came up to Louise. I can't believe you actually came, he said, as if they were to recognise each other. What a brilliant dress, oh and I love your bum. She pretended to understand his advances as the silliest come-on she had ever heard. I can't believe you are wearing Ray-Bans, she said, they are totally out of fashion. He pushed them into his slick-gelled dark gentleman-hair and grinned as if satisfied with her answer. Two Long Islands he indicated to the bar-man in sign-language. The bodyguards turned out to be random people he had given a lift, so he said. Bodyguards, he was astonished when she asked, don't be silly, I'm a martial artist myself. They kept suspiciously close to their encounter, however.

So you're the one, said he. And I said yep, how many letters did you have? You didn't think anyone was going to take your request seriously, were you? Next thing I did was go to the costume shop and hire a robe, so you like it then? You didn't just guess I have a fetish with bottoms, did you? He asked. No, I replied. Spot on. What do you want to do?

Can we just talk for a while and then decide? Talking is boring, he proclaimed and tackled his first Long Island. Right then, she said, took a sip and chatted to the bar-man, who on first sight, had given her more visual pleasure than Ray Bans and his bodyguards. So they sat next to each other for the entire date, while he was looking at her flirt with the not-too-busy bar-keeper. Or rather, looking at her skirt. You've got x-ray-eyes, haven't you, she said, one time, and he: Can I touch the material? My father is a famous designer, I know about materials! She shrugged. Ok, he stood up after his fourth cocktail, Let's go to a cocktail party, and took her hand and dragged her to his car. I didn't want to refuse and went, only to realise in the car that I had left the shoes behind in the bar. How uncomfortable. I'll let you try on a thousand pair of shoes, he said, and if one of them fits you in your dress, you are my Cinderella. She obliged, irrespective of the fact that she might not have wanted to become his Cinderella, and held hands with him until the driver stopped. Out, he ordered. But "out" was dark, muddy and no house in sight. Here? I asked surprised. Here, the son of the famous designer and the stretch-limo growled, which made it even more uncanny. Her naked foot in the mud, squelching, and staining her dress.

Musical

The sound of an angelic choir.

Louise entered the Christmas-mall, decorated in white, green and red. Round the corner, past Habitat she discovered that the singing had not just been in her head. Silver-dressed, blonde-wigged darlings, legs up to the neck, were singing, not your usual Christmas songs, but a kind of mass, accompanied by one electronic piano. "Confiteor." I confess. That's about all she could understand in Latin. She had to confess she was quite impressed by the force of the notes scattering literally into her face. The warm melody spread through her body like a constant, abstract thought about a loved-one who didn't exist. She shut her eyes and meditated on this feeling, imagining the music to penetrate her skin and move up and down inside her veins, bubbling with the blood, rippling through her. The melancholy of the minor-key "Kyrie" edged into her brain, making her sad, in a full sort of way, thoughtful. I'm not depressed, I'm happy. I confess. She started to cry as if the notes had struck a chord with her optic nerve. Her tear-filled vision merged the angels into one blonde mass. Turning away, looking around in the mall full of people, she was overcome by awe. How many lives crossed paths here, without realising. Remain untouched by each other. No, she cried out, vision regained, as the tears had rolled down her face and she'd wiped them off, You know we know each other. Look into each other's eyes when you walk by, look into faces, give a smile, and don't just fake one with your mouth. A smile travels form the feathers of your eyes into the pupil of the other person. We are in this together.

Preacher. Weirdo. Whispers. Screw loose. Who is she? What the hell is she talking about?

Leave me alone. She walked in circles among these people who had formed a semicircle around her to see what she was saying and whether it was funny. I need to be a clown, otherwise you won't listen. Comedy wins your hearts, am I right? No proclamation, no, no speaker's corner, really.

Hecklers.

Is that your honest opinion? If I was selling something, she walked up to an old man with a hat on, what would you buy off me? Without stepping back, the man grinned into her face, answering slyly. A bra. Your bra. Thought so, she replied. I fucking thought so. Everyone wants to sell you things through sex. It's not that sex is for sale, but things sell well with it. Did you just think of sex here? Right here, in front of me, of everybody? Are you a heterosexual at all? Now, the man was moving back slowly as Louise was spouting into his eyes, focusing on his brown pupils. Do you know you have a stain in your eye? A what? A stain, a grain of silver. I can read your eyes, your personality. The man pressing forward again, Do you think you scare me? I don't fucking think so.

Louise laughed, and laughed, and laughed until the whole mall had contracted laughter. Until everywhere in the mall people started to look into each other's eyes, laughing, and started to dance with each other like in old Hollywood musicals.

Adrian Cooper

Blood and Peeled Plum Tamato

The train surged clattered into its halt home. Metal-cot, metal-coffin, Ashley thought, sending his cells thinking up what happens to a carriage when its not needed anymore: crushed quarter size, endlife, newlife.

He waits in his seat until the shuffle and nudge have left, listening to the tap-toe army as it marches home. A constant pool of liquid hung in his eyes, the work of each twitch and glance had churned a sticky bud of yellow-white rheum down in to the corner of each socket. He'd earlier convinced himself it was an allergy. He'd spent enough summer afternoons sniffing and sneezing his way through double biology double maths, but the way carriage-yellow beams stabbed at his eye, the way his heavy limbs hung, joints ached; he knew what swam inside him wasn't going to pass. A deep snort growls through his nostrils, an intake of air trawling up the contents into his mouth. Then: spit result out of window: a white ball of foam, solid core, descends, joining hands with concrete.

Neon yawns across wet asphalt – mustard red blue – swallowing streets and alleys. Ashley's new hands and new feet make their way to a cab in the new City- 'Southover Street.' His cousin Amy had found the room. She'd been in the City a few years, working up steam after being plucked from University by some Law Firm. 'Why don't you stay with me Ash? It would make both our lives easier, I need an extra body to fill the spare room, you need somewhere to live'. He said he'd prefer to start on his own, get bearings, find Dailies that were his. Truth, but half of one. He loved Amy but thought her friends were a bunch of Arses (Different World Amy. Different world). She found the place through a pal-in-property- high rise, low rent: 'Its a box Ash. Its your decision'.

The flushes became constant. A Red Rage had worked its way through his blood and bones, pushing sweat from pores to slalom Ashley's young stubble and skin. He already had the keys- deposit, inventory, first month advance; 'Yes Mr Jones but until I get some work its going to have to come from Benefit. And face it, there isn't a more reliable source around is there.' A trip last month had achieved all that; now he needn't mutter to a soul, just get to bed.

Sink full of cold water: dunk. Palm-full of Vitamin C's: swallow. A chill made its way down his spine, nibbling at nerves on its way. Horizontal, a relieved sigh leaves his lips, into air, chattering, making acquaintance with the existing breath of peoplepast. Blanket to mouth, barbs of wool scratching at body. He stretches his arm, fondling for the light switch.

Sleep, slee

Tins and packets stacked high in aisles. People and trolleys need to twist –'Uh, um scuse me' – turn degrees to avoid eye contact, conflict. Roberta heard the language that made her feel at home when she'd just passed cereal and was about to reach cat food. She'd noticed the two black girls last week, and only now remembered that she'd hatched a wonder of where they were from. Not a new ponder mind, the High Street's fruit store, booze place, Perfect Pizza, were all worked by kids from either the Caribbean or West Africa these days. But this time she knew the dialogue between Check Out One and Check Out Two. More, it shot vertigo into her M & S soles, wibble-wobble. A feeling of nostalgia flittered from jaw-line to stomach, and turned cardboard and plastic, tin and cellophane into a line of nandy-flames flowering violently next to jacaranda tree purple, disappearing to a vanishing point beyond Dairy and Meat where Weavers bend a branch with their nest. A can of Tesco's homegrown cat food, blue-stripe white-stripe, moves from shelf to basket, nestling against a bottle of Olive Oil (sunlight for blood). She doesn't have a cat but thought she'd start feeding the stray that curled spine and fur around her stockings whenever she fumbled with keys and locks.

The rivers of chatter motioning between the two Ugandan girls made more sense then any painting hanging from the walls of the Art Gallery, made more sense then the Woody Allen (he's a funny little man, isn't he) picture that she'd journeyed to see at the Multiplex last night. More sense. She freaked them out at first. The girls, synchronized, turn to look at Roberta and at each other. Shit, maybe all the mzungus in this place know what we say about them. Shit, maybe even Jehovah at the Check Out, with his spluttering prophecies of overconsumption, can of beans and Penguin packets under his coat, knew what they said about him (mind you he was madasacake, so it didn't matter).

Roberta started with questions of where in Uganda they were from, and how long they'd been in UK. They followed, a courteous flurry, Check Out Two talking between mouthfulls of customer arms and elbow, taking the three of them to a mutual landscape: a geography they yearned for, longed to see again, if it weren't for their sort-of-lives sculpted here and Shillings they'd borrowed there to get here. A growl and grunt came from the queue that built, brick-on-brick, behind Roberta: pay-up, pack-up. Olive Oil, semi-skimmed, onions, lemon squash, cat food.

And as the hiss of electric air lets her out into the High Street, Roberta decides that next Thursday she'll invite the girls to dinner. Start with a nice bit of proscuito on melon. Then sizzle some peppers-onion-garlic and serve with a thin slice of veal, melt-tongue Osobucco.

Sweat drenched back. Ashley is lying in the same position that had taken him to dreams the night before. His arms and hands pinned to his sides. Rigid. The woolen blanket still drawn to his neck. And though he slept, his eyes were open, in absolute stillness, hypnotised by the white-paint swirls in the ceiling's Ocean. Cu-Clonk clonk.

Knuckles on wood. Not the knock itself but its shadow, an echo of sound became a player in a nightmare he was having about two Pigeons. The two birds perched at the foot of his bed, fat Pigeon and not so fat Pigeon, discussing how best to remove his eyes: slice or peck? Cu-Clonk clonk. Knuckles never become a part of his room-world. Instead, freed by fever, he flicks backwards: 'Ashley sweet heart. Ash'.

The traffic was light. Roadway anxiety, fears of him missing the train, emptied out of his mother. In their place a new force started streaming from inside of her: mustell. There is never a right Time to Tell. Only A Time to Tell, a moment pegged either side by throwaway conversation. The station is still a good half-hour away, she thought. That's enough time, she carried on thinking. Unthreaded, words had to be sculpted, chipped at, ejected into the car to mingle with upholstery. Sentences that made sense, to him. He should know. Maybe-maybe. Yes. Better, before he leaves. Time to think. It's a Good Time, he'll understand, life isn't easier then it's meant to be: 'Ashley sweet heart. Ash.' Straight is best. 'Your mother, she didn't really want you to know. You know you're adopted, yes?' Respin old stories first, confirm known truths, send a bright yellow flare into night sky: warn him about what's to come, help her find her way. 'No Mum. I haven't forgotten.' A fragment like this doesn't dissolve by day, something this shape doesn't decay in memory soil. If anything it grows, silently twists that-way-this, wraps itself until: 'Darling heart. Your mum, your real mum that is. She was a young girl when she met Him, on holiday with her girlfriends. Your father, your real dad, was living there, a foreign chap. Greek or Spanish, something Mediterranean.'

Silence doesn't really exist. Every place has movement, waves, sounds that flick and patter. Voices maybe, just the whispers. Motorways are constant like the Sea.

'Are you angry with me Ashley?'

'When you were young, summertime at school. Do you remember? You'd ask me why you were always darker then the other boys, had such a good tan?' Yes, and she used to tell him he was lucky because every body wants a good tan. He also remembered that the true source of his adolescent inquisition wasn't seasonal, wasn't a summertime thing. But he couldn't tell her that. Say his mates took the piss during PE on Monday, Games on Thursday. He was the only one, apart from Adip and Paul C, who it was natural for given their skin was darkish all over. He was the only one, nearly whiteboy, with a black-brown dick. A prick for a birthmark. Bastards, they can all fuck right off.

High rise, low rent. Ashley lets a laugh loose. A solitary hysteria that only him and him in the whole wide universe can understand. His mum, not real mum, tried so hard but never touched the ground. His laugh evolves into heaving, dredging clots of phlegm from deep inside his lungs. Retching, wearing his blanket as cloak, he makes his way to the sink. His corneas are completely red, burning away the dark browns of his iris. Blood vessels scream.

Richard and Judy had concluded their morning philanthropy, saving the British Isles from personal trauma with a cup of Lapsang and sticks of shortbread, leaving a void for regional news, and other stories. Roberta thought she'd try again. The trays she'd left outside 62 yesterday and day before hadn't been touched. Maybe he's dead, she thought. He looked close to it the night he arrived, staggering, suitcase sliding behind, passing her without so much as Hello. Maybe the police will have to come round and bash the door down with that heavy thing. Maybe.

I'll phone them when he starts to smell.

She tries tomato soup this time. More Universal. Campbell's, not Tesco's own. She scrapes away the burnt layer, spraying black particles, carbon crumbs into the bottom of the sink. Dollop of margarine, leave it to melt. Slice, corner to corner, she arranges the toast in a circle around the bowl. Each edge touching the one next to it, Unity. She wopps in a tablespoon of semi-skimmed into the soup, thinking along the same vitamin lines as the glass of concentrated orange juice. A banana too, still cold from the fridge. And 'Allora, andiamo', she shuffles to her door, one free hand, one balancing hand: 'Bloody thing. Open'. Through the door and along the corridor, her slippers making music with the cold stone floor: skis through snow. Number 56, 58, 60. She gives her three-knock recital, bumps the tray down and back to 55.

Cu-Clonk clonk. 'Fuck off', he mumbles into his blanket, barbs on lips. The paranoia that each nock, each day had instilled — new Ash in a new City — is replaced by a kind of courage — new Ash, new City. Up, he reaches for the door. Along the corridor he sees a short hunched body dissappear behind a wall into a flat. Clu-clunk. 61-59-57, his bare feet stick to the cold stone floor. "55: RS VITRANI". He rings the bell.

Roberta is hardly inside when her buzzer goes.

'You Alive'.

Ashley's Privacy speech sinks to sand. 'Yes.'

'Good. I won't need to call the police'

'Nno'

'Go put clothes on. You'll freeze standing here.'

Cloak sliding behind his heels, he heads back to 62. 'And eatsome food too. You need some strength. You look bloodyshit.' A curl of steam draws his eyes to the soup, bread, bruised banana and juice. Tomato, he thinks to himself, arching to pick up the tray.

Cli-clunk.

Ashley's invitation to cook Roberta dinner the following week, 'a thank you meal for all the ones I let go cold', didn't quite go as he'd intended. 'finefine but you haven't got anything to cook on, or with'. True. 'You buy what you want to cook. Come to my flat, and cook. Okay.'

OKAY. Ash went to work on the onions. Not a classical technique, but it looked well enough rehearsed. Roberta let him carry on. Fine pieces of onion sharing a plate with thin slices of garlic, red-pepper chunks in a bowl next door: a structure. The abc, 1-2-3 of it shapes a higher order: the addition of each ingredient to Sauce. She wasn't sure about peppers though, too sweet; but okay. Let him keep going.

'I couldn't get any smoky bacon', the Olive Oil spat and crackled.

'Listen, why not wait to do the garlic, it'll burn now you've put it in with the onion.'

'0'

'Later you'll need some chicken stock to thicken the sauce', she gifts him a jug of steaming water, crumbling a Knorr cube from its golden wrapper.

It was clear to both of them what was best. Roberta rescued the wooden spoon from its temporary hostage, and Ashley shot to Threshers to get some Red Stuff. Tia Maria too. He'd noticed a bottle, three-quarter gone, white crust marking the rim below the lid, next to half-a-dozen yogurt pots filled with peeled plum tomatoes and a plume of basil wrapped roughly in tin foil.

'Do you miss your home Roberta?'

'This is my home.'

'You're lucky to have lived somewhere else, abroad you know.'

Taglaitelle with a red sauce, mild cheddar instead of parmeagano. Roberta and Ashley sit at opposite ends of a small mahogany table, both of them working their forks round and round, digging deep into their food mountains. A screech of metal on porcelain.

'As soon as I've earned enough cash I'm going to leave this country. Getaway. Not just travelling around. I've got friends who've done that. It seems the only reason they went was to come back.' Roberta fills his quarter-empty glass with more wine. She always stayed on lemon squash while she ate.

'I want to actually live somewhere else, you know'.

'This isn't such a bad place to live Ashley'

'Maybe that's just the point. It's not bad. So middle, All right. The Citys abuzz when you arrive – people making money, going out doing things, you know. Livings good here compared to a lot a places. But I can't see anyone struggling, all the unhappy stuff stays behind walls, pretending smiles. I'm not talking about the struggles of earning a living, successes and failures. That's different, that's ambition. I'm thinking daily.'

Roberta didn't really understand him. She could sense what he meant by the fire that burned when he spoke. But when he spoke, the words tumbled, overlapped. A new sentence would start before his last idea could breathe. 'I'm not sure I get you Ashley.'

He swallows a mouthful of Red Stuff, shards of onion and layers of sauce wash around in his mouth and then disappear down his gullet.

'Look at you lot. Your generation had so much more to deal with. Daily. Two wars, your lives were much more uncertain. You didn't know whether your family would eat or starve. That's got to teach you. Give you perspectives, tell you how to value life.' She drops the bread basket next to his plate. Takes a piece herself and swoops and mops whatever else is left on her plate.

'I'm shy with my money, I know that.' He copies, turning a piece of bread over and over until all the sauce has soaked in and turned the slice limp in his hand. 'No I don't mean that.'

'What you have to remember, Ashley, is that those things happened the wars – so our children, our grand-children, you wouldn't have them'

'But if its't all easy, you never learn anything. Just end up worrying about things that aren't really there. There might be a token cause here and there, 3-Pint revolution and all that, then its over. And I think values change when you're too secure, when lifes easy like that.' He sucks in a breath, 'I don't know. I just reckon that if there wasn't so many choices, things to believe in, ways-to-live; then maybe we'd all look a little harder to find them'.

The Red Stuff always tied his words in a knot. Made him think clearer, but made people who listened to him squint their eyes and look away at clock-hands or reach for an itch on their neck. Roberta listened. She might not understand it all, but she absorbed it, made an effort to untwist the wreckage, attach meaning to whatever he said.

'Let me show you.'

Behind Ashley is a window. A view stretching over the City, lights winking. Next to the window is a bookshelf, where Roberta hovers. Her eyes scanning the titles – Murder Inc., a Picasso biography, World Atlas – the possibilities making her forget, temporarily, why she is actually there. She reaches in and pulls a red-leather bound book from the shelves, as thick as a fist and battered by use. 'This is my album.' She sits on the couch and summons Ash with a glance. 'Have you seen my glasses?' He didn't even know she wore glasses. 'A. Here they are', she leans her body to one side and plucks a plastic case from under the pillow she's sitting on.

'I was born in Varesse, Lombardia, northern Italy. This is my mother.' A grey and white image, eyes reaching through the page: a young women, thick curls of black hair etching their way around a thin pale face. In her arms a baby, stunned by the photographer's flash, wearing trousers to the knee and a sprawling bonnet. 'My father was a drunkman. My mother kicked him out when I was eight years. I don't have any pictures.'

'Who's that?'

'My Uncle, Ermano. He looked after me and my mother. That's his shop. He was a sculptor really, but he had to make the plates and tiles because nobody ever bought his sculptures.'

'Is that his?' Ashley points to a china statuette on the bookshelf. A dancer, one leg lifted off the ground, an arm stretches above her head. A hand clutching something high in the air. But whatever it was she'd held for so many years, like the fading pastle colours of her body, had been rubbed away by a life of crates and suitcases.

'No. All his things were destroyed after the second war. They hung him too. Said he was Fascista. But he wasn't, he was a sculptor'.

'This is the boat I took to Addis Ababa. Me and friend went there to find work.' Ashley listens. But doesn't look at pictures anymore. Instead, his eyes are out the window, blinking at the lights. He lets her stories carry him, each description a feather, each new person a warm current of rising air.

He wasn't sure when he fell asleep. Maybe Dar-es-Salaam, a house with green shutters and washed walls; a market street below, bubbling voices and clanking metal, a barking dog. Roberta didn't know either. Didn't see his sleep-snapped neck fall, didn't notice the thin line of drying wine around his lips. She never took a breath away from the album until she felt the weight of her own head. Heavy. She only just managed to put the album on the floor, then dig an orange blanket from under a small table next to the couch. She stretches its wool across Ashley, and then herself. A radiator autumn night.

She watches his peace. A blotchy layer marks his cheeks, pink-rose dust, blood and wine boiling. An eye flickers behind its lid. She kisses him on the forehead, between fringe and skin. A smile moves to her lips, spreading across her face into her eyes. Tears well, never fall. A sigh circles as she leans her head into the couch and switches off the light. Rustle and twitch, one of Roberta's hands searches wool. She finds his, squeezes her fingers through forefinger and thumb, resting in his palm.

No one would ever notice the moisture that built between their crooked fingers, twisted roots, that night. Not even Ashley. Who, attempting to stand, cracking bones and dislodging knots, is first to wake. Dribbling wreck, he thinks to himself about himself. He notices Roberta's album on the floor by her feet, half-covered by blanket. He picks it up, wanting to establish where in the world he'd fallen asleep. Clearing plates stained with pink crumbs to the opposite side of the table, he sits and opens the heavy cover.

He remembers the boat to Addis; her job selling clothes in a hotel boutique; the party pictures – empty wine bottles and glowing faces. And then is lost. Pictures of a safari, mountaineering trip, picnic, a row of young tranquil faces lined with fighter-jacket fur; all mean nothing to him.

It was later into the book, without Roberta's narration to string threads between each image, give character to each face, that Ashley started to realise. Disjointed. The stories she'd carved in the air of her flat that night were hers, they had tumbled from her mouth after all. But the pictures and pastings that covered each page of the album weren't. The dried flowers and ticket stubs, spider letters scrawled in black ink under each image were undoubtedly hers too; but the faces, lives she'd entered through her own history never surfaced more then once. Inconsistent. The families that grinned and laughed; people marrying giving birth getting drunk. Random clippings, articles – people winning football trophies, scholarships, businesssswoman of the year – cut from magazines, tabloids, broadsheets. Each scene ruptured by unconnected faces, people she couldn't have known, strangers.

Ashley looks across at Roberta. The weight of pages has twisted and numbed his wrist against wood. He closes the album, stands, bends to put it on the couch. He notices a hair on her lower lip stuck to lipstick, quivering with each breath. He find a pen near the telephone and starts to write her a note. He stops, screws the paper napkin into a tight ball and puts the words into his trouser pocket.

He walks to the door. It doesn't open at first. Bloody thing. Then out, into the corridor.

Cli-clunk.

Adam LT Hays

In The Guts of a Tick

1

The plan was my baby. It wasn't genius, but it was simple, and effective.

Feature: Amsterdam in November time. Waiting at the east end of the Warmoesstraat, past where the neon beams failed to reach, past where the dark shoe polish canals turned the corner and left us alone in a cobbled black dead end. Next to me, Dane, my gringo partner, shivered and sniffed violently, then we simultaneously turned up our collars against a curled fist of wind. The rain battered our heads coldly, so hard you could smell it.

I arranged the meet with the others for eight-thirty. It was now ten to nine, and only Dane had showed up. I clenched my fists in my pocket, and tried hard not to grind my teeth.

There were five of us in the crew, and part of the plan involved flying out from London under assumed names. We had all booked the break separately: different hotels, different seats on the same flight. It was a loophole, basically, to guarantee that no hard evidence was left anywhere that implied any of us knew the other. Like I said, simple but effective. Except the downside of this idea was that you had to work out a rendezvous for the other side. And like I was finding out, words flowed easier than actions.

We were there for a dope deal, which in itself was nothing hardcore, nothing like a major complication, till people started turning up late. We were only moving light stuff, nothing to worry about till we got out of the country. I don't like admitting it, but we're not anything like an empire. More like a high street retail chain. We're still at the stage where we've got to smuggle the shit through the airport. A bit more money our way we might be able to move it over water, save a lot of necks on the line. But you've got to start somewhere.

Dane shuffled his feet next to me. He was nervous. I didn't blame him. It was his first time with me, but he's good. He was staring at the pills in his hand he had just bought off a canal rat. He looked shameful.

"Idiot. A hundred guilders, what's that? Thirty-three quid?"

"Four tablets!"

"They're probably aspirin. You could be a Jap tourist the way you stick out. Jesus."

"I don't look like a tourist."

"None of the natives buy from these guys. They go to the proper dealers."

He threw two of the tablets he was convinced were E's down his gullet.

"Fuck you too," I said. "How do you feel?"

A snort. "Obviously they're not going to kick in yet."

"You'll get more of a buzz from one of my Extra Strong Mints," I sang.

Snort. I don't touch drugs, ever, so Dane, being sooo typically bourgeoisie in a way that most hopheads are, likes to talk down to me whenever I talk about any of his hobbies. He sees me as an easy target. He's the same with anything he thinks he knows more about than I do. But I'm used to it. I just make it sound like I always know what I'm talking about, and that's the trick in this life, isn't it?

"Where are the others?" I was getting itchy. After making sure we had all arrived safely, I had set up a meet with Leroy Merlin, and I didn't want to be late.

"You want to walk back down through the district?"

I looked at him for a second, then stomped off back down the Warmoesstraat.

"Where is Vincent?" I asked as he caught up.

"I told you. He just took off to look around, you know, case the place. He'll be here. Where are Natalie and Henry staying?"

"At the Eden Hotel. It's on the river."

"Do you think he's sleeping with her?" he pondered, with all of his seasoned innocence. I lit a JPS Light.

"Right now? I should hope not."

"I think he's sweet on her."

"Good. We wanna keep up appearances."

We walked on rigid legs, sauntered on down the Warmoesstraat towards the garish neon. We had been talking in a very dark spot, probably unwise, but we're big lads, and Dane was made up with the switchblade I bought him.

"These canals all look the same. How do you know where you're going?"

"This is the red light district. Just follow your nose." I pointed to the gathering throng. We plunged into the mass. A man in a tux and long overcoat gesticulated wildly with a silver-topped cane from the leopard-skinned lobby of a strip club.

"Boys! My boys! Come in, for much show! Come in! Only fifty guilders for real anal penetration!" We walked past. His accent was spot on, like it belonged to a wealthy Sussex lord. Fitted right in with the words he was saying.

A car shuffled down the narrow cobbled road. He couldn't get through, despite furious revving and much hooting of the horn. A man leaned out of the passenger window and swore furiously in Dutch. At least, it sounded like swearing. He could have been politely asking everyone to move out of the way. You never can tell with Dutch. We moved over and the car pushed slowly on.

At the next bridge, a black man, almost identical in size and attire to the one that had sold Dane the fake E's, approached me. I didn't change pace, or look at him, but he walked with us anyway. He was short, and had trouble keeping up. He looked put out. We were the only ones on the Warmoesstraat walking at this speed. He had a go anyway. Something in the air – natives and ex-pats alike have the same outlook on life. That "what have I got to lose?" mindset. Then you're only a step away from "what's the fucking point, lets up the dosage till we redline."

"Hey man, charlie?"

"No, I think you must have me mistaken for someone else." I kept looking straight ahead as I spoke, and I heard Dane snicker next to me.

"Get you good gear, man, you want uppers, downers, pills, poppers, wizz?"

"Get the fuck outta here before I get upset." I turned to him and glared, and he scurried off. We were central now, the neon signs illuminating the place almost as bright as day. We hung around on the corner by the water, outside a sex boutique. I leaned on the window, Dane stood in front of me, shifting from foot to foot. He kept looking past me, at the paraphernalia displayed, Debenhams-style, in the window.

"When can we hit the coffeeshops?"

"Not yet. I want to make sure we're all here first."

"I know. You think they're all right? None of them speaks Dutch."

"None of them have to. Look around. Every fucker here speaks English, probably better than you do." I flicked my cigarette over some heads, and watched it land on the cobbles.

"There's Vincent." I looked to where Dane was pointing, and saw Vincent approaching us. He was short, thin, and had a smug glint in his eye, as if he had a quip ready on his lips every second of the day. He was a cheeky fucker, the sort of person that someone in an authoritative position would want to victimise. And that was why I had chosen him.

He punched Dane on the shoulder, and they shook hands in their townie mock-ghetto fashion. They were good at their roles, mainly because they were halfway there in real life anyway.

"Good flight?" I asked, looking over at a patrol black-and-white trying to cruise past the punters.

"You should know, you were on the same plane. Where are the love-birds?"

"We don't know," said Dane. "They haven't shown up yet."

"Come on, we walk," I said. We started off back in the direction we had come.

"Try not to look at anyone, Vince. You'll get thumped," said Dane.

"Fuck you very much," he grinned. "I'm safe here. Everyone's just mellow."

"Not if some buck-arsed pimp lays claims of ownership upon you, rent boy," I said.

"Look. Who's that?" Dane pointed ahead to where we had been standing a few minutes before. A man and a woman. They saw us and walked, arm in arm, towards us. They smiled as we approached. They looked like a young, dignified, happy couple of newlyweds. Which was the desired effect. When we all congregated together and they had all said their hellos, I spoke.

"You're nearly an hour late. I should bollock you, but I believe in democracy, so I'll just be nice and make you feel guilty about it instead." There were mumbled apologies and foot shuffling.

"Sorry," Henry muttered. He was a big man, but gentle-looking, harmless. And the beard was now fully-fledged. Bang on.

"Sorry Kenley," Natalie said, and smiled slightly sheepishly. She always called me by my surname; I don't know why.

"Now we're here, we don't need to be quite so secretive. Ground rules. Don't visit or telephone each other's hotels. Don't use cheques or credit cards. Pay cash for everything. If anyone needs money, say so now." There was silence.

"We'll meet at Short's of London in the Rembrandtsplein, tomorrow at midnight. All news can wait till then. If it is really urgent, then call the cafe and leave a message. But I don't want to hear from any of you prematurely unless one of us dies, or worse.

"Vince, tomorrow I want you to find us a secure lock-up of some description where we can rendezvous and make preparations for return. Dane and I will go and meet with Leroy Merlin and close the deal. Natalie, Henry, you make like a couple of tourists and keep your senses tuned for anything we should be aware of. Use the trams, they really work. Don't get yourselves arrested. We're in Amsterdam, so enjoy yourselves, but do it discreetly. Any questions?"

Nothing.

"Then go have fun."

2

After the meet, I walked back to my hotel, the Europa. It was on the Constantijn Huygensstraat, not far from the Vondelpark. Unassuming place; simple, quiet, cigarette machine near the room.

I showered and changed, then headed down to the bar to kill a few before I caught the tram back into the city to meet Dane for a drink. We were here on business, but you can mix pleasure. Just in moderation, like the poem goes.

I met him in the Leidseplein, not far from my hotel. He looked lost, and stepped out into the street excitedly when he saw me.

I chuckled and waved when he collided with the cyclist, and watched from afar as the apologies and apportioning of blame was reduced to grunts and knuckle-scraping gestures. Eventually the cyclist accepted the blame when I appeared at Dane's side and she fucked off sheepishly, never to be seen again. We were outside a steak house. Dane was shifting from foot to foot, itching to get going. It was only the second time he'd been abroad, and he was determined to enjoy himself. I wanted to stick to him while he did, because he sometimes has trouble saying when.

The tram lines cut through the square, which was dotted with cafes, coffeeshops, jazz bars and restaurants. The vertical neon signs jutted out from the buildings, jostling for position along the walk.

"Let's go in there." Dane pointed to a public house on the east side of the square called The Bulldog. It was the largest pub in the square, the name brightly lit by halogens above the windows, framed either side by eponymous cartoon effigies.

"You've got to be joking," I said. "You can hear the scousers from here."

"Just to see what it's like," Dane protested.

"Don't you want to sample a bit of Dutch culture?" I asked. "Second holiday ever, and you want to go where all the tourists go."

"Just to see what it's like," he repeated.

"Come on. Let's go down there." I took his arm and began steering him down an alley adjacent to The Bulldog. It was crammed with pool halls, clubs and bars, more tightly packed than in the rest of the square. And it seemed darker.

"Will there be cafes?" Dane asked.

"You mean coffeeshops," I corrected. "Cafes are cafes, coffeeshops are where they sell the stuff you're after."

He pouted. "Maybe I want to go to a cafe."

"You on the wagon?" I raised one eyebrow at him. He tutted. "I didn't think so."

We walked past evil looking places, black and dingy, with satanic faces on the doors. Dutch thrash metal bellowed out of any available escape route.

"How about here?" I suggested, pointing to a coffeeshop on the left. It looked pretty homely, a large cannabis leaf painted on the door, pasty white pseudo Rastas lying in the gutter. They looked like polytechnic undergrads.

We went in, and the warm smell of dope hit us straight away. It was quiet, only three or four of the tables were occupied. The place was lit by an amber haze, and spinning spotlights casually cruised the walls. A Santana track mellowed its way out of the speakers, all crybaby guitars and laconic vocals.

Dane made for the bar, and asked to see the smoking menu. The barman obliged nonchalantly, and he meticulously made his choice, and bought the bag full of brown that looked like cat shite. I ordered a scotch with chaser, and joined him at a table in the corner, near the pool table.

The stoner marvelled, Rizlas and books of roaches were there on the table, where you'd normally find the salt and pepper. After Dane had smoked half of his peace pipe, he offered it to me. I pointedly took out my cigarettes and lit one. He shrugged and resumed normal service.

"When are you meeting this guy?" Dane asked.

"Leroy Merlin? Midnight." I looked at my watch. It was ten forty-five.

"What is he?"

"A fucking animal."

"In relation to you."

"Dealer/bagman/fence. Take your pick."

"You used him before?"

"Twice. He's cool." Dane inhaled deeply, and hacked violently. "Go easy, you fucking hippy. I don't want you too wasted. I may need some muscle."

"Thought you said he was cool."

"He's beer cool, but there's a first time for everything. And I don't trust him as far as I can throw him."

"Why do you use him, then?"

"He's got the best prices in town. And you don't do yourself any favours if you suddenly defect to the competition."

"Fuck them. That's up to us. If he puts his prices up, then we've every right to shop over the road."

"You're a man of principles, Dane. It'll be the death of you." I nodded towards the pool table. "Want to shoot some?"

"Okay, man," he said, milking the vibe for all it was worth. He racked them up, and we sunk some frames for an hour or two. He lost.

He got hungry. We needed fresh air. We walked back along the alley towards the Leidseplein, and then caught the tram into the district.

On the tram was an old guy wearing beat clothes and a knackered hat. He was sitting behind Dane, eating dinner, which consisted of a sandwich and a can of Orangina.

When he had finished, he took a plastic bag out of his pocket and removed the toothbrush it contained. He made a loud point of cleaning his teeth, retching and coughing bile up, spitting bits of the sandwich he had just eaten onto the floor. Dane came and sat next to me.

The guy got up, and staggered to the exit doors. He jabbed the stop strip. He was six foot two, three, and couldn't have been more than eight stone. He began leering incomprehensibly at a middle aged woman near us. She shouted at him in Dutch and made a shooing motion with her hand.

He continued to jabber and wail. I listened hard – he didn't sound Dutch. When he got off at the next stop, I heard him say, "Don't you want to be like me?" to some teenagers. He was British. Fucking typical.

We headed into the red light district. Dane wanted to get laid.

We walked up and down the district, watching the girls in the windows. The more experienced, older ones winked and swayed their hips coquettishly. A fantastically-breasted blonde pointed a finger at me and beckoned with a painted fingernail, a wicked smile on her face. I grinned and walked on.

The younger girls tried to smile, though they looked nervous.

Closer inspection – I'm convinced they were shivering.

A fat Chinese man, sixty, chinless, loitered outside the window of a particularly young brunette. She looked straight ahead, and winked urgently at Dane. The Chinese man blabbered loudly, and opened the door. I thought I saw her shoulders slump a little, then she turned to him and smiled. Her teeth blinded in the ultra-violet light, and the Chinese man jabbered again, excitedly. He shook hands vigorously, and then the girl led him into a room behind a curtain. Inside was all red. Just red, and the UV strips along the tops and bottoms of the windows.

We walked past a window below street level. The bargain basement. This wench had at least four of her own teeth, madly giving it the come-on-then. She had to be into some kind of Oedipal fetish scene – she was pushing sixty. I silently gave it five to one on coming out without at least one new strain of the clap.

There was a murmur of noise flowing over the whole street. A steady hum, broken occasionally by gangs of men roaring as they paraded down the canal. If you strained your ears to hear them speak between yells, nine times out of ten you could pick out "Faaaaaaack you!" or "'Ave summa dat!" In the lulls a jazz saxophone floated along the crowd.

I felt a hand on my shoulder. My naturally wary reflexes had doubled since touching down at Schipol, and I spun round, fists clenched and spring-loaded. The man put his hands up in the universal white-flag gesture. He offered a pacifying smile.

"Look, man." He pointed to the girls on the other side of the canal. "See them hookers, man? Them all chicks with dicks, man! You get good woman here, but over there, nah-nah."

Dane and I continued past the array of sex. We passed a window higher than the others. In it sat a black girl, with long, wavy tresses of hair. She had on a white bra and panties, and a pair of black spectacles to aid her in the book she was reading. She chewed a pencil as she did so, and looked at us, expressionless, as we walked past her window.

Dane slowed to a halt just past her window. He looked back at her, then at me. I lit a cigarette.

"I've always wanted…" he murmured, half to himself, "…to make love to a black girl."

"So go on," I said. "What's stopping you?"

"'What's stopping you?' the man says. I'm about to pay for sex. What do you think is stopping me? I've never done it before. I mean, of course I've done it before, but I've never paid for it before."

"Think of it as something to tell your grandchildren."

"I'm not waiting for you to talk me into it. I'm going to do it, I just…"

"So why are you out here freezing your balls off? You'll need them. What are you waiting for?"

"Stop nagging me!"

I sighed loudly and irritably. He snapped to glare at me with an angry look in his eye. I stared him back, blank. He knew I was winding him up, but it still worked.

"Fine. I'm going." He didn't move.

I turned to look behind me. "You're still here." I saw an elderly couple grinning at a girl. They seemed very happy. I turned back. Dane had gone. I looked around quickly. He was not to be seen. I looked up at the window of the black girl. She was gone.

I wondered how long he got. Assuming he didn't bust the groove in a couple of minutes, how long would his money last? Twenty minutes? Fifteen? I leaned against a wall and smoked, watching the greed go by. I checked my watch. Time seemed to be slowing as I got colder. I hoped he wasn't too long. Leroy Merlin was not likely to be on time, but I wanted to be there first.

I went for a walk to keep warm. I dug my hands into my pocket and walked around the market. The jazz seemed louder – "Night Train." I tried to find the source of the music. It was sparse now, stripped of sax and guitar. Just a trio of piano, drums and goosed-up bass, echoing around the city.

I walked past a doorway, where a girl wearing tight leathers and a policeman's cap stood smoking, leaning on the doorframe. She was double-hard, the only one braving the sub-zero temperatures. She clutched a whip in her left hand. I caught her eye as I passed, and she shot me a dirty look. I toyed with the idea for a nanosecond, then walked quickly on. Err, no thanks.

I passed a window, and stopped. I had already passed it once, but it had been empty. Now a blonde girl sat in the window, talking on a mobile phone. Eleven steps led up to her door. I tilted my head up to look at her. There was less than eight yards between us, but she looked straight ahead, over the top of my head, as she talked.

She was beautiful. She was wearing an aquamarine bra and panties, and black leather boots. Her mouth just quivered as she talked, her body could have melted stone. I turned back, and saw that Dane's girl was now back on display. I walked away from the blonde's window and went in search of Dane.

I saw him walking dejectedly towards me over a bridge. Dickhead nearly got run over again.

"Well? How was she?"

He sighed like he had been punctured. "Fucking great."

"I think you're lying to me."

"I couldn't get it in her, man. I almost didn't get it up at all. She was too tight, and it hurt. Then she told me I wasn't doing it properly, said I had to fuck her like a man."

"Ouch. How much did you pay for that abuse?"

"Two hundred guilders. Then she got up and started getting dressed, and I had to jerk myself off just to finish the job."

"You should have gone to the S&M girl down the street. She probably would have been kinder."

"Yeah, I saw her. She looked like one of the Village People. Fuck, that was horrible."

"Oh well. It was an experience, wasn't it? And now you've achieved one of your lifelong ambitions."

"I didn't think it would be quite like that."

"Fuck, you look like you're going to cry."

"Shut up. Where are we meeting your guy?"

"The Amstel Café. Come on. They play jazz there. It'll cheer you up."

The Amstel Cafe was just off the Rembrandtsplein, an inconspicuous exterior hiding behind the pulsating neon of the rest of the square. It was busy inside. We took a table by the window, and watched the band. They were good. I looked at the lights outside, saxophone and bass soundtracking mute frozen-breath conversations.

Leroy Merlin sauntered in with his entourage at twelve minutes past midnight. He brought a girl, whom I recognised immediately as the blonde whore in the window I had been admiring. He also had some hired help with him; two guys, looked like ex-ex-cons. I wasn't expecting that.

He clocked me at the table, and strolled over with the posse, greeting us with open arms and keyboard cracked grins that smacked of one too many personality disorders.

"Mr K, how pleasing to see you!" Big fucker, two-sixty, two-seventy. He put all of it behind the handshake; gave me the standard bonecrusher.

"How you doing, Leroy?" I nodded at the two gorillas. "Got yourself some insurance there?"

He squinted at me for a second, then giggled. "Of course, Mr K. Business is busting, and success inspires jealousy in one's rivals. I must not be too careful." His English was brilliant fun – throaty thespo art-school drivelling one moment, broken playschool sentences the next.

"Very true. Buy you and your men a drink?"

He nodded curtly. I rose and went to the bar, leaving Dane looking uncomfortable at the table. I returned with a tray of drinks, introductions were exchanged, then we talked shop. There wasn't much to negotiate – we were going to do a repeat deal on the last batch. The meet was just a procedure, for each to make sure the other wasn't going to sodomise him. Ordinarily, a big time dealer wouldn't communicate directly with small time buyers without a middleman, but I had known him a while, and I knew his ego thrived on trying to impress the small fry. I guessed the bodyguards were more for show than anything else.

"So, Mr K, you are interested in a repeat batch. Or perhaps you would like to increase the bulkload?"

"Like to, Leroy, but no can do. Don't have the means by which to move it. Give me eight or nine months and maybe we can up the ante."

He frowned, big gastropod brows dancing autonomously over his eyes.

"Mr K, you are selling yourself short. The weed is perfect for, ah..." he waved his hand while searching for the word. "...the recreational user, but you could only do well from purchasing some heavier shit." He leaned forward and winked. His blonde escort excused herself silently and headed for the ladies room. I watched her go.

"Thanks, Leroy, but my resources don't stretch far enough to smuggle horse through the airports. Too risky. Like I said, soon I'll be able to shift it over water, then we can talk big."

He frowned again. "Mr K, you misunderstand. I am offering you favours by selling you shitty little loads of hash. I am a legitimate wholesaler. I sell the hash only to licensed premises. To the man without a license, it is only contraband. I am taking considerable risks by selling to feeble street vendors like yourself."

"I'm not sure I like that description."

"Mr K, let me be clearing. I can do you this deal once more, but next time I need you to buy more. To make me worthwhile I need to set a minimum price on your account, or else," – he stood up – "we can do no more business."

One of the goons cracked his knuckles. I flinched – too late to check myself. Then he smiled.

"Mr K, it is a good investment. Think about it."

"I always do. Can we arrange the usual test drive?"

"Mr K, do not be thinking I would fuck you over. I offend easily."

"No offence intended, Leroy. Just a formality. We can't be too careful, like you said."

He beamed. The man had more faces than a dodecahedron.

"Of course, Mr K. Come to my nursery, tomorrow at nine. We shall arrange some testing."

The girl returned from the bathroom. I watched her walk over. Leroy Merlin noticed.

"You like her, eh?"

"She's beautiful."

He leaned close with a broken smile, bursting with pride.

"She is my own."

She arrived and loitered around the table, not wishing to sit, itching to get going. Leroy Merlin sensed this. He rose.

"Tomorrow at nine, Mr K. Enjoy yourselves." He nodded blankly, and the gang left the cafe. They walked outside to the car parked out front, and climbed in. I squinted. A Land Rover Discovery. Jesus-fucking-Christ. A clear advertisement that if the truth was known, Leroy Merlin probably barely had a pot to piss in.

Dane expelled air, like he had been holding it in since Leroy Merlin arrived.

"Well," he murmured. "That didn't sound good. What's his problem?"

"He's a greedy fucker, plain and simple."

"What was he on about – it's too risky for him?"

"That's bullshit. That guy runs every Class 'A' chemical you can think of from the street. Contraband worries are not top of his list."

"Oh."

I rose. "Get some rest, Dane. It's been a long day."

"No thanks. I'm on holiday. I'm going to a club and get myself a good old fashioned freebie."

I punched him on the shoulder and left the bar.

Walking back down through the district again, I wound up outside the window of Leroy's arm glitter. She had clocked in for another shift, sitting in the window talking to a friend/colleague.

I felt a surge of something in my stomach, and walked up the steps. I tapped on the window, and she turned briefly, then pressed the buzzer to let me in, still talking to the girl.

I stepped in. The red hallway was wonderfully warm. I felt my face glow. She opened the door and smiled at me, making no sign of having recognised me. I leaned on the doorframe, and smiled back.

"How much?"

"One hundred guilders for fuck and suck."

"Okay."

"Great." She got up and stepped into the hall. She pointed up the stairs to a red room. "Go up there and make yourself comfortable. I'll be up shortly." Her superb English was an accented slant of American and Dutch.

I walked up the stairs to the room. It looked like a normal bedsit, except for the powerful red light and the mirror that took up the whole right hand wall, next to the single bed. The floor was heavily varnished wood with a flat weave rug sitting on it. A rickety chest of drawers, cheval mirror, small chair and wardrobe completed the ensemble. Glamour it was not. Except for the red, and except for the mirror.

The girl followed me in and closed the door. I turned to her, smiling. She returned the smile and held out a hand.

"My name is Nancy."

"How do you do?" I replied, holding out my hand. She took it, and looked shocked.

"My, you are so cold!" She rubbed my hand with both of hers. "Is it raining outside?"

"It has been."

"I don't like the rain. I don't like the cold either, unless of course it snows. But it never snows in Amsterdam. You are British?"

"Yes."

"I like the British. They are all gentlemen. Does it snow in Britain?"

"Not very often."

"I went to Switzerland last year. I love the mountains. I had snowball fights with my sister. She is seven." She removed her bra, and took out a condom from the chest of drawers.

"You must pay me in advance."

I took out my wallet and handed her a C-note. She smiled thanks and put it in a purse in the bottom drawer.

"Please take off your clothes and put them on the chair," she said, slipping off her panties.

I stripped naked, and sat on the bed. I played it submissive, thinking of all the shitbirds she must have been with. Aren't I a fucking saint?

She sat down beside me. "The important thing is that you must relax. Don't worry." Her tone was soothing. "Would you like to lie down?"

I lay down on my back and looked at her in the mirror. She slid down between my legs, and got busy. She knew what she was doing.

"Do you like that?" she said, between mouthfuls.

"Yes," I murmured. I looked at the ceiling. For an awful moment I thought I wasn't going to be able to get it up, and then she stroked my tummy, and it was easy.

"You are hard enough to enter me now," she said, and got off the bed, motioning me to do the same. She lay down where I had been, and guided me into her. "Is it all right for me to place one of my legs on your shoulder?"

"Of course it is."

"Thank you. Be careful of my boots. I do not want to make you impotent."

I slid into her. I took it slow, looking at her face. Her eyes were shut, she was *ooh that's it come on baby* running on autopilot, but it still felt good. I marvelled at her body as we fucked.

"Am I allowed to kiss your breasts?" I whispered.

"No," she said. "But thank you for asking."

"I want you to go on top."

"Another fifty guilders to change position."

"Now?" I asked, withdrawing.

"No, not now. It spoils the flow, don't you think?"

We swapped places, and she straddled me. She shut her eyes again, craned her neck back and moved back and forth expertly.

"Tell me when you are coming," she said, "and I will speed up."

She only opened her eyes to look at me at the last moment. I couldn't help biting my lip for those few seconds of wilful vulnerability, and then it was over. I caught my breath, and she quickly dismounted, removed and tied off the condom, and then gently stroked me dry with a Kleenex.

I got up and dressed, then settled the account. She wiped herself, and talked as she put on her underwear.

"You are here long?"

"Just for the weekend."

"On business or pleasure?" She fed me the line. I didn't miss it.

"Well, what do you think?" I said, grinning.

"Business for me, pleasure for you."

"Isn't that the way of the world?"

"I hope you enjoy your stay. Do you like nightclubs? For the house music?"

"Nah, not really. I like jazz."

"Really? I am surprised. I love jazz. None of my friends like jazz. I have trouble finding time to go and enjoy it, because whenever I do, I am always approached by awful men. Wherever I go."

"Perks of the job, I suppose."

"The Amstel Cafe in the Rembrandtsplein is the best place to go for jazz. They have good music."

"Good. I'll go there."

"There is also The Cotton Club down by the marketplace, but it is small, and not as nice. Amsterdam is not great for jazz. New York is the best place to go for jazz."

"Have you been?"

"Of course I have. You should go if you like jazz."

"I intend to."

She held out a hand. I took it. "Enjoy Amsterdam. Do not take drugs. They are bad for you. Especially the spacecakes. You have one and feel nothing, so you have two more and then you are gone."

"I know. Thank you, Nancy." God, I sounded sickening. I'd overdone the deferential bit, but then realised I hadn't been playing it at all.

She walked me to the door, held it open for me. The outside chill blasted me in the face. I had almost forgotten everything else, forgotten any notion of talking to her about Leroy Merlin. She shook my hand again.

"Goodbye."

"Bye."

I trotted down the steps and headed back towards my hotel, streets quiet, the air damp with the threat of midnight rain.

3

The plan was thus: Flight BA79290 touched down at Gatwick around noon local time on the Sunday, two days after Dane and I met Leroy Merlin on the Friday.

Ex-euro baggage reclaim was at its quietest at mid-Sunday, same story at Schipol. Couple of customs officers at the gate, quick frisk, golden gateway, have a nice day. Yeah, they've got dogs, but not always. Dogs aren't cheap, neither is an armed guard. I'd cased the rota system for the past three months, and was pretty sure I could lay my money on there being little hassle on Sunday. Even if we had a little canine intrusion, Natalie was gonna carry some of those herbal fruit teabags with one 'accidentally' torn open. They smell like buggery, and the dogs go nuts for it.

Besides which, if you wanna get technical in a court of law, the Dutch militia don't give a fuck about you taking the stuff away, it's when you hit the tarmac on the island and try to bring it in that the trouble starts.

Right, so, we come in off the plane and make for baggage reclaim. First off: Vincent and Dane are the bait. Diversionary tactic. They swing out in the wideboy garb, giving it the mouth and the swagger. Two young kids still high on a weekend in the Amstel – the knock officers would be queuing up to pull them over. They'd both have to endure the cold fingers of a full body cavity search by H.M. Customs & Excise, but they weren't actually gonna be carrying anything, so at worst they'd be walking bandy-legged for a week.

So while they're causing a ruckus in the green channel, Natalie and Henry would walk through at the same time with the pushchair, a happy young couple in love. Fake baggage tickets would inform anyone in a uniform that they'd just come back from a blissful fortnight in Malaga. The kid in the pushchair was the real culprit, a six-month-old bonny bugger, borrowed from a friend of Natalie's, with a pound of the shit in the lining of his nappy.

Right behind Natalie and Henry, or Mr & Mrs Burns, as the passports showed, would be yours truly. Decked out in a double-breasted Savile Row pinstripe number, I was gonna be carrying the bulk of the shit, taped in strips to my body. Pains had been taken to get a convincing effect, and I had sweated over accessories. I had the digital clasp briefcase containing important looking spreadsheets, the

Weekend FT and white bread sandwiches. I also had a slim cellular telephone in my right inside jacket pocket, a breath freshener spray in the left, and an expensive looking watch with matching cufflinks. I had even added some grey streaks to my hair to get a more mature look. I was the perfect ponce. And with Vincent and Dane demanding all the spotlight, the three of us would saunter straight through. The final rendezvous was at midnight that night in a safe house in Kent. That was the plan. We had done it similarly twice before with no problems. But there's a first time for everything.

I met Dane for breakfast in a tiny place just off the Leidseplein. Red-and-white gingham tablecloths, candles in bottles covered in congealed wax, Dutch radio. We were the only ones in it. I ordered a couple of pancakes and some coffee, and we sat at the back. A radio squeaked tinny europop at us, and even the morning DJ sounded exhausted.

"It's deserted." Dane looked around him.

"Late town. No-one will be about till ten, maybe later. Only the weirdo tourists get up early. So what did you do last night?"

"Found Vincent, queued up for forty-five minutes to get into a nightclub, got turned away, went to a coffeeshop, smoked till two, went to bed."

"Jesus, you still look miserable as fuck. You didn't get in?"

"Members only."

"That hurts." He didn't say anything else.

We finished breakfast, then took a tram to Leroy Merlin's showroom. He met us at the door, arms open, beaming smiles that didn't reach his eyes. He made my skin crawl.

His nursery was in the basement of a house overlooking a canal. Typically Euro; tall, narrow, and Dane, probably on some sort of comedown, was convinced the houses were leaning forward alarmingly. "They're falling! They're ... fuck! ... gonna fall on us!" Leroy Merlin said something about the smallest house in the world, and then spat on the ground.

He took us into the house through the front door. Dane kept looking over his shoulder. I tried to reassure him that the whole deal was legal until we touched down at Gatwick, but he just twitched.

Downstairs was a large garden like a tarpaulin railway tunnel, half inside, half out. The place reeked of maryjane. Tucked discreetly behind a row of budding plants was a pallet stacked high with polythene bags, each packed full of brown resin and bearing a small coloured label.

I motioned Dane to come over. Leroy Merlin cut a small lump from one of the bags and gave it to Dane. Dane sniffed it, then flicked his Zippo and heated the lump. It crumbled in between his fingers, and he smiled.

Leroy Merlin and I shook hands. "As we agreed," I said.

"Of course, Mr K. Ten ounces Ketama, ten Super Polm, ten Moroccan Blonde. I shall cut more for your artist to sample tonight."

"Well done. We'll be around Sunday morning at seven to pick it up. Okay?"

"Yeah, it is okay."

He cut three more lumps from different labelled bags, and handed them to Dane, who tucked them into his cigarette packet. We shook hands again, and Leroy Merlin showed us out, making the usual post-deal banter: damn weather, the euro, AFC Ajax recent home form. It seemed tinged with relief. Without the gorillas he seemed nervous, meek. Maybe I read it wrong; intended meanings often get lost in translation. But he walked us to the tram pick-up point, and even waved to us as we pulled away.

Midnight came around. Dane and I waited for the rest of the crew in Short's of London. We got there at fifteen minutes to, and took a table by the window, looking out onto the semi-real neon java of the Rembrandtsplein.

I looked at the band. The chalkboard claimed it was jazz night, though the Dutch band's interpretation of the term was so broad it included a cover of "Y.M.C.A." Dane sat still, concentrating on rolling a joint with the tasters.

They rolled in, bang on time, got drinks, and joined us at the table. I thought Natalie looked flushed, even in the dark. I thought about what Dane had said. Was she fucking Henry? I shook it out of my head, thinking he was welcome to her, knowing I was lying, feeling better for pretending I wasn't.

"So, what do we have?" I leaned forward and rested on my elbows. The jive filtered out. Vincent spoke up, disco lights bouncing off his newly-shaven head.

"I got the lock-up." He lit a cigarette. "Ideal location. Three miles south of the airport, less than half a mile from the train station. On the main line from Centraal Station to the airport."

"Cost?" I asked.

"Peanuts. One hundred guilders for the week. All cash up front, the old guy renting it thought it was his fucking birthday. I've got the key." He held up a ring dangling two padlock keys.

"Chance of witnesses?"

"Nothing. It's on a tiny industrial estate, but it looks like the last thing it was used for was building steam trains. Open land. Has to be, it's directly south of the airfield. The planes dump their fuel there. You can smell it."

"Good stuff. Dane and I secured the deal on appro of the sample shit. How's it taste?"

Dane looked at me with half-closed eyes, and nodded slightly through a haze of smoke.

"Good." I turned to Henry. "Tomorrow, you and Natalie get hold of a rental car. An estate. Hertz's number is in the hotel directory. Meet Dane, Vincent and me at this address tomorrow at nine." I handed Henry a slip of paper, which he eyeballed, then tucked away. He didn't speak much. I met him on the skids. He used to spar with my brother, and got himself a fiendish habit. He was desperately ashamed of it, and it had stunted his personality. But it made a good man out of him. He was eager to please, sometimes excessively so.

"We'll ship the stuff straight to Vincent's lock-up, and make plans for return when we get there."

"Bring coats – it's fucking freezing in there," Vincent added, killing his cigarette.

"Well," I spread my hands, "that's it. Be at the place on time. That's all I have to say."

I got up and went to the bar. They dispersed. I didn't see them go. I returned to the table with a scotch. Natalie was sitting where I had been. It was a dark corner – I didn't see her till I was about to sit down. I started, and nearly dropped the drink.

"I thought you'd gone."

"You didn't buy me one?"

I went back to the bar and returned with her port and lemon. She smiled thanks. I sat opposite her, and she moved round so she was sitting next to me.

"You know, Kenley, you conducted the whole of that very moving speech without once looking at me." I could smell her hair, her skin, her cheap roll-on. It warmed something in me, something I wasn't sure I liked.

"Like I said before, you and Henry don't come into play until we get to Schipol."

"Is that a reason to ignore me?"

"This is business."

"You said I could enjoy myself discreetly."

I sipped my drink and gazed at the band, now roaring their way through a Grease medley.

"What do you think of Henry?"

"That depends."

"On what?"

"On whether you mean professionally, or socially."

"You tell me what I mean."

"As a colleague? He's meticulous, focused and hard-working."

"And socially?"

"He's hung like a carthorse." She threw her head back and roared with laughter, doubling up when she saw the look on my face that I was trying, and failing, to hide. Slowly the laughter subsided, and she rested her chin on my shoulder, looking up at me with a smirk. She had got to me. I grinned at her. She moved closer.

"This is unprofessional, Nat. You're supposed to be married to Henry."

"We're in Amsterdam, Kenley. I did some background research on my character. She's a serial adulterer."

She placed her mouth on mine, and the warmth melted that something inside. I pulled her to me, and she whispered something I didn't catch.

Then she stood up, and held out her hand. I took it, and we walked out of the bar. We stood looking at each other outside in the square, jazz riffs and house beats merging in the air.

"We … we can't stay at the same hotel," I said.

"Yes, we can," she whispered.

We checked into a motel under two Dutch names, and paid cash for the room, overlooking the River Amstel. We made love until the breaking dawn blitzed the red neon motel sign buzzing on the wall outside.

4

We rose the following morning, and shared a comfortable silence. She wanted to get breakfast, but I refused, saying we were already taking too many risks. She fed off that, and made another move on me. Gentle but firm, I pushed her away, showered, and left the motel, telling her to check out an hour after I'd gone.

I spent the daylight hours wandering around the city, questioning what I was doing far more than was healthy. I strolled round the market, took in a canal ride, killed bullshit time until the dusk fell and I was comfortable.

It was dark by the time I got into the district, and the Saturday night crowds were already slavering through the streets. I did my window shopping, then tried to kid myself that I was surprised when I arrived at Nancy's window again.

She wasn't there. For a second I felt let down, then laughed out loud in the middle of the street. No heads turned. What the fuck was this? Dimestore pulp romantic cuts himself up when he falls for the hooker/drug kingpin's moll? How often have we heard that one?

I dawdled outside for fucking ages, bittersweet teen lusting colliding with hard-nosed icepick cynicism in the middle of my brain, the nuclear fallout it caused fucking my head more than any chemical Amsterdam had to offer.

Then she suddenly appeared in the window, though I didn't see her enter, and I could have sworn I hadn't taken my eyes off her empty chair.

She was wearing a black and red glam trash brassiere, eyebrows furrowed as she wrestled with the broadsheet. I bounded up the stairs, and knocked on the window. She glanced briefly, then let me in.

"Hello," I said. Good start.

"One hundred guilders for fuck and suck."

"You don't remember me?"

She frowned and looked at the ceiling as she thought, then smiled as she if she really gave a fuck.

"Oh yes, the jazz man. Sorry, but I have many customers every day."

"I can imagine."

"I doubt it."

"No, really. In fact I came over to ask if I could borrow your fishnets."

Lost, totally lost on her. Or she didn't think it funny. What the hell was I doing there?

"Please come in, you are letting in cold air."

"Sorry." I stepped in and shut the door. She motioned me upstairs without a word. I went obediently, and began taking my clothes off again. She followed, and conversation was sparse this time. The second timers had to be the worst: she couldn't use the same talk she had the first time, and didn't know me well enough to talk about anything else.

It was nearly a non-event, but I managed it in the end. I didn't know what I was expecting. I walked out of her place feeling somewhat fucking stupid, and saw Dane mooching around by the canal, watching a barge go past. He turned to me as I approached him.

"What are you doing here?" I asked. He looked past my shoulder and nodded at Nancy's window.

"What is she like?"

"She's great," I said in a monotone.

"Are you being sarcastic?"

"No."

He looked dejected, and shuffled from foot to foot. I sighed and palmed him a hundred guilders.

"Go on, go nuts. I'm sponsoring you." He beamed, and started to say something, but I stopped him with a wave, and pushed him off towards Nancy's door.

I walked around again, waiting for him, and the dusk bloomed into night, the neon coming into its own. The lights nuked my tender brain, and I felt all of a sudden that when I remembered this, I probably wouldn't believe myself. Amsterdam is like that.

Dane emerged into a quiet street twenty minutes later and walked towards me, wearing a shit-eating grin that stretched from 'ere to 'ere. The grin parted as he began to speak, just as the lump of four-by-two came out of nowhere and crashed down onto his head.

He crumpled at the knees, but he didn't go down. The fucker's as hard as concrete, and though the blood was streaming down his face, he got up, running on adrenaline, and faced his attacker. The cunt with the weapon looked mighty scared when instead of going down, Dane turned and went for him, pissed off big time. Dane got two body shots in, hard, to the kidneys. A third, a head shot, and the greaser went down. Too late, another shitkicker with a cosh appeared and attacked Dane. Outnumbered, bleeding like a fucker, couldn't win. Strength dying, the first cunt got up again.

I ran for him, but got the same treatment, from behind, out of thin fucking air. I went down heavy, and just had time to raise my head to see Dane bravely battling off his two opponents before I took a second clout and was bundled unceremoniously into heavy unconsciousness.

Daylight burrowed into my eyes, slowly brought round by open hand slaps to the face. I opened my eyes to acknowledge the pissant slapper, but couldn't focus. I got three more slaps, then tried to mumble "I'm awake now, thank you nurse" but my words stopped at the bundle of rag jammed into my mouth.

Slap. "He is waking, boss." Accented English, but I'm sure it sounded like Dane. Piece of shit! What was going on? "He is awake now." No, maybe it wasn't Dane. I wished my eyesight would hurry up and come back, being blind is not particularly fucking nice. Slap. Slap.

Tried to wiggle limbs and vital organs to make sure everything was still there. Slap. It all seemed to be there, but I was trussed like the girl in the playing cards I had bought the day before.

Smell. What was that smell? Recognised it, but my brain couldn't place it. Slap. Getting pissed off with Smart Julian now, forced myself to get with it. My eyes were streaming, but slowly the flow stopped and they sharpened up.

I was in some kind of damp cellar, on the floor, leaning against a cold stone wall, the ground wet and bitingly cold. Hoped to god I hadn't pissed myself.

Opposite me was Dane, in a hell of a state. Out for the count, blood streaming from a gash in his head. His face was puffed up like an ornate dessert, black clumps of clotted wounds suggesting they had been beating him for some time.

A big dude approached. Unmistakable – Leroy Merlin. The big fucker who was about to get some stick for the slaps yanked the gag from my mouth – I guessed he was one of Leroy's no-claims discounts.

"You fucking nonce, you slap like a girl!" I shouted at him. He recoiled, surprised. "If you're gonna hit someone, hit them fucking properly!"

Foolish words, really, because the punch nearly broke my fucking jaw. He'd have swung the other as well, but Leroy hurriedly pulled him to his feet and said "Enough." I tried my hardest not to black out again – hard work.

I got my sight back and breathed deeply, fighting off the urge to puke. Leroy crouched by me.

"Leroy! What the fuck are you doing? Why are you doing this? What's going on?"

"Mr K, I have considerable cause for concern."

"You and me both." I pointed at Dane with my chin. "Is he ... have you killed him?"

"No, Mr K, though Bruno can sometimes be difficult to restrain."

"What's going on?"

"I have received word, Mr K, that one of your little team, is a grass."

"A what?" I hoped he wasn't trying to be funny.

"A grass, Mr K. A pigeon. A canary. A snitch. Someone, Mr K, is telling tales to people on high." His English had improved in spades in the space of a weekend.

"That's bullshit, Leroy, and I consider it a fucking insult of the highest order as well."

"You are in no position to be offended. Someone somewhere knows more than they should, and one of your posse is responsible."

"Fuck you."

Bruno's next punch did break my jaw. It went with a bang, like someone had force-fed me a firecracker. I blacked out as well, though only for a few seconds, I think. I came around again, with the two bastards still peering into my face. I spat out some blood so I could talk.

"You've got a real nice bedside manner, Florence," I chuckled to myself, which descended into a coughing fit, and racked my body with pain.

"Someone in your position should exact more courtesy, Mr K."

"I've never been very bright." Then, not wanting to take another punch, I tried to be reasonable. "Okay, okay, look, why would one of us want to turn you over? And to who? We're small time."

"Because you're small time, Mr K. Today's rewards for weeding out the bad guy are likely to outweigh the tiny profit you make on the feeble little amount of dope that you peddle."

"But it makes no sense. If you've been turned over, how come you haven't been arrested?"

"I'm a suspicious creature, Mr K. It's what keeps me at the top. People asking questions, deliveries turning up late, extra crew members whom I've never seen before. It adds up."

"So your neanderthal just ruined my looks because you've got a hunch? I know you're not a pretentious man, Leroy, but if you're trying to make a point, believe me, I get it."

Dane stirred, and let out a choked groan. Bruno went over and squatted beside him. I kept Leroy talking, in the hope it would distract his attention from Dane. His body didn't look like it could cope with much more shit.

"But why us, Leroy? Why do you think it's us?"

"Mr K ..." That was as far as he got. A door on the far wall burst open, and three big fuckers of another chemical familia strode in, led by a tattooed besuited mountain of muscle. They stood, looking menacing. I was convinced, and I had yet to decide whether this interruption was going to work for or against us.

Leroy Merlin looked decidedly un-scared, and it suddenly dawned on me how in over our heads we had just become. They exchanged words; threats and fuck-yous, I guess, but they were in Dutch. Each of them laughed at least once.

They moved slowly toward each other. I didn't like this. Ah, the gut-wrenching tension of another Mexican stand-off. How I'd missed you. They always go on for far too long. Mistakes get made. Sweat fell in my eyes. I tried to shake it out. Fuck, one of them had to act quickly, or ...

And the chief invader did. He leaped forward like a pissed cat, an automatic firearm came out of nowhere, and Leroy Merlin was gunned down by spitting firepower. He jacknifed backwards with a sigh, open wounds slapping the stone floor. His goons parted like velociraptors, and went for the trio.

My brain was on long play – I didn't get details, only loud, really loud bangs, blinding muzzle flash roasting my headache, and the smell of blood in a human slaughterhouse. That was the smell I couldn't place before. Fresh, human blood. You smell it once, by the bucketload like that, you don't forget it.

When it was over, I realised I was sobbing. From the pain or the bloodbath I had witnessed, I didn't know. But it went quickly, displaced by the realisation that I had to shake it up and hightail it hell for leather.

After painful wriggling and jerking, I managed to get a hand free. I bellied over to one of the dead gorillas, hoping my splintered ribs wouldn't puncture a lung, and prised the knife from his hand. After much complicated twisting and double-jointing, I managed to cut myself free, though not without grazing myself several times. Thankfully I missed any arteries.

I hauled over to Dane and felt for a pulse. Weak, but still there. He's a heavy bastard, but I dragged him out of there, up dank stairs and into the daylight. I was worried we'd been blasted in a foreign basement miles from anywhere, but Leroy Merlin had been short sighted enough to take us to the house where he grew his shit. Cost the dickhead his life.

I jimmied open a Citroen parked outside, shoved an unconscious Dane in the back seat, and hotwired it away from there, trying to drive in a straight line. Harder than you might think.

We'd missed the midnight meet – it was the day of the return. The car clock read ten a.m., and suddenly I remembered we were originally meant to collect the shit three hours beforehand.

I weighed it up for about six seconds before I swung a U in a packed four lane urban street, and went back to Leroy Merlin's place. Fuck it. Career suicide it may have been, but what I had seen had already thickened my skin, and I wasn't about to chuck it away, despite the fact that it was only thirty ounces of plant resin.

It didn't take long to pick the stuff up. There was no law on the scene – basement must have been well soundproofed. I held my breath as I stepped over the bodies, their faces already beginning to caramelise with death. I collected the shit, then got on the gas again and headed for the town.

Round a corner, I saw a Discovery in the rear-view and got the shakes. It closed up. Nix: Leroy Merlin's was a three-door, this was a five.

They'd left a message at Short's of London, saying they'd already left for the lock-up, along with directions. Cheers, loves. Slightly risky, but still, a lot of shit had happened since the last meet.

I checked on Dane. He was breathing steadily, pulse getting stronger. Apart from the mess of his face, he could have been asleep. Getting some sense of reality back, I highballed it out of the Amstel and headed for the airfield.

5

Dane woke up in the back seat on the way there. He snapped out of it pretty quickly, so it looked like it was mainly bodywork damage, just one or two panels that looked like they needed beating out.

"What the fuck happened?" he groaned.

"Don't ask."

"Fuck ... my fucking head. Where are we?"

"On the way to the lock-up. Flight's in two hours."

"Do I look as bad as I feel?"

"Worse."

"Oh good. Have we got the stuff?"

"Yes. Don't talk. Get some rest."

It took an hour to get to the lock-up. It was one of a row of old bunkers in the middle of an ancient industrial estate that had been dead in a long time. An old factory with decayed brickwork and smashed windows lay south of the estate. Nothing around except an expanse of barren, flat field, and in the distance was the end of the runway at Schipol. Airliners screamed low over our heads every two fucking minutes.

Vincent emerged from the lock-up, and turned white when he saw us. I got out of the car.

"Stop standing there like a goldfish and help me get Dane out of the car."

Vincent closed his mouth and hurried over. We hauled Dane out of the seat. His protests went unheeded, till he shook us off with a pissed "I'm fine, fuck off!"

"What ... what happened?" asked a weak Vincent. We went into the lock-up, and Natalie and Henry put on carbon copy faces.

"Little going away present from Leroy and chums."

"What? What the fuck for?"

"He had a bee in his bonnet that one of us was a grass."

"Wanker!" This was Nat. The atmosphere got heavy: they were outraged, but even so, everybody gave everybody else a conspiratorial look.

"Don't sweat it. None of us is guilty. Leroy Merlin was one paranoid fuck."

"Was?"

"Yeah, he got in the way of some speeding bullets."

"I'm well confused now."

"Some rival cartel ran in and spoiled the party. Quite a show. Every fucker there got wasted, and just about saved our bollocks."

"Jesus."

"Never mind, we're all right. Plan goes ahead as normal." We closed the door of the lock-up and stood still in the semi-darkness.

"Are you sure?"

"Plan goes ahead as normal. Let's go over it one last time." I sat down heavily on a concrete block, and let my muscles go limp. It felt good. Nat walked over with some water. I sipped it gratefully, then she dabbed at my wounds with a damp cloth. I smiled thanks, then she kissed me on the forehead and went over to tend to Dane.

"Right, Vince, when you and Dane swing through past Customs, give it as much mouth as you can. And make it good, boys. If you don't get pulled, we're fucked. Now, you're each gonna have to endure a full body cavity search by the cold fingers of H.M. Customs & Excise."

Silence indicated assent. Vincent flared his Zippo and lit a cigarette.

"Be like every other Friday night."

There was a murmur of laughter.

"Nat, you got the baby?"

"Asleep in the back of the car."

"Good. When you attach the baggage tickets, do it out of sight. Make it look like you're seeing to the baby."

Dane rocked on his heels. "Isn't that a really obvious place to hide drugs? They do it all the time on the telly." He sat down heavily, allowing Nat to sooth the cut on his head.

"Doesn't happen. Unless they have word of a cartel sending over ten kays of horse, then they can't stand the grief that mothers give them when they make them take off a baby's nappy. Especially if it's just cacked itself.

"Then I'll walk through. Dane, Vince, it's important that you don't get called over and searched until I've gone past. If you're called to have your baggage checked and I haven't gone past yet, then it will give one of the other officers a chance to refocus on the other passengers. Just keep him talking in the channel until I've actually gone past. Vince, give it some lip, make him want to ruin your holiday."

"How many will there be?" Natalie's voice was calm.

"One, possibly two. Three at worst. Right, now remember, do not interact till we are at the house. You still don't know each other till you take your separate routes out of Gatwick. Dane, Vince, take the train. Nat, Henry, ditto, but take the Gatwick Express. I've got my car at Gatwick, so I'll pick it up, and we'll meet at the house at eleven tomorrow night, where we'll either celebrate or wonder if the fucker that got caught will grass the rest of us up."

Silence.

"That was a joke."

Someone – I think it was Dane – coughed.

"Right, that's pretty much everything. Anybody got any questions?"

I looked round at the others, tried to make out their faces in the gloom. Dane was now prostrate, huddled in a corner, blowing his hands furiously. Vince was smoking, a crack in the door cutting light across his face. Henry was standing in the shadows, motionless, probably the sort of guy who could sleep upright. Nat was sitting next to Dane, stroking his hair.

They were silent. I could feel their expectant eyes boring into me, placing faith in me, trusting me that it would all go smoothly. I hoped I wouldn't fuck it up.

"Okay then, that's that. Let's change."

Dane hauled himself up, pulled on his townie woolly hat, puffer jacket, earrings, and that was his costume complete. Vincent was similar, except he was sans hat, to show off the skinhead, and he also had his lower lip and tongue pierced. They looked great. Neither of them had shaved for a week, and they looked rough, boisterous, and hard as fuck. Dane's fucked up visage enhanced the image nicely. Perfect.

Henry had changed into a rollneck with a knitted tanktop over the top. He wore a corduroy blazer on top of that. His false passport showed him as the Reverend P. Burns, and with the bushy brown beard, the soft watery eyes he looked gentle, unassuming, and every bit the padre.

Nat already looked coy enough to be a nicely domesticated housebat, so she was sorted. I put on the trousers and shoes of the suit, then we began attaching the shit to my body. It was uncomfortable as buggery, but with the shirt and jacket, it didn't show.

"Okay, we set?" Heads nodded. "Let's go."

We walked out of the lock-up, across the barren estate, towards the train station. Nat linked her arm through mine as we walked.

"Kenley," she said softly. "It'll go all right, won't it?"

"Of course it will. Nobody's a grass."

6

Dutch customs: piece of piss. Laughing and joking, not even a frisk. Not a dog anywhere, nairy a firearm in sight. Small flight: out across the tarmac of the airfield onto the plane.

The second we hit Schipol we broke away from each other and would not utter another word till we were at the safe house. Different seats on the plane, everyone sinking into their role nicely. Dane turned to look at me once, but I lifted my briefcase lid so I couldn't see him.

My stomach lurched just as the plane began to begin its descent to Gatwick. I could feel myself breaking sweat. The rustle of the polythene below my shirt sounded deafening to me.

The landing was bumpy. I needed to piss real bad. Too late, no time. I got up quickly off the plane, and my seat at the front meant I was the first out. I heard the murmur of noise and activity behind me as people began to scrabble for the bits in the overhead lockers.

I marched to baggage claim, first there. Nervous, more nervous than I had been the first two times I had done it. The lag was catching up with me as well, lousy fucking timing. I felt like everybody was looking at my face, which they probably were, dammit.

I felt Dane and Vince approach round the other side of the conveyor, already mouthing off and attracting attention. Nice going, lads. Henry appeared a few feet away from me, waiting for the luggage. I guessed Nat was behind, out of sight of the green channel.

I cast a wary eye over to the only Customs officer. That was good news. He was leaning on the partition between freedom and underwear embarrassment, and looked bored as hell. I looked back to my luggage.

Henry's luggage came first. He took one bag, then let the other one circle till Dane and Vincent had theirs. My suitcase came round. I took it, and waited. Dane and Vincent had theirs. Waiting for Henry and Nat's last one. Dadadadadadum. Where is it?

There. He took it, then walked back out of sight, where he and Nat would attach the Malaga luggage labels. I checked the time and bent to do up my shoelaces. The signal. Dane and Vincent began singing drunkenly and lurched off towards the green channel.

The Customs officer stood upright as they approached. I hadn't moved yet – I wanted to make sure they got pulled. The Customs officer held up a hand to them.

"Just a minute, lads."

"Problem, Your Honour?" Vincent jeered.

"Where have you two been, then?"

"Amsterdam!" they chorused, then let out a bassy cheer in unison.

"On business or pleasure?"

"What the fuck do you think?" Dane hollered.

"What happened to your face, my friend?"

"Fucking Dutch cunts. Taught them a fucking lesson or two. Cunts."

"Would you lads mind if we took a look through your luggage?"

Paydirt. I made my move, praying Nat and Henry weren't too far behind.

"Yeah, fucking would mind, as it happens. What for? We ain't carrying anything."

"I'm afraid I'd like to see for myself."

I got closer. They timed it just right, don't know how, and capitulated at just the right time. I walked past. The Customs guy was oblivious.

"All right then, mate. But you're gonna be disappointed."

The Customs man gave a weary nod, then barked into his radio. Poor bastards. I really felt for them. Ever had your arse probed by these imperialisto sadists? It's horrible.

I walked through the empty channel, towards the double doors and freedom. The adrenaline surged.

Then, the Customs officer's relief came. A female, this time. A fucking female. She stood in my path, arms folded in a reckless intimidation posture.

I almost died right there.

Fuck.

Fuck.

I couldn't believe it.

Sure, her face was scrubbed of make-up. Sure, her blonde hair was tied up into a tight bun. Sure, she was wearing a dark govt. issue uniform, but there was absolutely no mistaking her. No mistaking Nancy, the prostitute who had sold her bounty to me.

ABOUT THE AUTHORS

Chantele Bigmore was born in 1978 and grew up in Surrey. After completing a creative writing degree in Chichester last year, she now works in television post production in London. Her work has appeared in several poetry anthologies. She has just completed her first feature film script. She was mentored by poet Selima Hill.

Clare Birchall teaches cultural studies and creative writing at the University of Sussex. She is a Brighton based writer working towards a collection of short stories. Her agent is AM Heath. She was mentored by poet, short story writer and novelist Tobias Hill.

Andrew Briscoe lives in Brighton. He was mentored by novelist and playwright Stella Duffy.

Suzanne Conway was born in 1976. She has published poetry in The Rialto and has an M.A in Language (Creative Writing), the Arts and Education. She is currently writing throughout Australia and Asia. She was mentored by poet and novelist John Burnside.

Adrian Cooper is a filmmaker. He was mentored by novelist and playwright Stella Duffy.

Eleanor Hartland began writing at the age of thirteen and some of her earliest memories were of reading The Brothers Grimm's complete works. From there it was a natural progression into the dark, surreal realm of Gothic literature and film. Amongst other jobs she has spent time as a photo-lab technician, a cosmetics manufacturer, and an anthropological archaeologist, before completing her first novel 'The Serpent Rose'. She currently lives in London and is studying herbalism as well as working on her second book. She was mentored by thriller/ horror writer Chaz Brenchley.

Adam Hays. After sixteen years trying to figure out what he'd done to deserve it, Adam Hays left school and went through a string of jobs with his eyes wide open, including furniture salesman, bandleader, van driver, planning and traffic advisor, roofer, hospital porter, and telemarketing consultant for a prominent brewery. Some would say romantic, others would just say sad, but, unable to face anything like real life and rejected by the police force as a direct result of it, he comes home every night and spends the small hours writing crime fiction because it's the only place to be, even though no-one's paying him for it yet. He was mentored by crimewriter Russell James.

Sonja Henrici is a filmmaker. She was mentored by poet Alan Brownjohn.

Daniel Hill was born in Brighton where he has lived most of his life. The piece of writing in this book was inspired by love and postmodern filmmaking as I then believed it to be called. While the latter was a vogue with, it seems, a highly limited shelflife, the former continues to inspire many even to this day. He was mentored by novelist Robert Edric.

Robin Hill (1974-) lost his job in Hollywood and returned to England seriously broke, embittered and disappointed. He remains superficially chipper, though, thanks to the hard work of his long-suffering girlfriend, that 'big-titted short something' described in this book. He lives in Brighton, wondering what tomorrow might hold. He has two beautiful pet rats, Milly and Poppy. They like cheese wedges and Bob Dylan. He was mentored by crimewriter Russell James.

Rowena Macdonald was born on the Isle of Wight in 1974. She grew up in the West Midlands before moving to Brighton and studying English at Sussex University. She has been a gallery technician, delivery driver, life model and secretary. After a stint as a reporter on the Sussex Express she spent a year in Montreal writing and working as a waitress and bartender. She was mentored by Shena Mackay.

Alan Morrison was born in Brighton in 1974. He has been writing poetry, plays and prose since he was 16. Although he is still seeking a publishing contract, he has had two poems published through competitions, one of which, Dance of the Dragonflies, has been put on the Internet. Poet Sophie Hannah believes he has "enormous potential".

Inspired chiefly by the Romantics, Blake and Keats, Morrison is also an admirer of Marvell, Emily Bronte, Wilfred Owen, Sassoon, WH Auden and Dylan Thomas, his style being a mixture of conventional rhyme and free verse – his themes often deeply personal or of a socio-political nature. He was mentored by poet Sophie Hannah.

Rosie Rogers lives in Brighton. She was mentored by novelist and short story writer Suzannah Dunn.

Matt Sparkes was born in London in 1973. Following a freak laboratory accident involving a radioactive chameleon he is now able to change colour at will and move his eyes 360 degrees to fight crime and bring justice to all. He lives in London. He was mentored by novelist Robert Edric.

Peter Guttridge is a critic and the author of five novels.